PRAISE FOR KAT~~~~
AND HER NOVELS

Also by Katie Ashley

Vicious Cycle
Redemption Road

LAST

MILE

A VICIOUS CYCLE NOVEL

KATIE ASHLEY

A SIGNET ECLIPSE BOOK

SIGNET ECLIPSE
Published by New American Library,
an imprint of Penguin Random House LLC
375 Hudson Street, New York, New York 10014

This book is an original publication of New American Library.

First Printing, May 2016

For more information about Penguin Random House, visit penguin.com.

LIBRARY OF CONGRESS CATALOGING-IN-PUBLICATION DATA:

Names: Ashley, Katie, author.
Title: Last mile: a Vicious cycle novel/Katie Ashley.
Description: New York City: Signet Eclipse, [2016] | Series: A Vicious cycle novel; 3 | "A Signet Eclipse book."
Identifiers: LCCN 2015047828 (print) | LCCN 2016001090 (ebook) | ISBN 9780451474933 (softcover) | ISBN 9780698192362 (ebook)
Subjects: LCSH: Motorcycle clubs—Fiction. | Motorcycle gangs—Fiction. | Undercover operations—Fiction. | Man-woman relationships—Fiction. | BISAC: FICTION/Romance/Contemporary. | FICTION/Contemporary Women. | FICTION/Romance/General. | GSAFD: Romantic suspense fiction. | Love stories.
Classification: LCC PS3601.S548 L37 2016 (print) | LCC PS3601.S548 (ebook) | DDC 813/.6—dc23
LC record available at http://lccn.loc.gov/2015047828

Printed in the United States of America
10 9 8 7 6 5 4 3 2 1

Penguin
Random
House

To my faithful readers who embrace me across genres:

I'm forever in your debt for the amazing blessings
you have bestowed on my life.
You have my sincerest and deepest love.

ACKNOWLEDGMENTS

My thanks first and foremost go to God, from whom all blessings flow, and my cup certainly runneth over personally and professionally.

To my agent extraordinaire, Jane Dystel, who always has my best interests at heart in both my personal and professional lives. Here's to many more successful years together.

To my NAL editor, Kerry Donovan, thank you for being such a pleasure to work with on this series. Thanks for ensuring the books were the best they could be, for allowing me to keep as much control of my "babies" as possible, and for being there when I needed you.

Thanks forever and always to Kim Bias for talking me down from the ledge, working me through the plot points and being my first reader, doing daily writing goal check-ins via text, and generally making my books and my life so much better. Love ya hard, woman!

To Marion Archer—I could not and would not put out a book without your amazing feedback. I'm forever shaking my head at your comments and wondering, "Now, why didn't I think of that?" Most of all, I thank you for your friendship. Your prayers and support from across the ocean get me through.

To my cousin Kim Holcombe, and my friends Kristi Hefner, Gwen McPherson, Kim Benefield, Tiffany Allred, Brittany Haught, and Michelle Eck—thank you so much for taking such good care of me and Olivia during the first days and weeks of her life. That tender care greatly enabled me to finish this book. I love you all so very, very much!

To Katie Brown and Stephanie Frady: Thanks for watching Olivia to give me some writing time . . . and some sleep!

To my babysitter, Robin Riddle, thanks for taking such great care of Olivia and me so that I could do all things writerly without worrying about Miss O.

Cris Hadarly, my dearest friend and greatest book supporter. We may be oceans apart, but I couldn't ask for a better person to be in my corner. I will forever be in your debt for your unfailing contributions to my writing career. Thanks for going along on the crazy roller-coaster ride that has been the past three years. I love you with all my heart.

Jen Gerchick, Jen Oreto, and Shannon Furhman: Thanks for your unfailing support of me and my books—it means so much that you've embraced us. Most of all, I appreciate your friendship, which sustains me during the good and bad times.

To my street team, Ashley's Angels, thanks for the love and support!

To the ladies of the Hot Ones—Karen Lawson, Amy Lineweater, Marion Archer, and Merci Arellano—thanks for your friendship, book support, naughty memes that make me laugh, and hours of Zoom chats. They mean the world to me.

ACKNOWLEDGMENTS

To my naughty sistas of the Smutty Mafia: Thanks for keeping me sane and making me laugh!

To Kristi Hefner, Gwen McPherson, Brittany Haught, Kim Benefield, Jamie Brock, and Erica Deese for being the bestest friends a gal could ever ask for. I thank God for having you all in my life for so long.

LAST MILE

PROLOGUE

Knives and forks clanging together mixed with idle conversation echoed through the dining room and grated on eight-year-old Samantha Vargas's last nerve. Peering out into the hallway, she eyed the golden hands of the antique grandfather clock for the millionth time. It was almost seven, and her father was now thirty minutes late. While her mother and siblings seemed unaffected by his tardiness, she was on pins and needles awaiting his presence in the house.

"Ignoring your food isn't going to make Daddy get home any sooner," her mother chided, motioning her fork at Sam's untouched plate. "Eat up."

With a sigh of frustration, Sam picked up her fork and started poking at the food that was usually her favorite but tonight held no appeal at all. She brought some of the arroz con pollo to her lips. Just as she was about to take a bite, her ears perked up at the hum of a car's motor. When a door slammed outside, Sam jerked her head up. "He's here!" she cried, flinging herself out of her chair.

As her black Converse tennis shoes beat a hot path out of the dining room, her mother called, "Samantha Eliana Vargas, get back here and finish your dinner!"

Ignoring her mother's command, she sprinted down the hallway and threw open the front door. She barreled forward off the porch and onto the path, where she jumped into her father's arms.

He dropped his briefcase onto the concrete, unable to juggle them both. He then chuckled at her enthusiasm. "I guess this means you're glad to see me, huh?"

"You've been gone almost a week," she protested as she tightened her arms around her father's neck. When she pressed herself flush against him, she could feel the gun holster through his suit, along with the steel of his gun. It might have freaked out most kids, but to her, it was comforting. It was how she identified her father. Like on television and in the movies, he was one of the good guys fighting against all the bad ones committing crimes.

"This case took a little longer than I thought, *mija*. But rest assured that after tomorrow, I'll be home now for a while."

"I'm so glad." She pulled back to stare into his dark brown eyes—the same ones she had inherited from him. Of course, she had inherited so much more from him than just his eye color. Unlike her older brother and sister, who favored their mother, she was her father's Mini-Me. She wanted to be just like him when she grew up. Law enforcement was in her blood. Her grandfather had been a detective with the Miami police, and then her father had become a DEA agent. She had a strong desire to beat the bad guys, just as they did. While other girls her age were playing with Barbies and other dolls, she was learning from her father's stories how to dismantle weapons and read body language.

"Come on. Let's go inside. Your mama promised to cook my favorite dinner tonight, and I'm starving."

Sam grinned. "She did."

"And that's why I love her so much. She might be a good Irish girl, but she tries her hardest to make her Cuban husband his favorite foods."

As they climbed the porch stairs, her mother and siblings were waiting in the doorway. Her father eased Sam down onto her feet so that he could give her fifteen-year-old brother, Steven, and thirteen-year-old sister, Sophie, each a hug. Being teenagers, Steven and Sophie didn't think it was cool to show the same kind of excitement for their father's return as she had done.

Drawing her mother into his arms, her father gave her a lingering kiss. "Mmm, I've missed you, Jenny."

Her mother smiled at her father. "I've missed you, too. Do we have you all to ourselves for a while?"

"I have one last thing to wrap up tonight around nine, but after that, I'll be chained to my desk for the next few weeks."

A relieved sigh escaped her mother's lips. "Since that's the safest place you could be, I'm glad to hear it."

After bestowing another kiss on her mother's lips, her father added, "You worry too much."

"Daddy, can I go with you tonight?" Sam asked. When he shook his head, she argued, "But it's Friday night. I don't have school tomorrow."

"There's a little too much heat on this one for you to come along." As disappointment clouded her face, he reached over to tweak her nose. "Next time, *mija*."

From her father's no-nonsense tone, Sam knew not to press the issue any further. Once he took his seat at the head of the table, she reluctantly sat down in her chair. Her dinner held a little more interest than it had before her father got home, and she managed to clean her plate because she knew it would please him.

It was during those last few bites that a brilliant idea formed in her head. She would prove to her father she wasn't too young to see a case with heat. If she was going to be an agent like him one day, she had to start somewhere. Just as with her siblings, he had started her off young by teaching her how to shoot a gun down at the range as well as demonstrating several self-defense moves.

Of course, if she was to succeed, she would have to be a little sneaky. That was where the idea came in.

"What's the grin for?" her father asked, bringing her out of her thoughts.

"Nothing," she murmured.

After the dinner dishes were washed and her siblings scattered off to their own Friday-night social events, Sam pretended to be interested by what was on television. When the clock ticked closer and closer to nine, she faked a few yawns and then claimed she was tired and turning in early. She held back a smile as she kissed her parents good night.

When she was sure they weren't paying attention, she slipped out the back door. She hustled around the side of the house to where her father's sedan was parked. Throwing open the car door, she dropped down onto the floorboard. She covered herself with her blanket. Her body trembled so hard with excitement that her teeth knocked together. She didn't know how long she waited before her ears perked up at the sound of her father coming up to the car. Once he was inside, she took shallow breaths, afraid that he might somehow hear her breathing over the car's engine.

After the car made a few turns, Sam knew they were getting on the interstate, and from there, she imagined they were heading from the suburbs into Miami. Her mind whirled with different scenarios of what her father had to do. Maybe he was going to meet with an informant or do some undercover work. Those thoughts sent excitement pounding through her veins.

It seemed like an eternity before the car pulled off the interstate. It coasted along at an even speed, and then they made another turn. At the way she was shaken about, she imagined they had abandoned the paved road for gravel. Once they came to a stop, Sam eased the blanket off her face, taking a deep breath of the fresh air.

Her father turned off the car and then fumbled around in the front seat. The unmistakable scratchy sound of a radio filled the silence. "This is Agent Vargas checking in at 1901 Liberty Avenue."

"Roger that, Vargas. Do you seek assistance?" another voice crackled over the frequency.

"No. Just a routine information exchange."

"Good luck. Ten-four."

"Ten-four."

A few minutes went by. The blaring of motorcycle pipes came from behind them, causing Sam to jump where she hid. She couldn't imagine what business her father could possibly have with a motorcycle gang. The last time they were in the city, a group of bikers had roared past them. The emblem on the back of their leather vests had frightened her even more than the noise had. It was a skull that looked as though it had an American Indian headdress. Her father had called it a "death's-head."

Wondering if this biker was part of the same scary group, Sam eased up to peer out the window. Out of the shadowy darkness, a man dismounted his bike and came strutting across the parking lot. As he grew closer, the lone streetlight allowed Sam to get a better look. Long, dark hair spilled over his broad shoulders, but she couldn't make out much of his face since it was covered in a beard. Even in the dark, he wore a pair of sunglasses, and Sam wondered how he could possibly see anything.

"Good to see you again, Willie. You have the location of the drop like you promised?"

"No," the man muttered in a gravelly voice.

A frustrated grunt came from her father. "I thought we had a deal. The location of the drop ensured the close of the case, but most of all, it kept you out of jail."

Willie shrugged. "All I have is a message."

"What is it?" her father questioned, both caution and apprehension filling his voice.

"People who fuck with the Rogues get put to ground."

"Oh shit!" her father muttered before he began frantically shifting in his seat.

An explosion like a cannon blast went off beside the car. Sam bit back her scream at both the noise and the fact that something warm and sticky showered over her in the backseat. A few seconds ticked agonizingly by . . . or was it minutes? Sam's heartbeat drummed so loudly in her ears she was sure her father and the man were going to hear.

After the roar of the motorcycle started up, she realized the biker was leaving. When she was sure that he was gone, she slowly rose into a sitting position. "D-Daddy?" she questioned in the silence. When she dared to look into the front seat, a scream tore through her chest, but after she opened her mouth, nothing would come out. Blinking furiously, she sat frozen in horror at the sight of the gaping wound in her father's head and the blood and something else spattered across the front seat and the dash.

Immediately, she knew he needed help. Someone had to come and put her father back together. With trembling fingers, she fumbled with the handle on the door. Once she got it open, her feet dropped onto the gravel, but her wobbly legs barely supported her as she went around the back of the car. After opening the passenger-side door, she slid inside.

She pried the radio from her father's hands. Her shaking fingers pressed down on the button he had taught her to use. Of course, they had just been playing around then. "H-hello?"

After she released the button, it seemed like an eternity before anyone responded. "Kid, this is a police frequency you're on. Get off it before you get yourself in trouble."

As if from instinct, her anger overrode her fear. "My name is Samantha Vargas. My father is Agent Antonio Vargas. He's been . . ." Glancing over at her father's lifeless body, she pinched her eyes shut. "My father has been shot."

"Jesus Christ!" came the reply. There was a flurry of activity on the other end. She dropped the radio, ignoring anything further that the dispatch might have to say. Taking her father's blood-slick hand, she cradled it in her own. She was still staring down at it when the police and paramedics arrived in a flood of flashing lights and wailing sirens.

Someone jerked open the passenger-side door. "Holy fucking shit," a voice muttered.

When a pair of arms reached out for her, Sam didn't fight them. Instead, she dropped a kiss onto her father's hand and then let herself be pulled into the person's arms. A kind female voice began talking soothingly to her. She didn't bother making out the words. After all, there was nothing anyone could say that would make her feel better.

Her father was dead.

ONE

BISHOP

The clang of the opening bell echoed through my ears, sending a jolt of electric energy surging through me. Adrenaline pumped through my bloodstream while muscles and ligaments tightened in anticipation when I came charging out of the corner of the ring. My gloved fists were positioned at chest level to either inflict harm or block a hit.

When you were facing down an opponent, timing was everything. Dodging in just a split second meant the difference between a right cross narrowly missing your jaw and one potentially knocking you senseless. Coming back from a block at just the right moment could also mean the difference in incapacitating your enemy and winning the fight.

I'd faced a lot of adversaries in my day. Most of the time, I was in crowded, noisy bars or in dimly lit back alleys. While I might use my fists defensively to protect my club brothers, I usually relied on other forms of weaponry. Tonight, however, found me under the bright lights of the boxing ring, facing down a fighter I'd never seen before. The one place I was most confident was in the ring. Between the ropes, I didn't need to count on guns or knives to save my ass—my hands and my body were the only weapons I needed. They could inflict great pain and suffering while making me a champion.

At twenty-five, I'd been fighting most of my life. My old man had gotten me started when I was just a kid as a way to release steam. Considering that he was a former felon turned holy-rolling preacher turned MC president, he had experience defusing hot tempers with intense physical activity. What he hadn't anticipated the day he brought me into his MC-owned gym was the natural talent I had when it came to boxing.

Tonight as I bobbed and weaved around the ring, throwing rights and jabs, I found my opponent ultimately to be such a pussy that I wondered if he hadn't been paid to take a dive, aka lose the fight. But then in the fifth round, he found his second wind and started pummeling my face. I felt the stinging burn of skin slicing open along my forehead and eyebrows. Blood trickled into my eyes, clouding my vision. Instead of becoming a handicap, it merely fueled my rage.

As the rounds continued, I began to wear my opponent down. Finally, after the ninth bell, I clocked him one to the jaw and then to the nose. He staggered back, collapsing to his knees and then falling forward onto his face.

The referee smacked the mat to confirm that my opponent was out. When he jumped to his feet, he grabbed me by the arm and jerked it over my head. The crowd clambered to their feet in a loud rush of noise. A cocky grin slunk across my face as I did a triumphant turn, raising both my arms over my head, which caused the crowd to roar their approval. After giving them a fist pump, I started to the corner of the ring, where Boone, the Raiders' official treasurer and my unofficial trainer, awaited me.

He thrust a bottle of water at me, which I gladly started gulping down. "Breakneck is AWOL tonight, so I texted Rev during that nasty fifth round to bring Annabel by to clean you up."

"Aw, fuck, man, the last thing I need is shit from Rev because his wife has to patch my bloodied ass up from a fight."

"Yeah, well, it was either Annabel or the emergency room." With a snort, Boone added, "Besides, we don't want to scar up that pretty puss of yours."

"Whatever," I grumbled as I snatched a towel off the ropes and started drying off some of the sweat on my chest.

"Need me to do that?" a voice purred behind me.

Glancing over my shoulder, I took in the scantily clad figure of a ring card girl. She was one of the hot-bodied women who walked around the boxing ring holding the numbered round cards above their heads. I had seen her around the last couple of fights. As she tilted her blond head, she gave me her best *come fuck me* smile. Regardless of the pain and the bloodied shape my face might've been in, my dick automatically responded to *her* call.

I turned around and took a step closer to her. "Think you could help me out once I get patched up?"

She pursed her red lips at me. "Maybe."

"I'll make it worth your while. Several times. I can promise you that."

Her gaze drifted down my body before her eyes met mine again. "Okay, champ. We'll see if you can have two knockouts tonight."

"Give me half an hour."

"Sounds good."

Boone's hand landed on my shoulder. "All right, lover boy. Let's get going."

When I hopped down, I came face-to-face with Rev. He grimaced at the sight of me. "Boone wasn't lying when he said you'd gotten pretty fucked up tonight."

"Doesn't feel any worse than usual."

Rev jerked his chin up at the ring, where my imminent piece of ass stood. "Doesn't look like it's affecting your ability to get laid, either."

I grinned. "Nothing but being dead or in a body cast will stop me from getting laid."

With a chuckle, Rev said, "You're a piece of work, brother."

We started through the crowd to the back hallway that led to the training rooms. Rev's phone rang. After grabbing it out of his pocket and glancing at the screen, he motioned for me to go on to the last door on the left. When I entered, Annabel had her back to me, digging through a bag of medical supplies.

After sneaking up behind her, I bellowed, "Hey there, sexy."

When the sound of my voice caused her to jump, I immediately felt bad. Although a year had passed since she was enslaved by a member of the Rodriguez drug cartel down in Mexico, she still had moments of being skittish when it came to men. "Sorry about that," I said sheepishly.

Without looking up from her bag, she replied, "I should be used to it by now." A smile curved her lips. "Or I should at least be used to you always acting like a dick."

I threw back my head with a laugh. "True. Very true."

As she glanced over at me, Annabel's green eyes widened in horror.

"Don't worry. The other fucker looks much worse," I said, hopping up on the massage table.

"I'll take your word for it," she said.

"You know, I'm kinda offended that I've got a lowly vet tech tending my wounds rather than an MD."

Annabel jerked her head up. She pursed her lips at me. "Yeah, well, I'm equally offended to have been dragged away from my date night to come down here to look after you."

Giving her a shit-eating grin, I said, "Sorry, sweetheart, but when you married my brother, you married the club as well."

"And for better or worse means skipping out on dessert to sew you up?" she asked teasingly.

"Sure as hell does." After drinking in her appearance in a sexy black dress that showed off her legs and her tits, I gave a low whistle. "Although I do have to say it's really better on my part because you're lookin' mighty fine tonight, Mrs. Malloy."

Pink dotted her cheeks as she put the necessary supplies down next to me. When Annabel finally looked me in the eye, she did smile. "Always the flatterer."

"Always. Of course, I would be a real dumb-ass to insult someone who is about to use a needle on me."

"For once, you are very wise."

As she started cleaning the cuts on my face and forehead, I asked, "So, exactly where the hell is Breakneck tonight that kept him from being here?"

"He's on a date." After a dramatic pause, she added, "With Kim."

My eyebrows shot up in extreme shock, causing me to hiss in pain. "Are you fucking serious?"

Annabel nodded as she tossed the bloodied gauze in the trash can beside the table. I couldn't say I was surprised that Breakneck was getting back in the saddle. The man had been divorced for years, and while he'd been known to hit it with a couple of the older club whores, he hadn't gotten serious with anyone inside or out of the club. But holy shit, he was stepping out with Kim, the widow of our former president Case. It had been more than a year since Case's murder, but for the most part, Kim still mourned him.

There had been no one else in the world for her since she was eighteen years old.

"That's the latest from the gossip mill, huh?" With a snort, I added, "You old ladies sure run your mouths."

"For your information, I found out from Rev, not Kim."

"Seriously?"

She nodded. "Apparently, Breakneck had asked Rev's advice about whether he should ask Kim out." She dabbed some antiseptic along my forehead cuts. While it stung like a motherfucker, I tried not to act like a pussy in front of Annabel. With a dreamy look on her face, she said, "Personally, I think it's a wonderful idea. They both need someone, and they're both in the club."

"Yeah, but boning your dead brother's old lady is complicated for a dude."

Annabel stared wide-eyed at me for a moment before grinning. "You have such a way with words."

"Thank you."

"Besides, I think it's about more than"—she swallowed hard—"*boning*, as you say."

"In the end, it all comes down to boning."

"To you, maybe, but there is more to a relationship than just that."

I winked at her. "Let's agree to disagree on that one."

"Fine with me." She opened up the suturing kit, and I braced myself to have my broken skin stitched back together. "So tell me something."

"What?" I asked.

"How exactly does your fighting fit in with the Raiders going legit?" When I gave her my best *I don't know shit about what you're talking about* look, she rolled her eyes. "Honestly, Bishop, I'm not an idiot. I know you're not fighting just to unload some steam, and I know there's big money on these fights. And before you accuse

Rev of always running his mouth to his old lady, he didn't tell me anything. I figured it out all on my own."

I chuckled as I shifted on the table. Both Deacon and Rev had picked strong, hardheaded women. The best kind of old ladies were the ones who just looked the other way, didn't ask questions, and kept their mouths shut. At the same time, you needed some strong-willed bitches to keep the other women in line, especially when it came to the president's wife. Annabel had been through enough to make her strong as steel, and with time, I knew she would become a woman all the others in the club would look up to as their leader's wife.

"You're right. I don't do it for shits and giggles. I do it for the prize money." I cursed under my breath as the needle pierced my skin.

"Do I dare ask what you're doing with all your winnings?"

I clenched my jaw through the pricking pain of the needle. "Although it's a legit way to earn a living, I don't always want to be a mechanic."

Annabel's hand stilled in her sewing. "What else is it that you want to do?" she questioned softly.

For a moment, I thought about blowing her off. I hadn't shared my long-term goal with anyone, really. Maybe Deacon and Rev had an idea from my weekend pursuits of buying broken-down bikes and refurbishing them, but it wasn't something I had actually come right out and said.

At my hesitation, Annabel continued stitching. "Oh. It's something you shouldn't tell me because it's illegal."

"Hell no. It's nothing like that." I drew in a deep breath. "I want to own a bike shop someday. I love rebuilding old bikes and restoring them."

"I think that's a wonderful idea."

"You do?"

Annabel nodded. "Of course I do. I think you can do anything you put your mind to, B."

It felt pretty fucking fabulous having her support. "Thanks. It means a lot."

As she finished stitching my eyebrow, her expression turned serious. "So you're totally on board with the new direction the club is taking?"

Although the question shocked the hell out of me, I tried to keep my face impassive. "I always support my brothers."

"That's a very diplomatic answer," she said as she snipped the suturing thread.

After a few moments of silence, I exhaled a deep breath. "I know some people—some brothers from other Raiders chapters—might think what we're doing is the coward's way out. That Deacon instigated going legit all because he was pussy-whipped by a woman. But that's not how it is."

"Exactly how is it, B?" Annabel questioned softly.

I gave a quick shake of my head. I didn't like to get serious with anyone about my world, least of all a woman. But in her own way, Annabel had earned her stripes. "In the last five years, I've lost my old man and then my president. Deacon almost got blown up, Rev was tortured and almost died, and even I got shot. I'm twenty-five years old, and if shit keeps going the way that it is, I won't live to see thirty. Each and every time you have to put a brother in the ground, it eats away at you. Even if I do make it past thirty, I sure as hell don't want to have to lose any more of my brothers, especially not Deacon and Rev. It's a vicious fucking cycle, and somewhere things have to change."

"Death is the greatest motivator for you," Annabel stated.

"Hell yeah."

"You don't worry about jail time?"

Shrugging, I replied, "I wouldn't want to do time, but at least there's an option to get out. You can come back to your family and your bike."

Annabel smiled. "Rev keeps quoting this MC president who turned his chapter around. He said, 'You can't ride a bike in jail.'"

"That's the fucking truth."

"And at the end of the day, that's really what is most important to you guys. Isn't it?"

"Bikin' and brotherhood is all that matters."

Rev appeared in the doorway then. "Putting Humpty Dumpty back together?" he asked with a grin.

Annabel laughed. "Yes. I just finished up."

"Good. Because he has some company waiting on him."

When Rev waggled his eyebrows, Annabel groaned. "I don't think I even want to know." She tossed the last of her supplies back into her bag. "I would recommend for the next twenty-four hours that you take some ibuprofen—" When I started to protest that I wasn't a pussy who needed anything for the pain, she held up her hand. "For the inflammation."

I grinned. "Yes, Doc."

My ring girl appeared in the doorway beside Rev. "You're looking better," she said, with a cat-that-ate-the-canary smile.

After Annabel took one look at my piece of ass, she rolled her eyes and grabbed her bag. "I would recommend icing your forehead as well, but I can imagine any further advice I give will fall on deaf ears."

"Pretty much."

She shook her head. "You Malloy men are stubborn to a fault."

Lowering my voice, I added, "We're also horny motherfuckers, so do yourself and my brother a favor by getting out of here and going home to bed."

"You're impossible," she muttered, but when she glanced over her shoulder at Rev, I knew he'd be getting some by the secretive smile Annabel wore when she gazed at him.

As soon as Annabel left my side, my ring card girl took her place. After Rev closed the door, she said, "My name's Candy, by the way."

I nodded. I wanted to assure her I wouldn't need to know her name because we wouldn't be hooking up again. The only reason why it might have mattered was to make sure I called out the right name when I came, because with all the women I'd been with, they managed to run together.

After making quick work of getting her and myself undressed, I showed her how a true champion can have multiple knockouts in one night.

TWO

SAMANTHA

Boiling summer heat radiated off the pavement, sending beads of sweat trickling down the backs of my legs. Even though the sun had set hours ago, there was no respite from the steamy onslaught. While I might've had plenty of ventilation in the black lace bustier and barely there black miniskirt, I waved my hand in front of my face, trying to salvage the makeup that I was sure was about to start sweating off. *How in the hell do some women do this day in and day out?*

A buzz from the communication device in my ear had me on alert. "Suspect has been spotted in the twelve-block radius. All teams on alert."

"Copy that," I murmured.

After I had made a quick visual sweep of the area, a crackling once again came in my ear. "ETA to Vargas is two minutes, thirty seconds."

"Look sharp, Sammie-Lou Hooker," came another voice in my ear. I fought the urge to glare across the street at the unmarked sedan. Sitting inside wearing a shit-eating grin was my partner, Gavin

McTavish. Since he was three years older than me, he was like an annoying older brother. He was more than just my partner—he was my best friend. We had met at the academy five years ago, and I'd shared more blood, sweat, and tears with him than with any other person in the world.

Even without having to be radioed, I knew the moment our suspect, Chuck Sutton, arrived on the scene. An awareness hummed through my bones, and I shifted into my chameleon persona. From his teenage days, Chuck had outsourced guns to some of the toughest Atlanta street gangs. After several prior convictions, he'd grown wiser in his older age, and he had learned how to evade our usual methods. We needed him in custody on a lesser charge so we could outwit him on the case we had been building.

That was where I came in. If Chuck had an Achilles' heel, it was women, especially ones he bought. There must've been something about the illicitness that he craved.

When I heard him behind me, I turned around. After giving him my sexiest smile, I said, "Hey there. You looking to have some fun tonight?"

He licked his lips, and I fought the urge to throw up. "Maybe." With slight apprehension in his eyes, he glanced around. "Is it just you tonight?"

I gave a quick nod. "I work for myself."

"I like that. I don't like middlemen."

I ran my hand up his arm before squeezing his shoulder. "That's just one of the things we have in common." To bust him, I had to have him agree to a price and start off with me. Dancing around the subject the way we were now wouldn't hold up for an arrest. "Wanna go somewhere so I can see what else you like?"

A slow smile spread across his face. "Yeah, I would. How much we talking about here?"

"A hundred for an hour whether you take that long or not." When I could see the flash in his eyes, I purred, "But I'm sure you'll last long enough to get your money's worth."

My petty compliment fueled his fire. "I've been known to be a big tipper if you make it worth my while."

"Of course I will, sugar." I dropped my hand from his shoulder to take his hand. "Your car okay, or you want to be a big spender and spring for the motel up the street?"

"My car is fine."

Just as he started to lead me to it, one of the other agents on the case pulled a dick move by jumping the gun and coming in early. The moment he stepped out of the shadows and Chuck got a look at him, the shit hit the fan.

Chuck not only dropped my hand, but he shoved me back, causing me to stumble on my heels and fall on my ass. Then he sprinted off down the opposite side of the street from where his car was parked. "Greenburg, you dumb fuck!" I grunted at the errant agent as I tried to get my bearings.

"We had enough to take him."

As I pulled myself to my feet, I glared at him. "Really? Then why the hell aren't we taking him?" I didn't bother waiting for a response. I hadn't just spent the last thirty minutes in mortifying attire, not to mention having to say the sick shit I did, to lose out on a suspect.

While my knowledge of the area was somewhat limited, I still knew of a way to catch up with Chuck. Pounding my heels into the pavement, I pushed myself to run as fast as I could go. Within my mind, I focused on the four-block radius on the map I had studied for days before the bust. After a split-second decision, I cut down a side alley.

Glancing around, I looked for something that could incapacitate Chuck. My eyes homed in on a discarded broom, which I quickly grabbed. I then sprinted toward the end of the alley. I made it there just as Chuck ran by. I swung the broom like a bat at the backs of his knees, sending him spiraling and finally skidding along the ground. I tossed the broom and then grabbed my gun. "Don't even think of moving!" I shouted as I pointed it at his head.

Chuck held up his shaking hands in surrender. I didn't bother alerting the team of my location, since they had me on GPS. After what seemed like only a few seconds, police sirens wailed down the street and screeched to a halt beside us.

At the sight of Greenburg, I said, "You can haul him in."

He gave a sheepish nod before beginning to work on Chuck. I was putting my gun back in my holster when I felt a hand on my shoulder. "You okay?" Gavin asked, his deep blue eyes filled with concern for me.

"Fucking fine and dandy now that I took out that douche bag."

With a shake of his head, Gavin asked, "Nothing really rattles you for long, does it?"

"Nope. Just dumb-asses pissing in my Cheerios," I replied, glaring at Greenburg.

"You mean people trying to steal your thunder," Gavin countered.

"Watch it, McTavish, or I'll take you out at the knees with a broom, too."

Gavin slipped an arm around my shoulder as we started to head back to the car. Pretending to be a prostitute in the scorching Atlanta heat was just one of the many masks I wore as an agent with the ATF—or Bureau of Alcohol, Tobacco, and Firearms. When my father was gunned down over the long-standing war on drugs between the feds and bikers, I lost all interest in following in his footsteps to the DEA. After I'd earned a criminal justice degree at FSU, my interest in the FBI eventually led me to the ATF, where I had spent the last four years as an agent. With the ATF, I was able to fulfill my childhood dream of putting away the bad guys, as well as feeding my need for a job that kept me on my toes.

When we reached the car, our superior, Grant Peterson, was leaned against it.

"Good evening," he said, with a smile.

"Evening," Gavin replied.

"Did you feel like slumming a bit tonight? I mean, you're used to your cushy office with its air-conditioning," I said. Although Peterson was my boss, we had a comfortable rapport with each other.

Peterson laughed. "A good general always stays in the trenches."

"I see."

"As always, nice work, Vargas."

"Thanks, sir," I said as I balanced on one leg to take off my heels. I groaned in ecstasy once my feet were freed from their stiletto prison.

Glancing between the two of us, Peterson asked, "You guys got anything else tonight?"

Gavin shook his head. "We were planning on working on the debriefing first thing tomorrow morning—if that's okay with you."

Peterson nodded in agreement. "Since you're free, why don't you two let me buy you some dinner?"

Gavin's and my eyebrows rose in unison. "Hmm, sounds like you've got something pretty heavy to talk to us about if you're offering dinner," I replied.

With a chuckle, Peterson said, "You know me too well."

I might've been exhausted, with my bed calling my name, but my stomach growled in approval of Peterson's offer. "Sounds good to me."

Gavin chuckled. "You think I'm ever going to pass up a meal on the bureau?"

"Don't hold your breath that it's going to be a fine dining experience. I see a Waffle House in our future," I teased.

"Oh, I'm way classier than that," Peterson argued.

"IHOP?"

He grinned. "Yep. How about the one off Exit 243 in ten?"

"Okay. We'll be there."

Peterson eyed my attire with a grimace. Before he could say anything, I held up a hand. "I have a change of clothes in the car. Okay?"

"Good. I didn't want to draw any unnecessary attention to us."

I batted my eyelashes at him. "Are you saying I'm a distraction dressed like this?"

He grinned. "Let's just say I don't think with you dressed like that, I could sit across from you and be able to hold a serious conversation without letting my mind wander."

Smacking his arm playfully, I replied, "You old perv."

"You know me too well. See ya in ten," he said before heading off down the street.

I followed Gavin across the street to the car. After we slipped inside, I asked, "What do you think is going on?"

Gavin appeared thoughtful as he cranked up. "Must be something pretty big, considering he's wanting to discuss this over dinner rather than waiting to do it in the morning at the office."

"That's what I was thinking. I don't think we've ever been propositioned for a case outside the bureau." I grabbed a T-shirt out of my bag and pulled it on over my bustier. "As long as it doesn't involve me in another ensemble like this, I'm game."

With a snicker, Gavin pulled out into the street. "You know, Vargas, you might not spend so many nights alone if you dressed like that more often."

I shot him a death glare before unbuttoning the flimsy skirt. As I shimmied it off my hips and down my thighs, I thought about Gavin's comment. While he might have been joking, there was a lot of truth to what he said. I did spend a lot of nights alone. It had been at least a year since my last long-term relationship. Each one seemed to end because of the same thing: I was married to my job. Although most men found my profession sexy at first, they soon were turned off by always taking second place. In the end, I couldn't blame them, because who really wants a relationship with a workaholic risk taker?

Shaking my head free of those thoughts, I pulled a pair of yoga pants on. I crumpled my hooker clothes into a ball and shoved them into my bag. The IHOP Peterson had chosen was in a better neighborhood than we had just been in. At the same time, it was pretty secluded, and there weren't many customers inside. At the hostess stand Peterson requested a place for us in the very back, away from everyone else.

I slid into the booth beside Gavin while Peterson took the spot across from us. After a waitress took our orders, Peterson dug into his briefcase and got down to business. "How much do you two know about the Hells Raiders MC?"

My stomach churned at the mere mention of an MC. In that moment, I was no longer a self-possessed thirty-year-old ATF agent. Instead, I was an eight-year-old kid peering out the car window at a man in a leather cut who was about to murder my father and shatter my once-perfect existence. Just the sound of motorcycle pipes was like a PTSD trigger. Of course, the agency didn't know that. You couldn't afford to have any form of emotional deficit when it came to cases.

"Never really heard of them," Gavin replied while I nodded in agreement.

"As far as the criminal element of one-percents goes, their Georgia club has a relatively small membership. Over the last few decades, they've flown under the radar. Compared to some clubs, they keep themselves pretty clean by only dealing with small-time gunrunning without a lot of assault weapons, interstate gambling, and a strip club with no backdoor prostitution."

"How admirable," I mused.

Peterson gave us a tight smile. "Because of the drugs and assault weapons that the Nordic Knights and the Gangbangers out of Techwood were pushing, our attention was kept elsewhere, while the Raiders weren't worth much of our time. Until recently."

"So what's changed?" I asked.

Peterson paused as the waitress returned with our drinks. Once she was gone, he said, "It appears the Raiders have made an alliance with the Rodriguez cartel."

"Holy shit," Gavin muttered.

I leaned forward on the table with my elbows. "Wait a minute. Didn't I hear of some hush-hush ATF and DEA presence at a takedown involving some bikers a few months ago?"

Peterson nodded. "A former lieutenant from the Rodriguez cartel became expendable—a man named Mendoza. A long-standing beef he had with the Raiders' president, Nathaniel 'Rev' Malloy, led to a hostage situation. Rev was tortured and shot by Mendoza, but he made a full recovery. From what I could gather from reading between the lines in the records, which are now black-lined confidential, it all stemmed from the human trafficking of Annabel Percy and her rescue by the Raiders."

My eyebrows shot up in surprise. "Rescue? Don't tell me the Raiders did something remotely heroic," I scoffed.

"They risked their lives and club to go in after a club member's daughter who had been abducted. While the member's daughter unfortunately got killed, they saved Annabel."

"She remained unscathed after her time with the Raiders?" I questioned skeptically.

Peterson chuckled. "She's married to Rev now."

I slowly shook my head back and forth. "You're telling me a former deb like Percy is married to some MC scum? She must've had one hell of a case of reverse Stockholm syndrome."

Gavin eyed me suspiciously. "Since when do you have such a hatred for MC gangs?"

With a shrug, I replied, "They're criminals who demean women and hide their violence behind an alleged love of motorcycle riding." I then turned my attention away from Gavin's inquisitiveness and started devouring my bacon cheeseburger. While he might've been my best friend and knew some of the details of my father's murder, I had never admitted that it was a biker who had killed my dad.

Peterson cleared his throat. "The bottom line is we could be on the precipice of one of the greatest interstate gun trafficking cases of my career. It's not just small-time sales to lowlifes and felons. We're talking about funding the cartel with weapons right here in our own backyard."

"I can assume that the bureau hasn't gotten shit with the usual methods of phone tapping and surveillance, and they want to get some agents inside. Correct?" Gavin asked.

With a nod, Peterson replied, "These bikers might be small-time gangsters, but they're smart gangsters. All business between them and the cartel has happened either face-to-face or on burner phones."

"So where do we come in?" I questioned.

"Gavin, you grew up working in your father's garage, didn't you?"

At the mention of his blue-collar roots, Gavin winced slightly. "Yeah, my dad and my grandfather were mechanics. I helped out there from the time I could tell a socket wrench from a combination wrench." He took a swig of his coffee. "I'm not sure how that knowledge has any bearing on this case."

Peterson flipped through his files before stopping at one. He took out a picture and put it on the table. "This is the Raiders' sergeant at arms, Benjamin 'Bishop' Malloy."

"Hmm, he's a looker," Gavin mused as he rubbed the stubble on his chin.

I nudged him under the table. "I'm pretty sure he doesn't bat for your team."

"Pity."

Peterson rolled his eyes at the two of us. "May I continue?"

"Yes," Gavin and I replied.

"Bishop has just taken a mechanics apprenticeship at a local garage—one that has no affiliations to the Raiders." At what had to be Gavin's and my identical expressions of surprise, Peterson added, "Apparently, he's looking to go legitimate in his career choice and have no help from the Raiders."

Straightening up in his seat, Gavin asked, "So you guys want to put me to work at this garage?"

Peterson nodded. "We're hoping you can gain his trust and become a hang-around for the club . . . maybe even work up to prospecting."

"I can do that. I might need a week or two to do a little refresher on mechanical terminology."

"We have you booked into a garage to do just that starting tomorrow. We won't put you into the one where Bishop works until after you've completed the refresher."

Gavin choked on the french fry he'd been chewing. "Tomorrow? Damn, Peterson, you guys sure as hell were banking on me saying yes."

"You're the only one with the credentials to do it. This case isn't just about someone who knows cars. It's also about motorcycles. Correct me if I'm wrong, but it's in your file that you ride your Harley every chance you get."

I couldn't hold back a snort of amusement. "He's at best what bikers call a 'weekend warrior.'"

Gavin glared at me. "I sure as hell could hold my own if I had to."

Picking up Bishop's picture, I waved it in front of his face. "You're telling me you could be BFFs with this guy and be convincing as a hard-ass biker?" When Gavin jerked his chin up defiantly at me, I merely smiled at Peterson. "For him to even remotely have a chance, you need to book him for one hell of a makeover—the best the bureau has when it comes to undercover. I'd start at the top, with weeding out the hair product, and then work my way down."

"Bitch," Gavin muttered under his breath, but then he winked at me.

After wiping his mouth with his napkin, Peterson said, "You also need to come up with a new last name. We don't want anything that can be traced back to you."

Gavin tilted his head in thought. After a few seconds, he said, "Marley."

Wrinkling my nose, I questioned, "Why Marley?"

"'Cause I love me some Bob Marley, and then my initials don't have to change just in case I draw a blank sometime."

I rolled my eyes but laughed in spite of myself. Jerking my chin at Peterson, I said, "So it sounds like you have Gavin all sorted out. I can't help asking where I come in."

Peterson shifted uncomfortably. "One of the last places you can be 'out' and be accepted is in the biker world." He stared straight at Gavin. "As an attractive man, you will immediately garner the attention of the sweet butts and club whores."

Gavin swept a hand to his chest. "Thanks for the compliment."

With a shake of his head, Peterson added, "But the first time one puts her tits in your face or grinds her ass on your dick and you don't rise to the occasion, so to speak, you're in big trouble."

"I could fake it," Gavin argued.

"Too much is riding on this case to put you in that position." His expression grew grave. "Although we have no proof that the Raiders have ever participated in this type of initiation, some prospects for other clubs have been forced to show their allegiance to a club by gang-raping women."

"Jesus," Gavin muttered.

"There's no way in hell we can have an ATF agent partake in such violence, and if you were to refuse, you could lose your life." His gaze flickered to mine. "That's why we're sending you in with him as his girlfriend."

With the tension high in the air, I couldn't help the nervous laugh that bubbled from my lips. "You're joking."

"No, I'm dead serious. With you at his side or on his lap, Gavin won't have to worry about female attention, nor will he be expected to partake in any illegal activity with women. At the same time, women can fly under the radar in MCs. If Gavin were to appear to be nosing around, he could get his ass kicked. No one suspects a woman who is just hanging around."

I nodded. "I understand."

Gavin smacked my thigh under the table. "Guess this means you'll be expanding your slutty wardrobe to be my babe."

When I realized what he meant, I groaned. "I'm going to have to wear spandex with my boobs hanging out, aren't I?"

Peterson laughed. "I'm afraid so. Although Gavin isn't an MC member, you will want to fit in with how the other women in the club dress."

"I highly doubt the president's wife and former deb dresses like a hooker."

"Yeah, well, you're not a former deb. You're just a simple mechanic's girlfriend," Gavin argued with a smile.

"Lucky me," I muttered.

As I listened to Peterson discuss the reading material and video the bureau expected us to submerge ourselves in, I took a few moments to get my head together. There was little I feared in this world—years of law enforcement training had toughened and hardened me. But bikers were my equivalent of a childhood bogeyman and an adult Grim Reaper.

Not even in my wildest dreams could I have imagined how much my life was about to change because of a biker named Bishop Malloy.

THREE

SAMANTHA

Just as I was adding an extra coat of eyeliner, the doorbell rang, causing me to jump and send a squiggly black line up my temple. "Fuck," I muttered before grabbing a tissue and rubbing off the liner. To say that I was slightly on edge tonight about my first meeting with the Raiders would have been a mild understatement. It pissed me off that I was letting them have an effect on me. After all, I'd taken down criminals who on paper were a hell of a lot more intimidating than a bunch of small-town bikers. But tonight it all really boiled down to the merging of my past and present.

Leaning out of the bathroom, I called, "It's open."

The beep of the security system went off as Gavin opened the door and stepped inside. "I know you've moved up to the East Side and all with a house in this posh neighborhood, but you still need to lock your door, for fuck's sake."

I grunted and stepped back in the bathroom. "I knew you were coming, dickhead."

He chuckled as he walked down the length of the hallway to meet me at the half bath. When I looked at his reflection in the mirror, he was doing a sweep of my attire—the practically painted-on black jeans, the skintight black top, and the knee-length leather boots. When he met my eye in the mirror, he winked at me. "Looking good, Vargas."

"So you won't be ashamed to call me your old lady?"

He waggled a finger at me. "Wrong terminology. Hang-arounds don't have old ladies—only full-patched members."

"Yeah, yeah," I muttered.

Gavin tsked at me. "Do I need to tell Peterson you're not doing your homework?"

"I've done my homework, asshole," I snapped, brushing past him out into the hallway. Normally, his ribbing wouldn't have gotten to me, but tonight was a different story altogether.

I didn't get too far before Gavin pulled me to him. "You wanna talk about it?"

"About what?"

"Whatever it is about this case that has you spooked."

A shiver went down my spine at his words, but I quickly recovered. "There is nothing about a bunch of beer-guzzling lowlifes that has me spooked." I wiggled out of his arms and once again started down the hall.

Just as I reached to grab my purse, his next words froze me from head to toe. "So a man named Willie Bates means nothing to you."

My eyes pinched shut as my chest heaved. There is no adequate way to describe the emotional shit storm that hits you when your past and present collide. I didn't even hear Gavin walk down the hall, but then suddenly he was at my side. "What do you know?" I questioned in a whisper so low my voice was barely audible.

"Everything." When I dared to look at him over my shoulder, he gave me a sad smile. "I'd never seen you react the way that you did when Peterson gave us this case, so I did a little digging."

"Does Peterson know?"

"No. Only me. And it's going to stay that way."

Although my heart swelled with the surge of love I had for Gavin and his loyalty, I still exhaled in defeat as I leaned back against the front door. "From what you've discovered, you should request that I be taken off the case." When Gavin started to shake his head, I held my hand up to silence whatever argument he had prepared. "I'm a deficit, and you can't afford a deficit out in the field."

He reached out to cup my face. "You could never be a deficit, Vargas. You're the only one I would ever want to work with. I know that no matter what happened to you when you were eight years old, when it comes down to it, you'll have your game face on and your shit together."

Although I hated myself for them, tears stung my eyes. "You really mean that?"

"Yeah, I do."

I swiped away some of my mascara-blackened tears. "I'm sorry I didn't tell you."

"I can understand why you didn't. That was some horrible shit done to your father and in turn to you. It's nobody's business, really."

Trying to lighten some of the tension in the air, I grabbed both of his biceps and squeezed hard before pushing him away. "Why, why can't you be straight?"

Gavin laughed heartily. "You and I make a great business partnership, Vargas, but there's no way in hell we could ever be married."

Cocking my head at him, I countered, "Is that right?"

"It is, and deep down, you know I'm right."

I did know Gavin was right. We were too much alike to ever make any relationship besides friendship work. In the end, we were closer than friends. We were more like brother and sister.

Waggling my eyebrows, I said, "Yeah, well, maybe I wasn't talking about us marrying. Maybe I meant for us to have hot, sweaty sex." At Gavin's horrified face, I couldn't help laughing. "Gotcha with that one."

"So not funny," he muttered.

"It's good to know how repulsed you are by the idea of having sex with me," I teased as I walked down the hall to the bathroom to fix my makeup.

"Oh, for fuck's sake, Vargas. It's not about having sex with you. It's about having sex with a vagina, period, that wigs me."

I snorted as I reapplied some powder to cover the tracks of my tears. Gavin appeared in the doorway.

"But regardless of all that, you're the only woman I would ever consider going straight for."

I smiled at his reflection in the mirror. "Aw, you can be awfully sweet when you want to, McTavish."

He came over and turned me around. After bestowing a kiss on my cheek, he winked. "Come on, hot stuff. Let's go show the bikers how it's done."

While I didn't share his confidence or enthusiasm, I nodded in agreement. After turning on the security system, I followed him out the front door. In my driveway was a motorcycle the bureau had provided for Gavin. On a lowly mechanic's salary, Gavin wouldn't have been able to afford the bikes that he owned, so instead, the bureau had gotten him one that would fit in better with his persona—which he of course hated.

"What a hunk of junk," I teased as I grabbed my helmet off the back.

"I fucking loathe and despise every moment on this piece of shit," Gavin replied.

"Looks like you could've lent yourself some street cred by pretending you had stolen one of your bikes."

As Gavin slid onto the worn leather seat, he grunted. "Don't think I didn't take that angle with Peterson."

I laughed as I climbed on behind him. My arms slid around his waist to grip him tight. Riding bitch on a motorcycle was something I hated almost as much as having to dress like a hooker. Gavin and I had spent several evenings riding together after work to make sure I looked like a natural on the back of his bike. But those had been only short trips around the neighborhood and in town. Tonight would be the farthest I had ever been on a bike.

We sped off into the night, leaving my house, my comfortable life, and my usual .40-caliber Glock behind. The Raiders clubhouse was a good forty-five minutes north of Marietta, the Atlanta suburb where I lived. After Gavin started scaring the hell out of me as he careened in and out of the Friday evening traffic, I closed my eyes and focused on the briefing we had had earlier in the day with Peterson.

Tonight was a huge opportunity for our case. Gavin had spent weeks slowly befriending Bishop Malloy, and it had finally culminated in Gavin—or Marley, as he was known to Bishop—being invited to a hang out at the clubhouse.

While Gavin was to keep his eyes and ears open with all members of the Raiders, not just Bishop, I was to focus my attention solely on Bishop. As the sergeant at arms, he would be the most connected to the gun trade, not counting the president and vice president. Because of the type of man he was known to be, I was to pull out all the stops when it came to using my feminine wiles. While his two brothers, Deacon and Rev, were settled down and married, Bishop was the epitome of a womanizer. His greatest joy in life outside the club was to flirt and fuck, and my intent was to use that against him. It was the old cliché of a woman driving a man to distraction, and that distraction being used to slip him up and eventually take him down.

When we got off the interstate, the terrain began to change. We started to wind around curvy roads and climb small hills. I could see the mountains off in the distance. It was hard to imagine an MC staking claim in the backwoods, but apparently that was where the Georgia chapter of the Raiders made their home.

I knew where the roadhouse was long before we reached it. Far off in the distance, I saw a building ablaze with lights, and bikes lining the parking lot. Gavin surprised me by not turning in but parking away from the others. But then I remembered something I had read, that only fully patched members parked their bikes together, and in turn, those bikes were watched over by a prospect. Everyone else was on his own.

After Gavin killed the engine, he glanced over his shoulder at me. "How are you doing?"

"Fine," I said—a lie, considering that my anxiety had spiked from zero to a hundred just from being on the Raiders' property.

When Gavin chuckled, I knew he saw through my line of bullshit. After he stood up and took off his helmet, he helped me. "You're going to be fine, Vargas."

I held up a hand. "Please. No more pep talking. I can't begin to tell you how thankful I am that we're not wired up tonight, because I would die a thousand deaths before I would want Peterson or the others to see me so fucking fragile."

"I promise no one will ever know my ball-busting bitch turned chickenshit. Okay?"

I laughed as I smacked his arm playfully. "Thanks."

"Okay. Let's do this."

We started across the parking lot toward the roadhouse. As I worked to control my breathing, Gavin slid a comforting arm around my waist. To others it would look like a possessive move to show ownership over me, but I knew in his mind he was doing it to try to put me at ease.

When we got to the front door, a burly tattooed guy with multiple piercings guarded the entrance. "Can I help you?"

Without missing a beat, Gavin said, "Yeah, we're here for the party."

Tattoo Guy smirked skeptically at Gavin. "Is that right?"

"It sure as hell is. Just ask Bishop."

"You Marley?" When Gavin nodded in acknowledgment, Tattoo Guy stepped aside. "Enjoy yourself."

"Thanks," Gavin said.

As we walked in the door, I somewhat expected everyone to turn and stare at us—confirmation of the true outsiders we were. But no one really looked our way, and if they did, we were greeted with a nod of acknowledgment. Across the room, a house band had music pumping out of the speakers, and couples danced on a makeshift dance floor. Others hung around the bar, sipping on beers and mixed drinks.

Gavin started to take a step forward, but I froze. Each time my gaze fell on a biker, he became my father's murderer standing in front of me. My heartbeat accelerated wildly in my chest, and I fought to breathe. Ducking my head, I pinched my eyes shut and started counting to ten in my mind.

"Sam, are you okay?" Gavin whispered in my ear. The fact that he called me by my first name meant he was truly worried.

"Bathroom. I need a bathroom," I gasped. When he started to lead me across the room, I jerked back and shook my head. "No. I do this on my own. You go on. I'll catch up to you."

Gavin's eyes widened. "Are you sure?"

"Yeah. Just give me ten to get my shit together."

He looked as though he wanted to argue with me, so I pulled away from him and started across the floor. At the food table, I spotted the vice president's wife, Alexandra, bouncing a dark-haired baby boy on her hip. I knew all about her from the files I had read, and just like with the president's wife, I had been surprised that someone like her, a teacher from a respected, middle-class family, would have taken up with a biker.

"Excuse me. Where's the bathroom?" I asked.

When her dark eyes met mine, a look of confusion came over her face, which wasn't too surprising. I was sure she knew all the old ladies, girlfriends, and sweet butts of the club. The expression was quickly replaced by a smile. "Just down the hall from the kitchen," she replied, motioning to the right.

"Thank you." Without a word to her or the other women, I made a beeline down the hall. I burst through the door that signified it was for women by a pair of giant carved boobs on it. It was packed full of scantily dressed women fighting for mirror time as they worked on their hair and makeup. I bypassed them and went into one of the stalls.

Once I was safely closed inside, I placed my palms flat against the graffiti-colored walls. I tucked my head to my chest and once again began taking deep, cleansing breaths in and out. In my head, I kept repeating the mantra I had adopted many years ago. *I am stronger than my fear. I am stronger than my fear. I am stronger than my fear.*

After what felt like an eternity but was probably only a few minutes, the overwhelming panic began to dissipate. I started slowly feeling like myself again—my strong, courageous kick-ass self. Pulling my head up, I rolled my shoulders to ease the tension the anxiety had brought on.

With my courage renewed, I focused on the task ahead of me.

Throwing open the stall door, I made my way out of the bathroom. After entering the main room, I didn't even falter when a hulking biker with gleaming silver piercings and arms covered in multi-colored tattoos bumped into me. "Sorry, sugar," he drawled.

I gave him my best smile before craning my neck to search for Gavin. I found him sitting alone at a table, nursing a beer. When I started to get near the table, he jerked his gaze to mine as if he had sensed me approaching.

After I took a seat next to him, he asked, "You okay?"

"Never better." Knocking his hand away, I took his beer and downed the rest in one foamy gulp. When Gavin's eyebrows shot up questioningly, I shook my head. "Look, it was exactly as I said. I just needed a minute to get my shit together. You have nothing to worry about."

He grinned at my forceful tone. "Never said I was worried."

"You didn't have to. I could tell by your face and the fact that you called me Sam."

Gavin took his beer back from me. "Ready?"

"More than ready. What happened while I was gone?"

"Bishop got me a beer on the house and told me to have a seat. I thought he was coming over to talk, but then he got called away."

My eyes narrowed in suspicion. "Some backdoor meeting?"

With a chuckle, Gavin replied, "More like some hot piece of ass with her tits hanging out of her top asked him to dance."

I rolled my eyes in a huff. "Men. Don't you ever think with anything besides your dicks?"

"Nope," Gavin replied with a wink.

Turning away from Gavin, I focused my gaze on the dance floor. It took only a second to spot Bishop through the crowd of other bikers. Gavin had adequately described the woman Bishop was with. At the moment, they were bumping and grinding to where they might as well have been having sex on the floor. Out of nowhere a flush of warmth spread over me, the same way Bishop's hands ran over the woman's body. It seemed to get even hotter when I watched the expert way his hips pumped against hers.

Leaning forward in my chair, I continued to study my target. The pictures the bureau had shown me didn't quite do Bishop justice. Although it should have been the last thing on my mind, I couldn't help thinking he was far more good-looking in person. He certainly appeared more built—his muscles more defined, his chest broader, and his thighs thicker. His body exuded power and strength—two things that came in handy for him as a boxer and the sergeant at arms.

I couldn't help snorting at how I felt like an airhead sorority girl with these lustful thoughts running through my mind.

"He's completely fuckable, isn't he?" Gavin asked in a low voice.

Oh hell yes. Very, very fuckable, I thought as I fought the urge to squirm in my seat. Needing to hide my illicit thoughts from Gavin, I said, "Just what the hell are you talking about?"

Gavin waggled his eyebrows. "Don't think I didn't notice the way you were just looking at him."

"I was assessing the target, smart-ass."

"Bullshit. Your panties were getting wet as you thought about what it would be like if you were that woman."

What woman wouldn't? "You're out of your fucking mind," I countered.

Leaning in to whisper in my ear, Gavin said, "I may bat for the other team, but I still know when a woman is hot for a man."

Rolling my eyes, I shoved him away. In a low voice, I growled, "He is the target in our case—not to mention the enemy."

"Yeah, and hate sex can be hot as hell."

"You are impossible."

Gavin grinned wickedly at me. "Even though it's frowned upon, I see nothing wrong with getting a good fuck or two out of him to gain information."

"I would slap the hell out of you right now if we weren't supposed to look like a loving couple."

After bestowing a kiss on my cheek, Gavin winked at me. "There's nothing more I love in life than to irritate the hell out of you."

"Asshole," I replied, although I smiled in spite of myself.

Nodding at Bishop, Gavin asked, "When he finishes humping that chick, you want me to get the ball rolling and introduce you?" When I cocked my eyebrows at him, he held up a hand. "I meant the ball rolling for the case, not for you to actually get busy with him. Jeez, Vargas, I can be serious when I have to be."

"Yeah, and part of you really enjoyed the double meaning in all that."

Gavin grinned. "Maybe." The song started to wind down. "So, do we make a move now?"

My gaze once again returned to Bishop. "No. Not yet."

"You got something in mind?" Gavin questioned.

I finally tore my gaze from Bishop to look at Gavin. "I need to unsettle him a bit before I make my move."

"Sounds like a good plan."

"I wouldn't exactly call it a plan." Looking back at Bishop, I smiled. "It's more like a game. One that I know just how to play to win."

With a wink, Gavin said, "You know your game, Vargas. Go roll the dice."

FOUR

BISHOP

For the hundredth fucking time, I felt eyes on me, stalking my every move. The extra scrutiny sent the hair on the backs of my arms tingling. If I had been anywhere else but inside the safety of the clubhouse and among my brothers, the freaky feeling would have had me reaching inside my cut to palm my gun. But in this case, I knew I wasn't in any real danger.

Casually, I glanced over my shoulder to take in the crowd. The clubhouse was at full capacity for a Saturday night. The house band was cranking out tunes, and couples were in the middle of the floor bumping and grinding. With Rev gone on his honeymoon and Deacon off on a Brownies' camping trip with his daughter, Willow, I was the only Malloy in residence. Though our president and vice president were gone, it didn't stop the remaining Raiders from having one of our weekend parties.

Even without looking, I could have guessed who was eyeballing me. A month ago, a new mechanic had started at the garage where

I was apprenticing. His name was Marley, and he was former army. That alone made me respect the hell out of him, but then that respect grew one day when we were eating lunch and shooting the shit. I discovered he was a motorcycle enthusiast whose knowledge of bikes could put some of the Raiders to shame. Then a week ago he gained my complete and total respect by saving my ass.

I was doing an oil change on a Dodge Challenger when a man came stalking up. He looked vaguely familiar, as though I might've seen him at the garage before. "Can I help you?"

"Yeah, you're the fucker who screwed up my car."

"Excuse me?"

"The transmission is shot to hell now. I realize you're new and everything, but I don't know how the fuck you managed to screw it up so bad."

"Sir, your car was fine when you left. I don't know how you could possibly think I did something wrong."

The man's face darkened. "I don't give a rat's ass what you think. Get me your boss. Now."

I bit my tongue to tell the man he could go fuck himself, which would have been the way I once handled the situation. But since I was trying to turn over a new leaf, I grumbled, "One second." I brushed past Marley, who had come out from underneath the car he had been working on. Knocking on my boss's door, I called, "Rick?"

He glanced up from a pile of invoices. "Yeah?"

"There's a dude who wants to see you." When Rick raised his eyebrows questioningly, I sighed. "He thinks I fucked up his car."

"Did you?"

"Hell no. It was just a standard oil change and tire rotation. When I told him his check-engine light was on, he told me it was because of the oil."

After grunting in frustration, Rick rose out of his chair. I stepped aside for him to come out the door and then I followed him down the hall. Once the man saw him, he started ranting and raving about how during the oil change I had screwed up his transmission.

He was halfway through his tirade when Marley stepped forward. "You're full of shit."

The man's jaw dropped. "Excuse me?" he demanded.

Crossing his arms over his chest, Marley said, "There's no way in hell Bishop could have done the damage you're talking about."

"Is that so?"

Marley nodded and then looked at Rick. "The guy came in here with a car wheezing like a two-pack-a-day smoker. Anything wrong with his transmission was already there, with the car wheezing like that."

Rick glanced from Marley to me. "Did you notice the noise, too?"

I grimaced. "No, I didn't."

"In Bishop's defense, he was in the back when the guy pulled up. He wouldn't have been able to diagnose that," Marley said.

It was my turn for my jaw to drop at Marley stretching the truth for me. Yeah, I had been doing inventory, but I still should have heard the noise when the guy drove away. I didn't know where in the hell my head had been that day to miss something like that. When I met Marley's gaze, he cocked his head at me as if daring me to go against his story. I bobbed my head in agreement.

The man sputtered with indignation. "That doesn't mean shit. He still fucked up my car!"

Rick narrowed his eyes. "You must think I'm an idiot if you really think you can screw up a transmission that bad through a simple oil change. Get the hell out of here, and don't ever come around here trying to scam me again."

After the man left and Rick went back to his office, Marley and I were alone. When he started to go back to work, I stopped him. "Why did you lie for me?"

"I wouldn't exactly call it lying—it was more like stretching the truth."

"Then why did you stretch the truth for me?"

Marley smiled. "We've all been the new guy once. Yeah, you probably should have noticed the wheezing when he pulled out of here, but maybe you were just having an off day. Maybe your mind was somewhere else. Hell, maybe you had to take a leak or a dump really bad and couldn't think of anything else."

"Hey, now." I laughed.

With a chuckle, Marley added, "That one little fact doesn't mean you aren't a damn good mechanic who knows his cars."

"I never would have fucked up with a motorcycle," I grumbled.

"That's probably true, considering what a hard-on you have for bikes, but I guarantee you'll never miss a transmission issue ever again."

"Fuck no." I held out my hand to him. "Thanks, man. I owe you one."

He pumped my hand up and down. "You're welcome." After dropping my hand, he started back to the car he had been working on. Staring at his back, I thought about what kind of man he was and couldn't help thinking he would make a great member of the Raiders one day. After everything that had gone down with Mendoza, we were actively looking to bring in a few new guys to steady things until the heat wore off. We were still slowly and surely moving toward being legitimate, and Marley's character would certainly fit in with our new direction.

All it had taken was a call to my brother during my next break. Rev had answered on the third ring. "What's up, B?" he'd asked.

"I wanted to run something by you."

"Shoot."

"I think I got a lead on a good hang-around."

"Really?"

"Yeah." Then I'd given Rev the lowdown on Marley. "Think it'd be okay to invite him to a party so we can feel him out?"

"Sure. Why not? We'll put Archer on his ass pronto. You know how he thinks he can sniff out rats."

I laughed. "Okay. Sounds good."

After I'd hung up with Rev, I put my phone back in my pocket and went inside. Marley was underneath a car that was up on the hydraulics.

"Hey, you ever think about joining a motorcycle club?" I asked.

Marley had glanced at me over his shoulder. "Maybe. Why?"

"I just happen to be part of one. Actually, I'm a little more than a part of one. I'm an officer in the Hells Raiders."

"I think I might've heard of them."

"You probably didn't hear anything too good about them."

Turning around, Marley had said, "Heard a bit."

My eyebrows rose at his summation. "Yeah, well, maybe everything you heard wasn't true."

"I'm listening."

I'd walked over to him so I could lower my voice. "It's a long process to join. You have to start at the very bottom as a hang-around. Then if everyone agrees, we could let you prospect. That's the hardest part of joining because you basically get treated like everyone's bitch."

Marley had smiled and shrugged. "Yeah, I've heard some shit about the prospecting period. To be honest, I've never really given the whole club scene a lot of thought. I just love to ride."

"That's what the club is really all about."

Marley had appeared thoughtful for a couple of minutes. "Maybe I could give it a try."

"I'm glad to hear you say that." I'd made sure we were completely alone before saying anything further. "Look, we're having a party this Saturday night. Why don't you come and see what you think?"

Marley had seemed to weigh my words for a few moments before he nodded. "Okay. That sounds good."

From his table across the room in the clubhouse, Marley worked on draining another beer. I'd found him the table earlier and insisted on buying him a beer. I owed him at least that much for saving my ass. I'd introduced him to several of the guys, and he seemed to be enjoying himself. I'd meant to sit down with him, but my newest piece of ass had come up and insisted we dance. My dick couldn't seem to tell her no.

But the stares I was getting weren't coming from Marley. In fact, he hadn't glanced in my direction all night. No, it was the fine-as-hell woman beside him who had been doing her best at eye-fucking me.

Tonight was the first night I had had the pleasure and the pain of meeting Marley's girlfriend. He'd mentioned her in passing during our lunchtime conversations. I hadn't paid too close attention, so I couldn't remember if her name was Sandy or Samantha. Since she was his age, she had at least five years on me, and that fact made me want to volunteer to be her cougar cub.

If there was one word to describe her looks, it was exotic. Sure, she was probably more an ethnic mutt than anything, but it made for one hell of an attractive combination. She looked more Hispanic than anything else, but her almond-shaped eyes gave her an Asian appearance. I hadn't failed to notice that she had turned the heads of more than one of my brothers tonight. I just hoped the leering looks hadn't pissed off Marley.

When she realized I was looking at her, a catlike smile curved her ruby-red lips. She tossed some strands of her silky jet-black hair over her shoulder. Sitting beside her, Marley didn't act as if he noticed anything that she was doing.

Even though he wasn't a patch-wearing brother, I still shouldn't have been giving her the eye. You didn't fuck around with women who belonged to your brothers. It usually led to trouble of the fist-flying kind. And even though there were more than enough hot pieces of available ass here, I couldn't help letting my mind wander to places it shouldn't with that woman.

My ears perked up at the sound of a baby's cry. I knew the cry very well, since it belonged to my nephew, Wyatt. As I headed across the main room of the roadhouse, I could see Alexandra in the doorway to the kitchen, walking around, trying to pacify the fussy baby.

"What's wrong with the little man?" I asked.

Alexandra huffed out a frustrated breath. "I have no idea. He's just been fed and had his diaper changed, but he insists on being whiny." She kissed the top of her son's dark-haired head. "Truth be told, I think he's sick of me. With Deacon gone camping with Willow, he's had no one else to amuse him the past three days."

"Here, let me take him."

Alexandra's eyebrows rose in surprise. "Really?" When I nodded, she passed him into my waiting arms. He immediately dried up the sniffling and gazed into my face. "Who knew you were so good with babies?" Alexandra mused.

With a wink, I added, "Nah, it's more about the fact that he's had too much tit time. He needs to be with some men for a while."

"You're terrible," she replied, smacking my arm playfully.

"You love me, though," I teased.

Alexandra leaned over and bestowed a kiss on my cheek. "Yes, I do. Very much." Patting Wyatt's back, she then said, "Bring him to me when you get tired of him or he gets tired of you."

"Sure thing."

As I walked Wyatt around the main room, several of my brothers stopped to talk to us while their old ladies or girlfriends cooed at Wyatt. Although he was all Alexandra when it came to looks, Wyatt was like his old man and knew how to work a crowd. He grinned and waved his hands, drawing smiles from everyone we talked to.

"What a little cutie," a voice said behind me.

I turned around to find my eye-fucker standing behind me. Damn, she was even more smokin' hot up close. "Thanks."

"Is he yours?" she asked.

"Oh hell no. He's my brother's."

She smiled as she reached out to stroke Wyatt's chubby cheek. "I take it you don't have any of your own."

"That would once again be a hell no."

"You're awfully good with him."

"I like kids just as long as they belong to someone else," I answered honestly. When Wyatt reached for her, she looked at me to gauge my response. "Sure. You can hold him."

Wyatt happily dove into her waiting arms. "Aren't you a charmer?" she murmured, to which Wyatt gurgled happily.

"I don't think we've met," I said as she sweet-talked Wyatt.

"I'm Samantha."

Extending my hand, I said, "I'm Bishop."

"Nice to meet you," she said as she balanced Wyatt in one arm and shook my hand with the other.

From her introduction, I knew she was as new to the MC lifestyle as Marley was. Most of the women we associated with knew that when introducing themselves, they were to say which man they belonged to and, depending on the type of party, which chapter her man belonged to. "You're Marley's girlfriend."

She nodded. "I am."

"I've heard lots about you."

Her dark eyebrows rose in suspicion. "You have?"

With a wink, I replied, "It was all good. I promise."

Samantha smiled. "I'm glad to hear that."

"I take it this is your first MC party?"

"Yeah. It is."

"And what do you think about it?"

After glancing around the room, she answered, "It's interesting."

I laughed. "This one is pretty tame. Wait until you go to a rally."

"How's a rally different?"

"Well, it's more of a drunken free-for-all with lots of half-naked people hooking up in the broad daylight." When she widened her eyes, I added, "It has to be seen to be believed."

After wrinkling her nose, she said, "Somehow I don't know if I like the sound of that."

"You'll get used to it. Especially if Marley becomes a prospect."

She nodded. "I mean, don't get me wrong. I do love a good party. I'm just not sure I want to see a bunch of naked strangers getting it on." With a grin, she added, "I can see better porn from the comfort of my own home."

I laughed. "I like your way of thinking."

It was at that moment Marley appeared. "Hey, B, I see you finally got to meet my girl."

"You're a lucky man," I replied.

Marley shot me a broad grin before leaning over to plant a smacking kiss on Samantha's lips, which caused her to jerk back slightly. Her reaction seemed a little weird, but then she gave him a beaming smile. "I guess I better hand over this cutie," she said. After I took Wyatt back from her, she said, "Thanks for letting me hold him."

"Anytime."

She then slid her arm around Marley's waist as they started away from me. Just as they got halfway across the room, she glanced over her shoulder at me, giving me that catlike smile again. I jerked my chin up at her in acknowledgment.

When she turned her head, I groaned, which caused Wyatt to glance up at me in surprise. I smiled at him. "Little Man, your uncle is in deep shit."

I spent the rest of the evening trying not to think, least of all fantasize, about Samantha. It was a losing battle. Even as I tried occupying my mind by making the rounds and talking to other club members, I couldn't stop thinking about her. Most of the thoughts involved having her on her back while pounding her senseless.

After about an hour of trying to avoid her and my out-of-control sexual thoughts, I somehow managed to end up at the pool table where she and Marley were playing. Just as I thought about running away, Marley handed me his stick. "Why don't you try a round? I'm getting my ass kicked and my wallet fleeced at the moment."

With a chuckle, I motioned to one of our newest patch members, Crazy Ace. "He's a real hustler."

Marley groaned. "Don't I know it?"

Motioning to the pool table, I said, "Rack 'em up. Let's see if you can do any better against me."

Samantha shook her head. "He's just going to end up embarrassing himself by having to bum money off me."

"Hey, now," Marley countered with a smile.

"Truth hurts, babe," Samantha said before leaning up to kiss Marley. I fought the urge to toss my stick on the table and walk away. Instead, I took the chalk and rubbed some on my cue.

A tap on my shoulder had me whirling around. It was Joe Casterini, or Jolting Joe, our newest prospect. He was also the bartender when we had parties. "Hey, B, we're just about out of beer on tap."

I nodded. "Take one of the other prospects and run down to the warehouse. There should be some kegs there."

"Sounds like a plan, except I'm the only prospect here tonight," Joe replied.

"Shit. That's right."

Holding up his hand, Joe said, "I can totally handle it alone."

Even if he couldn't make it up the hill with the steel keg, he knew as a prospect he shouldn't try to pussy out of a situation. I glanced over at Marley. "Hey, man, want to help out?"

He grinned as he set his beer down on the pool table's edge. "You bet your ass I'm down for anything that involves more beer."

With a laugh, I said, "Glad you're so eager to help."

"Seriously, though. I've been thinking about what you said about joining up with the club. Figure that helping out and pitching in is all part of it, right?" Marley asked.

"Yeah. It sure as hell is."

"Then I'm always down for that."

I smacked him on the back. "Can see that one."

Joe waved his hand. "Come on, man. Let's get this shit taken care of before the natives get restless."

"Okay," Marley said. He then followed Joe out of the roadhouse. When I turned back to the others, I noticed it wasn't just Crazy Ace and Samantha anymore. One of the newest sweet butts appeared to be glued to Crazy Ace's side. As she whispered in his ear, his eyes got glassy, and I knew that pool was the last thing on his mind. "See ya later, B," he said as he let the girl lead him away to one of the back rooms.

That left me all alone with Samantha. We stood in awkward silence for a few seconds before I held out a stick to her. "You play?"

She shrugged. "A little."

"Then let's have a go."

Samantha took the stick. "Just promise you'll go easy on me."

"I'll try," I said.

"Good."

As I racked up the balls, I said, "Marley hasn't told me too much about you."

"Glad to know he's keeping my secrets."

I cocked my head at her. "You got secrets?"

She shrugged. "Maybe . . . maybe not." After tossing her long dark hair over her shoulder, she pinned me with a stare. "Don't we all have secrets?"

"I guess so."

"It's been my observation that everyone has his or her own set of personal secrets. Hell, we even have some professional ones along the way."

"That's an interesting thought." Placing my palms on the edge of the table, I smiled at her. "Wanna trade some secrets?"

"What did you have in mind?"

I jerked my chin at the table. "For every ball the winner sinks, the loser has to give up something about himself."

"Sounds interesting."

"I thought as much."

Samantha leaned in on her cue, swaying her hips as she looked at me. "How can I be sure the odds aren't stacked against me? You know, since I'm new to the game and all."

"I said I would go easy on you."

She gave me a skeptical look. "Hmm, we'll see."

"How about this? To demonstrate my good intentions, I'll let you go first."

"Aren't you being sweet?" she teased.

"I try."

She took me off guard when she asked, "Stripes or solids?"

"Huh?"

With a grin, Samantha replied, "I was asking which balls you wanted—stripes or solids?"

"If I were really being sweet, it should be lady's choice, shouldn't it?"

"My, my, you sure are a gentleman," she mused as she brushed past me. It didn't go unnoticed how her breasts felt as they made brief contact with my chest. I was still thinking about her fabulous tits when she said, "I'll take solids, then."

I cleared my throat while I also tried clearing my mind. "Sounds good."

When I had suggested playing with her, I hadn't stopped long enough to think about what she was going to look like bent over the pool table. If I'd had any idea what a vision of pure sex she would look like, I would have tucked my tail between my legs and headed for the hills. Samantha's tight-as-hell pants gave me a great view of her perfectly rounded ass cheeks—the kind that when you were fucking doggy-style, you wanted to smack until you left a red handprint. When I leaned forward, I saw how her almost-double-D tits were spilling out the front of her shirt. There was no doubt I was going to end the night with balls as blue as some of the ones on the table.

When Samantha called, "Blue ten. Corner left pocket," I couldn't help noticing the irony. After she knocked the ball effortlessly across the table and into the pocket, my mouth dropped open in utter shock.

"Why am I thinking that wasn't beginner's luck and you've been hustling me?" I asked.

She batted her eyes innocently at me. "I don't know what you're talking about."

"I think I'll start calling you Fast Eddie."

"Ah, after Edward Felson?"

My jaw dropped in surprise. "You know Fast Eddie, the pool hustler?"

Samantha laughed. "Actually, it's more like I know my Paul Newman, and since he played Fast Eddie in *The Hustler* and *The Color of Money*, I know the character."

"I see." Closing the gap between us, I asked, "How did you learn to play pool?"

"Uh, uh, uh. I believe by the rules of your game, *I'm* the one who gets to ask the question."

I grunted in frustration. "Fine. Ask away."

Samantha drummed her bloodred nails on the edge of the pool table. "Hmm, this is harder than I thought it would be. I feel a little pressure to not ask some bullshit question."

"You can always forfeit and let me go."

"Oh no, you're not getting off that easy."

"Damn. At least I tried."

After momentarily closing her eyes, she opened them. "Okay. I have one."

"I can't wait to see what you came up with."

"What's something you're good at that I wouldn't be able to guess?"

With a smirk, I replied, "I don't think you really want me to answer that."

While I expected her to roll her eyes in exasperation when she got my meaning, she surprised me by pursing her lips. "I would think you being good at fucking would be a given. Right?"

I laughed. "Damn straight."

"So, what's something else—something that sets you apart from your MC brothers?"

After thinking for a moment, I answered, "Boxing."

"Interesting."

"I like to think so."

"Do you do it as an amateur or professionally?"

"Professionally. Or I used to."

"Why aren't you doing it anymore?"

"Whoa, I thought this was a one-ball, one-question kinda thing?"

Samantha hopped up on the table edge as if she was settling in to hear a long story. Swinging her legs back and forth, she said, "I've never known any real-life boxers before, so you can't fault me for being intrigued."

I tapped the bottom of my cue stick on the floor. I had never talked to anyone outside the club or the gym about boxing. None of the women I had dated, or I guess I should say fucked, gave two shits about it. Mama Beth wanted nothing to do with it, considering that it was a blood sport that got her baby boy injured. But for reasons I couldn't possibly imagine, Samantha seemed seriously interested.

"The main reason I'm not doing it so much anymore is I'm ready to do something else. It doesn't hold the same excitement for me that it once did. I guess you could say I want to do more with my life than beat the shit out of dudes."

"I think wanting to do something else besides fighting is totally understandable—if not commendable. I'm just not sure how you'll be able to do that with the lifestyle you're in."

"Why do you say that?"

"Isn't throwing punches all part of being in an MC?"

"Ah, I see you're subscribing to the shitty image most people have of bikers."

"I'm sorry if it sounded like I was stereotyping you. I guess I'm just ignorant when it comes to what real MC men are like."

Leaning in closer to her, I said, "Since Marley is considering joining an MC, it's probably a good idea if you take the time to really know what you're talking about. We're not all gun-wielding hell-raisers who terrorize towns."

"You're not?"

From her tone and expression, I didn't know whether she was serious or teasing me. "Last time I checked, we get along pretty well with most of the people here in town—you know, the law-abiding ones."

"Bishop—"

"As for a weapon, I would ask you to pat me down to check for one, but I don't think that would be appropriate."

"No. It wouldn't."

"At least I offered."

With a genuinely apologetic look, Samantha said, "I'm sorry if I insulted you and your club."

I shrugged. "It's okay. It's not like I'm not used to it by now. Even before I patched in to the club myself, I saw the way some people treated my dad. Then as soon as they heard I was John Malloy's son, they treated me differently, too. That kinda shit happened from the time I was in school."

"That was a really shitty thing to do to a kid just because of who his dad was."

Staring down at the floor, I replied, "Yeah, when I was young, I got my feelings hurt easily. By the time I got to be a teenager, I probably gave them a reason to judge me by having a chip on my shoulder." When I dared to look at Samantha, she was looking at me with respect.

"How did you get over it?"

"I finally decided that I didn't give a shit what people thought about us, because deep down, I knew who we really were." After Samantha and I stared at each other for a few seconds, I shook my head at her. "Damn, five minutes alone with you and I'm singing like a canary with all my secrets."

Samantha chuckled. "I'd hardly say you're giving away anything too revealing—like the club's secret handshake."

"True. It's more like I don't usually talk like this to women."

"Let me guess. You don't do a lot of talking period when you're with a woman."

"Pretty much."

"I can't say I'm too surprised by that." She hopped down off the table. "So since you said you were always beating the shit out of guys, I guess it's safe to say that you were pretty good at boxing, huh?"

"I won a lot of division titles back in the day."

"Were you as good as José Legrá?"

I widened my eyes in surprise. "How the hell do you know who José Legrá is?"

"Don't all women know their Cuban boxers?"

"Fuck no."

"Truth is that I wouldn't know my boxers if it hadn't been for my father. He always watched the Friday-night fights. Even if he was working, he would tape them. He was a huge fan of Legrá as well as Luis Manuel Rodríguez, Kid Gavilán, Sugar Ramos—"

"The fourth greatest boxer named Sugar *after* Robinson, Leonard, and Mosley."

Samantha smiled. "I'm not sure my father would have agreed with you on that one."

"Give me a chance, and I would set him straight."

Samantha's expression darkened. "He passed away."

Fuck. I had a special gift for being an insensitive asshole. "I'm sorry."

"It's okay. You didn't know."

"Well, I sorta know what it feels like to lose your old man." When she stared expectantly at me, I said, "My dad was killed six years ago."

She surprised the hell out of me by forgoing the usual bullshit "I'm sorry for your loss." Instead, she looked me straight in the eye and said something so few had ever said to me. "You must miss him."

I nodded as the familiar ache of grief clenched in my chest. No matter how old you are or how big a man you think you are, there's nothing like losing your father. "I miss him each and every day. The years go by, but it doesn't really get easier, even though people love to spout that 'time heals all wounds' bullshit."

"I know what you mean," Samantha murmured.

Wanting to change the subject, I said, "Unless you have any more boxing questions, looks like it's my turn."

"Nope. I think I'm good. Of course, if you're ever in the ring again, I'd love to come see you in action."

"Seriously?"

Cocking her head at me, she countered, "What? Don't I look like the kind of woman who would enjoy a good fight?"

I grinned. "Not exactly."

Samantha wagged a finger at me. "Now you're the one using stereotypes."

With a snort, I replied, "Whatever. Most of the chicks have to be dragged by their old man to watch a fight."

"Trust me. If you were going to be there, no one would have to drag me."

The conviction in her tone had me licking my lips in anticipation. "I'll keep that in mind."

Then she cut me off at the knees when she said, "I'm sure Marley would love to see you, too."

Somehow among all the talk of boxing and flirting, I had forgotten all about him. On the one hand, I felt like a complete and total bastard for wanting him out of the picture so I could have Samantha all to myself, and on the other, I resented him for being Samantha's boyfriend. I wanted to believe he wasn't good for her—that he probably cheated on her or mistreated her. But knowing Marley as I did, I couldn't imagine him doing anything like that. He might be a tough talker, but he was a grown-up Boy Scout at heart.

To get my mind off Marley and lusting after his girlfriend, I leaned over the table and positioned my cue. Needing to prove myself, I said, "Orange five. Left corner pocket."

"Going for a challenge right out of the gate?" she asked innocently.

"Damn straight."

After sinking the ball with ease, I righted myself and met Samantha's expectant gaze. I knew I needed to find a question that didn't sound remotely like I was coming on to her. "So, what's your family background like?"

Her eyes widened as if my question had taken her off guard. "Excuse me?"

"I mean, like I'm a little English and Scottish with maybe some German thrown in way back in there. But you look like you have an exotic background."

"Ah, I see what you're asking now. Actually, when it comes down to it, I'm more a mutt than anything."

"Funny, that was what I was thinking, but I sure as hell wasn't going to call you that."

Samantha laughed. "Wise choice there." After shifting the cue in her hand, she said, "Let's see. I'm pretty much pure Cuban on my dad's side. Then my mom's family is mostly Irish Catholic."

"You're not as much of a mutt as I thought you were."

"I guess not." With a wink, she added, "Thanks for the compliment about being exotic-looking."

"I just call it as I see it."

"Well, I like the way you see it. No one has ever called me exotic before."

I shifted on my feet as electricity seemed to pop and crackle all around us. For a moment, I questioned if it was because I truly wanted Samantha, or if it was more that I wanted what I knew I couldn't have.

Waving my cue stick at Samantha, I said, "You're up again."

She once again effortlessly sank her ball. After lifting her gaze to the ceiling and appearing deep in thought, she asked, "If you could have one dream come true, what would it be?"

With a grunt, I replied, "Wow, that's the fucking cheesiest question I've ever heard."

She poked me in the shoulder with the end of the cue stick. "Oh no, you don't get to judge the question. By the rules of your game, you have to answer it."

I held up a hand. "Fine, then. I'll answer your hokey little question."

"I'm waiting," she said while tapping the toe of her boots. Damn, if it wasn't both cute and sexy.

After fighting the urge to growl at her, I decided to answer her honestly. "The one dream I want to come true is to open my own motorcycle shop."

Samantha blinked at me in surprise. "Really?"

"Yeah, really. What did you expect I would say? That I wanted a threesome with two *Playboy* models or to have a ten-inch dick?"

"Well, you can't blame me for being surprised after your initial response to my first question."

"That's true."

"And you mean you don't have a ten-inch dick?" she questioned teasingly.

I laughed. "Wouldn't you like to know?"

She grinned. "I'll admit that my curiosity is certainly piqued."

"Let's just say the size of my dick will stay a secret for now."

"Such a pity," Samantha replied, before winking at me.

Since I knew we needed to get off the subject of my dick, I leaned over the table and positioned my cue. "My turn again."

"Wait a minute."

Glancing over my shoulder, I questioned, "What?"

"I want to know more about the motorcycle shop you want to open."

I shook my head. "I said we had to tell a secret, not go into a bunch of bullshit detail about the secret."

"But you answered my questions about boxing. Why won't you answer this one?" Stepping closer to me, she said, "Is the big, bad biker boy afraid to share?"

"I share myself just fine," I countered with a smirk.

"Physically I bet you spread yourself around, but I'm talking about emotionally. Would it really kill you to explain to me why you want to open your own shop?"

I narrowed my eyes at her. "You're shitting me, right?"

"I'm not exactly sure what 'shitting' is, but I'm pretty sure I'm being sincere when I say that I want to hear about the shop."

Bringing my free hand to my face, I scratched my chin in surprise.

Having a woman interested in something about me other than fucking was certainly a first. From the start of our conversation, Sam had seemed genuinely interested in my life. I couldn't imagine she was pulling my chain. "You really mean it?"

Samantha grinned. "Yeah, I do."

I drew in a deep breath. "Okay, then, here it is. I love rebuilding old, broken-down bikes. I love making some former pile of junk into something amazing. So I want to open a shop where I can sell these rebuilt bikes. You know, something that is just mine—nothing to do with my brothers or the club." Once I finished, I couldn't bring myself to look her in the eye. I almost jumped when I felt her hand on my shoulder. When I dared to meet her gaze, I found that she was smiling sincerely at me.

"I don't know why you didn't want to tell me about that. It sounds like a fantastic idea—one that you could make money at as well as doing what you love."

I bit my tongue to ask her once again if she was shitting me. Instead, I returned her smile. "Thank you. It means a lot when people take me seriously. I haven't gotten a whole lot of that from my family over the years. Of course, sometimes I haven't given them a whole lot of reasons to take me seriously."

"Being the youngest means you get shit on a lot, huh?"

"How did you know I was the youngest?"

Samantha waved her hand dismissively. "Oh, Marley told me about your brothers, Deacon and Rev, when he was telling me all about the club. He's really interested in the club and maybe one day patching in. He's talked about it a lot to me."

"I'm glad to hear he's interested. He'll need to keep up his spirits to get through the prospect phase."

"It's a pretty shitty period, huh?"

"Oh yeah, the worst. Especially when your dad is the president and your two older brothers are officers. You tend to catch even more hell to prove yourself."

"Poor baby of the family."

"You the youngest, too?"

Shaking her head, Samantha said, "I probably shouldn't answer your question unless you sink a ball. I hate being a rule breaker."

I groaned. "I'm regretting coming up with this damn game." I then leaned over the table. "Red eleven." Once the ball was securely in the pocket, I turned back to her. "Now answer my question."

"I understand where you're coming from because I'm the youngest of my family, too."

"Go on," I instructed.

She tossed her hair over her shoulder. "Fine. I have an older brother and sister. Growing up, I was never taken seriously by them. Whenever I said what I wanted to do in life, they would tell me I would never make it."

"Why?"

"Because I was a girl."

"What did you want to do that being a girl mattered?"

Samantha's face suddenly flushed, and she ducked her head. It was almost as if she was embarrassed that she had told me so much, which seemed out of place for the confident woman she was.

When she finally looked at me, she smiled. "Your turn."

"Oh, no. Not until you answer me about what you wanted to do in life. And don't think you're getting out of the emotional stuff."

She twisted the pool cue between her hands while simultaneously twisting her lip between her teeth. "More than anything in the world, I wanted to be like my dad."

At her vague response, I prompted, "And what did he do?"

Staring into my eyes, she replied, "He took out the bad guys."

"So you wanted to be a cop?" When she bobbed her head, I said, "I take it you aren't one."

"No. I do the books for a construction company."

The answer she gave felt almost rehearsed, and I could tell she had no passion for the job the way she had for law enforcement.

"A secretary sounds like a good profession. Maybe not as noble as cop, but it's still important."

"Interesting to hear you say that."

"Because I'm supposed to be an outlaw who hates cops, right?"

"I didn't say that," she protested.

"While I should be pissed at you for your small worldview of bikers, I'm going to let you off the hook."

Her eyebrows rose in surprise. "You are?"

"Yep. Going to bust my ass to prove to you how wrong you are."

"Is that right?"

"It sure as hell is."

After staring at me skeptically, Samantha smiled. "Okay. I'll take your challenge and let you try to change my mind."

"Should we shake on it?"

She shifted the pool cue to her left hand and then offered me her right. As we shook hands, I couldn't help shuddering at the soft feel of her skin against mine. When we were done, Sam said, "I guess it's my turn again?"

"This game is bullshit."

Samantha snorted. "Yeah, well, it's your bullshit, since you came up with it."

I tossed my cue onto the table and crossed my arms over my chest. "Then as the creator of this game, I say it's all bullshit, and we should answer each other's questions without earning them."

Samantha laughed. "I never pegged you for a quitter."

"I'm not a quitter. Just curious about you."

Tilting her head at me, Samantha asked, "Why?"

"Because I find you very interesting."

"You find *me* interesting or you find my *tits* and *ass* interesting?"

My jaw dropped at her audacity. Not wanting to let her get the upper hand, I replied, "If I had to answer truthfully, I would have to say it's a toss-up between you and your assets."

"An honest man. How refreshing," she mused.

"Admit it. You've enjoyed getting to know me and my emotional shit."

Samantha grinned. "Yes, I have. But there could be even more under the surface. Like how you're so in touch with your feelings that you cry at sad movies."

I wagged a finger at her. "Actually, it's that sad-as-hell ASPCA commercial with the pitiful-looking dogs and cats that gets me crying." *Jesus, did I actually just admit that?* This woman could make me sing like a canary if she wanted to.

Samantha's dark eyes widened. "Really? I cry at that, too. I have to change the channel the minute I hear the depressing piano music."

"I guess it's safe to say that one thing we have in common is a love for animals."

"That's right."

"Next time you come here, I'll have to take you to see Poe."

"Who is Poe?" Samantha asked curiously.

"He's a deer that Rev and his wife, Annabel, raised after his mother was killed."

"That is too crazy."

"Yep. He's an adult now, but he's so spoiled he still comes around to get attention . . . and some ground corn."

Samantha laughed. "I would love to see him."

"Then it's a date."

Just as Samantha stared at me in surprise, Marley asked, "What's a date?"

I whirled around to see he had finally returned from getting the keg with Joe. "Oh, Samantha wanted to see my brother's pet deer."

Marley grinned. "No shit. A pet *deer*? For real?"

"Yeah, for real."

"You need to count me in, too."

"Then it's a double date," I said. *A double date? What the hell are you thinking, you douche?*

"That would be more like a threesome than a double date, wouldn't it?" Samantha asked. When my gaze snapped to hers, a tantalizing look twinkled in her eyes. It was the kind of look that had the ability to make me feel like a fumbling teenage boy instead of a very experienced man.

After clearing my throat, I replied, "I guess so."

Marley chuckled. "Leave it to my Sam to say something inappropriate." He then slid his arm around Sam's waist and drew her closer to him. "My girl is something else, isn't she?"

I felt the heat of Samantha's gaze on me as I replied, "Yeah, she is."

"I'm glad. I hoped you would get along."

Samantha smiled up at him. "You have nothing to worry about, babe, because Bishop and I get along really well." She pinned me with her dark eyes. "Don't we?"

"Yeah, we do." With my mouth feeling unusually dry, I said, "Why don't we go try out the new keg?"

"Sure," Marley replied.

We ambled over to the bar, and Joe quickly filled us three foamy beers. Holding his glass up, Marley said, "Here's a toast to new friends."

Samantha snickered. "You can be such a lame ass sometimes."

"But you like me anyway," Marley countered.

The word "like" surprised me. I wondered why he hadn't said "love" instead. Maybe their relationship wasn't as serious as I thought it was. Of course that still didn't give me the right to be lusting after Samantha.

"True," she said as she raised her glass.

When I brought my mug up to clink with theirs, a feeling of dread pricked its way over my skin. Deep down, I knew this friendship would bring nothing but trouble and heartache. But in spite of all that, I drank to it.

FIVE

SAMANTHA

The ride back from the Raiders clubhouse held an entirely different sense of anxiousness than I had felt earlier in the night. Part of my job was always preparing for the unexpected—to have a plan B and C to execute in case plan A failed. But after all the research and all the profiling, Bishop Malloy had been the epitome of unexpected, and that fact unnerved me completely.

As I held tight to Gavin's well-defined abs, I pictured Bishop's toned muscles flexing as he took a shot at the pool table. Although he was quite a sight to behold, it wasn't Bishop's physical attributes that had my mind reeling. It was discovering that he had a deeply caring side. As sergeant at arms in the Raiders, he was called upon to deliver punishment from the club, I knew. While his body was built for being an executioner, his eyes had held such kindness and compassion as we spoke. And *that* was not at all what I had been expecting or prepared for.

Seeing him holding his nephew had momentarily thrown me

off my game. Anyone would find a hardened biker cooing over a baby a little disconcerting. Couple that with the fact that most women find a man with a baby the equivalent of emotional kryptonite, and it was no wonder I had been unnerved. Recognizing Bishop's paternal side was probably the first time I allowed myself to really see him as a person—one whose love for his family and friends was the reasoning he used to justify some of the illegal and immoral things he did.

Somehow I had managed to get my game face back on. He had taken the bait when I played him like a fool by overtly coming on to him, but he seemed conflicted by an inner turmoil. I had expected him to be the type of man who didn't give two shits about whether a woman was already involved with someone else—that he would see nothing wrong with taking me from Marley. After all, Bishop was an officer in the club, and to the Raiders, Gavin was no one. I'd read sickening articles where some MCs ordered prospects to let them "break in" their wives and girlfriends. If they didn't comply, then they were thrown out. In the back of my mind, I had built up an image of Bishop being that despicable.

But Bishop had surprised me by backing off as many times as he did. I had to spend only five minutes with him to realize he could never be as horrible as I had envisioned him. In the end, he would be tougher to break than I thought because he possessed a moral compass I hadn't originally anticipated.

It was that very moral compass that unnerved me. For the first time in my career, I had encountered a tiny amount of dread in the pit of my stomach about continuing the case. Usually, after I spent a few hours undercover, I was champing at the bit to get back in the field to bring the bad guy down. In my mind, tonight had somewhat blurred the lines, and I knew that I needed to get ahold of myself pronto. I had to remember that while Bishop had somehow evaded jail time with just probation, he was still a criminal, and criminals had to be punished.

Gavin eased the bike off the main road into the almost-deserted Waffle House parking lot. Through the window, we could see where Peterson sat at a booth—his shirt and tie slightly disheveled after the long day. Since we hadn't been wired, Peterson had set up this late-night debriefing to ensure that nothing, not even the smallest detail, went unanalyzed.

After I slid off the back of the bike and took off my helmet, I turned around to find Gavin staring expectantly at me. "What?" I demanded.

"You've been awfully quiet since we left the clubhouse."

"Excuse me for not realizing I needed to converse with you. For fuck's sake, I've been on a motorcycle going sixty down a country road. If I'd opened my mouth, I would have caught a bunch of bugs in my teeth."

When I started for the building, Gavin didn't follow me. Whirling around, I growled, "You're seriously starting to piss me off, McTavish!"

"I just want to hear you say it before we go in."

Crossing my arms over my chest, I asked, "And what is it exactly that I'm supposed to say? If it's 'thank you' for earlier, then by all means thank you for letting me get my shit together and for not ratting me out to Peterson."

Gavin closed the gap between us. "Nope. That's not it at all."

"Then what is it?" I eyed him suspiciously. "Did they slip something into your drink at the roadhouse to make you act so fucking weird?"

The corners of Gavin's lips twitched as though he was fighting a smile. "Admit it. You liked Bishop."

My heartbeat drummed so loudly in my chest that I was sure

Gavin must have heard it. How the hell had he been able to sense my dilemma? Playing it cool, I questioned, "Excuse me?"

"You heard me."

"Yes, but I'm trying to process why in the hell you would say such a thing out of nowhere."

"The reason you were so quiet on the way over here is that your mind was racing. I can always tell when you're overanalyzing something."

With an eye roll, I said, "You're so full of shit."

"After all that thinking, you realized that at the end of the day, you found Bishop Malloy completely different from how you had perceived him. And though you were on a job, you still found that you enjoyed yourself there tonight."

I slowly shook my head in disbelief. While my anxiety sent a cold rush pricking down my spine, I masked any inner turmoil I felt with a totally impassive expression on the outside. Although Gavin and I both knew each other inside and out, I still couldn't believe he had been able to guess what I was feeling so easily. I sure as hell hoped I wasn't becoming transparent, because the last thing I needed was for Peterson to ride my ass about it.

"Once again, you're full of shit," I said.

Holding up his hands defensively, Gavin said, "Look, it's all right to like him, Sam. He's a helluva likable guy with a good sense of humor. I've seen that for myself since I've been spending time with him."

"But it's different for you."

Gavin's brow furrowed in confusion. "What do you mean?"

I sighed and kicked one of the loose pieces of gravel with my boot. "If I like him, there's a different set of issues than there is for you."

"Because he's straight, and you're coming on to him to get the job done?"

"Yep. That pretty much sums it up."

Gavin grinned at me. "I just said you liked the guy, Vargas, not that you were ready to have his babies."

I couldn't help laughing at Gavin's summation. "The situation's escalated pretty quickly if I'm ready to have his babies."

"You know what I meant." He nudged his shoulder against mine. "So quit worrying, 'kay?"

"The thing is, I let myself get too comfortable with him while we were talking."

Gavin's smile faded. "What do you mean?"

Groaning, I covered my eyes with my hands. "We were playing this stupid get-to-know-you game, and when trying to connect with him about being the youngest of the family, I let it slip that my siblings didn't think I could do what I wanted when I grew up. When I realized what I'd done, I covered my ass by saying I wanted to be a cop."

When I dared to look at Gavin, he was once again grinning at me. "Jesus, Sam, you're entirely too hard on yourself. For a minute, I thought you had given him your badge number or some bullshit. That was barely a slipup."

"You're too forgiving when it comes to me."

"Fine. You want the truth?"

Now it was my turn to groan as he did the familiar bit with me from *A Few Good Men*. "Yeah, I can handle the truth."

"My first undercover case, I let it slip where I really lived—almost blew the whole damn thing."

I widened my eyes in disbelief. "You never told me that."

"Maybe I didn't want to look bad in front of my new partner," he said with a wink.

"Thanks for telling me now."

"You're welcome. Now we better get inside before Peterson wonders what the hell we're doing out here."

As Gavin started for the door, I blurted, "He's not a monster."

Glancing back at me over his shoulder, Gavin looked confused. "Who, Peterson?"

I shook my head. "No. Bishop."

"I'm glad you figured that one out."

"But I'm not. You know it just makes the case harder if he's really a decent guy," I argued.

"That's true. But at the end of the day, what we're doing doesn't mean sending Bishop to prison and throwing away the key. There are a lot of parameters in this case. He and his brothers play their cards right, and they won't be locked up forever."

While I nodded, I didn't tell Gavin what I was really feeling. The truth was in that moment, I had a hard time imagining seeing Bishop punished. In my mind, I hoped there was some way he could cop a deal and plead out of any charges. If they were truly giving their guns to the cartel, then the bureau would be much more interested in taking the cartel down if the Raiders would help.

"Stop overthinking, Vargas. I'm starving for some fucking waffles," Gavin said, bringing me out of my internal tirade.

I laughed and let him lead me into the restaurant. At the sight of us, Peterson waved us over. The place was fairly empty, with only a few sleepy-eyed truckers as the other patrons.

When we reached the booth, Peterson's gaze roamed over my heavy makeup and skintight attire. "We really have to stop meeting like this, Vargas."

I snorted as I slid into the seat across from him. "I have a feeling a burlap sack wouldn't stop you from ogling me, you old pervert."

Peterson threw his head back and laughed. "I'm never able to get one over on you."

"And you never will," I said as I picked up the grease-encrusted menu.

After the waitress got our order, Peterson asked, "So, how did your first MC party go?"

Although my mind still spun from trying to process all I had seen and heard, I gave an apathetic shrug of my shoulder. "Meh, it was okay, I guess."

Peterson's bushy salt-and-pepper eyebrows shot up. "Just 'okay'?"

"Actually, it was pretty tame. Apparently, all the exhibitionist sex and nudity happens at the rallies, not the parties," I replied.

"Did you find that out from some of the old ladies?" Peterson asked.

"Actually, Bishop was the one who let me in on that little secret."

"Ah, you had a little chat with the target. What's your take on him?"

At the insinuation of getting to know Bishop, I jerked my gaze up from the menu to stare at him. When I saw he wasn't suspicious, I replied, "Yeah. I did. I found him to be quite the fount of information about certain things." I didn't dare look at Gavin. Instead, I glanced back at the menu.

"You find out anything else besides the party-versus-rally info?" Peterson questioned.

"Not anything good that we can use in the case, but I did really well when it came to rattling him. We had a long time alone together while Gavin helped a prospect get a keg in the warehouse."

At the mention of the warehouse, Peterson forgot all about me. Instead, he turned his bright eyes to Gavin. "I had no idea you would get inside there so quickly. See anything useful?"

Gavin shook his head. "Nope. It was a total bust on physical evidence. No suspicious crates or boxes, no empty spaces where a shipment might've been or was about to be. If the Raiders are still running guns, I don't see how it's possible they're doing it out of that warehouse. Maybe they've got something going off the property."

When Peterson gave a frustrated grunt, Gavin held up his hand. "I said I didn't get any good physical evidence, but the word of mouth from the prospect, Joe, was pretty good."

"So the old adage that a frustrated prospect is your first point of club knowledge rang true?" Peterson asked with a grin.

"Yeah, it certainly helped." He leaned forward in the booth and lowered his voice. "Apparently, there's a big powwow coming up between the Southeast chapters of the Raiders. Louisiana all the way to the Carolinas are meeting at the chapter headquarters in Virginia."

"When?"

"The end of the month. The prospect was a little vague on the actual date."

"We need you at that meeting. Think you can work on Bishop in the next few weeks for an invitation?"

Gavin nodded. "From what Joe was saying, the other guy that's also prospecting really isn't working out. He fucks up one more time, and he's out. Joe was bitching about the fact that if this dude gets kicked out before the meeting in Virginia, he'll be running his ass off for everyone as the lone prospect. They'll need someone reliable to go along. I'm thinking it might be me."

"Good. You keep working that angle." Peterson then looked at me. "You'll be along for this one, too, Vargas."

"I figured as much."

"We need you front and center with Bishop. If we can have him rattled, we're likely to get more information about what's going on at the meeting."

"So more revealing clothes and whorish behavior?" I questioned humorlessly.

"Not entirely."

Intrigued, I asked, "What exactly do you need me to do?"

Before he answered me, Peterson downed the rest of his coffee and then waved the waitress over. Once we were alone again, he said, "Ideally, you need to be his shadow. More than anything, we need you on the back of that bike. As a hang-around, Gavin won't be allowed in the inner circle for any briefings before or after the meeting. If we have you there, you can pick up everything—from each time they stop to take a piss to before they meet up with the other Raiders."

"Jesus, Peterson, from the way you talk you want me standing beside them in the urinals."

"I would totally be down for that," Peterson replied with a wink.

"I'll try my best, but you can forget me being anywhere near germ-infested urinals."

Gavin glanced between us. "While that sounds great in theory, just how do we get Sam on the back of Bishop's bike? I mean, do I suddenly have a malfunction with the bitch seat on mine?"

I shook my head. "As a hang-around, you won't be taking your bike."

"Huh?" Gavin asked.

Leaning forward in my seat, I replied, "Prospects and hang-arounds don't get to ride their bikes on a run. Because they haven't earned full privileges yet, they end up driving a truck or car, which inevitably makes them stand out even more." At both Gavin's and Peterson's surprised looks, I rolled my eyes. "Don't tell me you guys didn't read up on that part?"

"I'm sure I read it—I just forgot it," Gavin mumbled.

"Do you mean to tell me the mighty McTavish actually forgot something?" I teased. He responded by maturely throwing a wadded-up napkin at me.

"So if Gavin is driving or riding with Joe, we just need a way to get you onto that bike," Peterson said.

"No need to worry about it. I'll get on that bike."

"How?" Gavin asked.

"I don't know exactly at the moment, but I'll figure it out."

"Yeah, well, I don't think this fly-by-the-seat-of-your-pants attitude is good. We need a plan."

"The plan is simple. I use my assets and our newfound friendship. It needs to happen in the moment. Anything too rehearsed will look suspicious."

"I guess you're right."

I grinned. "Oh, I know I'm right." I turned to Peterson. "Now, how about the bureau footing the bill for some waffles? Being a femme fatale has made me work up quite an appetite."

Peterson chuckled before turning to Gavin. "When it comes to Vargas, I don't think we have anything to worry about."

"Damn straight," I muttered.

SIX

BISHOP

There were a lot of things that brought me pleasure in life—sex, boxing, time with my family—but none of them quite compared to the feeling of taking my bike out on the open road. The sheer exhilaration of the wind rippling your clothes, the way the world melted into a blur of colors, and the freeing isolation of there being nothing but you and the road. Those were the reasons that called to all types of men, from the weekend warrior with his nine-to-five office job to the upstart desperate to stick it to the man. Preacher Man had called it a balm for his soul, and I couldn't have agreed with him more.

I didn't have to glance at my watch to know we were making good time. Since we made the trek yearly, I knew the route to the Virginia headquarters of the Raiders by heart. Each of the Southeast chapters was summoned to meet once a year to take care of necessary club business. While the actual meeting lasted an hour at best, the better part of the weekend was spent hanging out, getting drunk, and catching up with our other brothers. And fucking. Lots of fucking fresh ass.

But this year's trip had a different feel than usual. It was because of what our chapter planned to discuss at the meeting. While we might have already been unofficially legitimate, we needed to have the approval of the board to make it official. For the most part, what we were doing was uncharted territory, so we weren't sure how our other brothers were going to take it.

There had certainly been a tense feeling in the air as we packed up this morning. The blinding glare of gleaming chrome filled the Raiders parking lot when I stepped out of the clubhouse. Raiders from all over north Georgia had come out for the run. I spoke to a few of the out-of-town guys as I made my way to the bike.

Since I was a less-is-more kind of guy when it came to packing, I finished with my rucksack earlier than the others. Leaning back against the seat of my bike, I watched as my brothers and their old ladies, girlfriends, and sweet butts scurried around.

Across from me, Deacon had squatted down to address a pouting Willow. "Do you really have to go, Daddy?" she asked.

"I'm sorry, but I do." He cupped her chin. "But don't be sad. You'll barely have time to miss me, since I'll be back at the end of the weekend."

"Promise?"

Deacon smiled as he pulled Willow into his arms. "I promise."

"And you'll bring me something back, right, Daddy?"

I chuckled at her request. All of us knew Willow's expectations for presents if we were gone more than a day. We wouldn't dream of disappointing her, so we always got her something.

Deacon pulled away to eye Willow. "You're a spoiled little shit, you know that?"

"Deacon!" Alexandra's voice admonished him from behind them. She bounced baby Wyatt in her arms as she gave Deacon a disapproving look.

"Sorry, babe," he replied, smirking.

Although the trip was primarily about business, it didn't mean that the women were excluded. Since she had the baby, Alexandra would be staying behind, along with Annabel, who had some vet school work. She was currently wrapped in Rev's arms, gazing up at him and smiling. I fought the urge to roll my eyes at the utter domesticated pussies Rev and Deacon had become.

But there was a part of me—one I didn't much like to admit to—that kinda envied them. In our world that seemed to constantly tilt and turn, it would be nice to have someone you could count on who wasn't one of your brothers. Considering that I ran like hell when it came to commitment, I didn't hold out much hope of me having what my brothers had. It didn't help matters that the one woman lately who got my blood up and running was fucking unattainable.

Searching through the crowd, I easily spotted Samantha's jet-black hair shining in the early-morning light. It was the first time I had seen her since the night we met. Even though I hadn't seen her, she had certainly been on my mind. She looked just as good in person again as she did in my fantasies. I shifted my dick in my pants at the sight of her body in the painted-on jeans, a skintight black AC/DC T-shirt, and knee-high boots. With a cup of coffee in hand, she watched Joe and Marley as they double-checked the van. It was almost as if she sensed me looking at her, because she jerked her head and met my gaze. As I threw up a hand, she rewarded me with a smile and a wave.

Wishing to put her out of my mind, I pushed off my bike and walked over to my brothers.

"Are we ready?" I asked Rev.

Without taking his eyes off Annabel, he replied, "Archer's doing the final run-through. Once he clears us, we're ready to go."

I nodded. Before I was made sergeant at arms, I had been the road captain, as Archer was now. Big runs like today's were always such a pain in the ass to coordinate. You had to plan ahead where your stops would be, because with such a large group, you couldn't just make a stop out of nowhere, and there was always the factor of finding biker-friendly places.

A few minutes later Archer strode up to us. "All set. Everyone knows the route formation and the stops."

Rev reluctantly pulled away from Annabel to pat Archer on the back. "You're a good man." He then turned to the waiting crowd. Raising a hand over his head, he called, "All right, boys, we're pulling out."

Cheers and catcalls rang out among the guys, followed by the gunning of motorcycle engines. I waved to my sisters-in-law, gave Willow and Mama Beth a hug, and then slid onto the back of my bike. Once Rev and Deacon pulled out into the road, our secretary and treasurer, Mac and Boone, followed them. Then it was my turn, followed by the next-ranking member, which in this case was Breakneck because of both his age and his years in the club.

Although it had been a number of years since Breakneck went on a run, he had felt his presence was required on this one. If he was needed, he fully intended to testify in front of the officers about what had happened to his daughter, Sarah, which led to us going after Annabel and our deal with the Rodriguez cartel. I was glad to see that Kim was going along with him. On the outside, they had little in common—the doctor and the former stripper. But they were bound together by the MC world and the tragic shit that had happened to them. While they hadn't been together long, he probably thought she would be good moral support, not to mention a good time, since Kim was fun as hell.

At the very end of the line was Archer, who had to ride last as road captain, and then pulling up the rear was the van that held Jolting Joe, Marley, and Samantha.

We pulled into Stuckey's, one of our Tennessee favorites, at a little before ten. The mom-and-pop diner was a favorite among truckers as well as bikers. After grabbing a quick breakfast and taking a break to piss, we assembled back outside.

When I got to my bike, Samantha stood waiting on me with a bright smile. "Hey there."

"Hey yourself."

"It's good to see you again. Marley and I sure had a good time the other night."

"So did I."

She ran her hands over the handlebars of my bike. "You have a real sweet ride."

I couldn't help beaming at her praise. "Thanks. I rebuilt this one."

Samantha's dark eyes widened. "Get out."

"No. I really did."

Shaking her head slowly, she said, "You do have a talent."

"I appreciate you saying that." With a grin, I added, "Although I can't help being a little surprised that you know a hunk of junk from a sweet ride."

She laughed. "You can blame Marley for that one. He bores me to tears sometimes talking about bikes." Glancing over her shoulder at him, she sighed. "I'm sure he wishes he could be out on his bike now. It sucks seeing all the beauty of the road from inside the van."

"You've never been this way on a bike?"

"No. I haven't really gotten to take a good ride before. We're always cooped up in town."

"You mean, you've never really been out on the open road before."

"Nope. I'm an open-road virgin," she replied, then winked.

I chuckled. "That's a pity." As she continued to stare longingly at my bike, an idea popped into my head, and I acted on it before I really thought it through. "What do you say about riding along with me the rest of the way?"

Her eyes lit up. "Really?"

"Sure. Why not?" Once again I remembered that she had a boyfriend. The last thing I wanted to do was piss Marley off, so I quickly added, "As long as it's okay with Marley."

"I don't think he would mind, but let me ask." She waved Marley over and then asked him.

He glanced from her to me before grinning. "Of course it's all right with me. Then I won't have to hear her bitching about how much longer it is till we get there. I swear, she turns into such a whiny kid when we go on a road trip." He slapped me on the back. "She can be your problem, buddy."

"Asshole," Samantha muttered before leaning up to kiss Marley's cheek.

"Yo, Marley, let's go!" Joe called from over by the van.

"Well, I'm being paged. See ya next stop."

"See ya, man," I said.

As we started loading up, I handed Samantha my helmet. After she slipped it on, she smiled. "Thanks again for letting me ride with you."

"You're welcome. Of course, you might be cursing me when we start around the winding mountain roads going ninety."

Her face paled. "Seriously?"

Cocking my head at her, I asked, "Having second thoughts?"

She swallowed hard. "No. I'll be fine."

I laughed as I got on my bike. "Don't worry, sweetheart. I'll take good care of you."

"You better. If I end up roadkill, I'll find a way to haunt you as punishment," she said as she slid on behind me.

"That's a real threat." Glancing behind me, I gave her a reassuring smile. "Believe me when I say that nothing is going to happen to you."

"Okay. I believe you."

"Good. Hold on tight."

As I gunned the engine, Samantha's arms came around my waist. When I squealed out of my space and onto the road, her arms squeezed me with a deathlike grip. We rode like that for several minutes before she finally got used to the speed and eased up a bit. I knew she had finally gotten comfortable when she leaned in closer and propped her chin on my shoulder. It was the first time I'd ever had a girl on my bike who was as tall as me.

"Pretty amazing, huh?" I called.

"Yeah. It is," she shouted back.

After another two hours, we stopped to gas up. I guessed Samantha was still unsure around us, because she stuck like glue to me at the station. The only time she left my side was when I went to the bathroom. When I came out, she was waiting on me. "You up for the rest of the trip?"

"I am if you are."

I sure as hell am, I thought. I grinned. "Sure."

"Good. I'm glad to hear it."

The rest of the trip to Virginia was uneventful. Well, as long as you considered having the legs of a smoking-hot chick clamped against your thighs uneventful. I tried hard not to think about that fact. Of course, it didn't help to get a whiff of her perfume or to feel her tits pressed against my back. I sure as hell hoped there were some fresh sweet butts at the party tonight. While I hadn't had a hard time hooking up at the meetings before, I hadn't needed them as badly as I did now.

Between all the stops, we pulled into Remington at a little before five. It was outside Richmond, and just like where we lived, it was a small town. Because the Virginia chapter was the original one in the Southeast, they had chosen the location for the meetings. They had set up their headquarters in a somewhat run-down motel. It was owned by one of the Virginia brothers, so there was no worry of its being bugged by the FBI or ATF. Even though there wasn't that fear, we were still expected to be patted down at any time. Whenever officers went into the meeting room, their cell phones were taken and checked for wires. The Raiders took security very seriously.

Officers and their families were afforded the small number of rooms, while the other members camped out in the field down below the motel. All meals were provided and served in the dining hall.

When I turned off the engine, Samantha hopped off. "I guess I better go see what Marley is up to."

"Most likely he's already been made someone's errand bitch."

Samantha laughed. "I figured as much." As she handed me her helmet, she said, "Thanks again for the ride."

"You're welcome. I'll see you at dinner."

"You're not roughing it?" Sam asked.

I chuckled. "If you consider sleeping on the floor of Rev and Deacon's room roughing it, then yes, I am."

She wrinkled her nose. "Considering that you'll have indoor plumbing, I don't think it's really roughing it."

"Sorry. Just some of the perks of being an officer . . . or being an officer's brother."

"Just please tell me there's a communal bathroom where we can shower?"

Kim appeared at our side. She patted Sam on the back. "Oh, honey, do you think I would be going anywhere there wasn't a shower?"

"I would hope not," Samantha replied.

With a grin, Kim said, "Just stick with me. I'll show you the ropes."

"Thanks. I appreciate that. Especially since I doubt I'll be seeing much of Marley this weekend."

"Yep. Your boy is going to be ridden hard. The only thing you can do to make it easier on him is stay out of the way, get him food and water when he's allowed, and give him a blow job for moral support."

While Samantha gave a nervous laugh at Kim's remark, I didn't find the images running through my mind very funny. Wanting to put distance between myself and them, I said, "I'll see you, ladies."

Kim leaned over to plant a kiss on my cheek. "Bye, sweet thing. If I see any available ass, I'll send it your way."

"Thanks, Kim. You know me too well." When I dared to look at Samantha, I found she was staring down at the ground. I couldn't help wondering if the idea of me with another woman bothered her. No sooner had the thought crossed my mind than I wanted to kick myself in the balls for being such a bastard. Inwardly, I groaned because I knew it was going to be a long, long weekend.

SEVEN

BISHOP

At the party in the field, I managed not to be alone with Samantha.
Although she was on her own with Marley running around for all
the guys, she stuck close with Kim and the other women. She
seemed to get along well with all the girls, which if Marley did patch
in would be in his favor. No man wanted a woman who was trouble
with the other club women, because in the end, it caused him too
much grief.

I shot the shit with the guys and drank way too much, but I didn't
end up searching out a piece of ass. Instead, I crashed, or maybe
passed out, on the floor around five a.m. The next morning had us
rising early. I wasn't sure whose bright idea it was to have the meeting
at ten after a night of drinking and partying. Although we were usually
quiet when we were hungover, we were especially quiet that morning.
I think we all felt the heaviness of the situation pressing down on us.
So we slurped down black coffee and tried eating some from the buf-
fet. When it was almost ten, we headed over to the boardroom. Since

only presidents and vice presidents were allowed in on the meeting, Rev and Deacon slipped inside while we were to wait to be called in when it came time for our motion to be heard.

As we stood outside the meeting room door, a nervous energy popped and crackled around us. Of course, none of us would have admitted to being nervous. That would have meant we were nothing but a bunch of pussies. Raiders would rather die than show fear. Each of us tried in our own way to mask our anxiety—Boone shuffled the coins in his pocket to the tune of *Bonanza* while Mac chain-smoked so fast he lit one cigarette off the other. As for me, I walked around the cramped hallway.

"Would you stop pacing?" Mac grunted.

Boone chuckled. "Forget it. B always paces before a fight."

I gave the two of them a sheepish grin. "I didn't even realize I was doing it."

Mac stubbed out another cigarette. "I sure as hell wish this was just a fistfight. Somehow I think we would have better odds than waiting around to chitchat."

"With you smoking like a fucking chimney, you'd be passed out in the first round," Boone quipped.

"Shut up, fucker," Mac snapped before taking another long drag on his cigarette.

As I chuckled, I felt some welcome relief from the tension. Unfortunately, the feeling didn't last long, because just then one of the Virginia Raiders stuck his head out the door. "All right, boys, you're up."

Mac cursed under his breath as he threw his half-smoked cigarette to the floor. After stomping it out, he made the sign of the cross and muttered, "Amen."

After exchanging a surprised look with me, Boone reached out to stop Mac as he started for the door. "Seriously?" Boone questioned.

"Frankly, we need all the help we can get," Mac replied matter-of-factly.

"Good to know we've got such a good Catholic boy on our side," Boone mused.

The moment we stepped inside the room, the door closed and locked behind us. Smoke hung heavy along with the smell of stale alcohol and sweaty road-worn men. Around the massive mahogany table sat the presidents and vice presidents for the Southeast states. While we represented the north Georgia chapter, there were also chapters from central and south Georgia as well. Boone, Mac, and I squeezed in to stand behind the chairs where Rev and Deacon sat.

At the head of the table sat the Southeast president, Rory "Rambo" Smithwick. With his long white hair and beard, he could almost pass for Santa Claus—if it weren't for multicolored ink all over his neck, arms, and chest. We'd never had any issues with Rambo. Back in the day, he and Preacher Man had gotten along really well. Their bond was cemented over the fact that they had both been in the army during Vietnam. Although they were in different units, there was something to be said for a shared experience of being in combat. It made strangers into a band of brothers.

Rambo let his gaze flicker around the table for a moment before clearing his throat. "The next item to discuss is a request by the north Georgia chapter." He paused almost dramatically. "It is their wish to go legitimate."

At the word "legitimate," you could have heard a pin drop in the room. I certainly had anticipated an uproar, but the silence that echoed around us took me by surprise. Rambo peered around the table. "This isn't the first time a charter has requested to be identified as legitimate."

"Just the first one in the Southeast, right?" Rev said with a smile.

Rambo nodded. "There's two northern California chapters, one Utah, and one Oklahoma." He eyed the men around the table again. "It's certainly not something unprecedented."

As a sergeant at arms, I wasn't used to being in on the meeting, so I didn't know any of the officers well. The only way I could identify them was by the patch on the front of their cut or the rocker on the back.

North Carolina's president raised a finger to speak. After Rambo had acknowledged him, he asked, "I assume you will still wear your Raiders patch and attend Raiders events?"

"Of course. We're not asking to disband, and trust me, we sure as hell don't intend to give up our patches," Rev replied.

"You intend to be present even at events where there are gun or drug deals?" east Tennessee's president asked.

Rev leaned forward in his chair. "Look, we would never judge our brothers. What your chapters choose to do is your business. For us, the heat we received is no longer worth the risk. We've lost too many good men to keep going at this pace. We love the Raiders brotherhood, and we'll always defend the patch. We just want to earn our living in a different way."

Deacon rapped his knuckles on the table. "I'm sure a lot of you think we're a bunch of pussies for doing this. While our business ventures will change, nothing will change who we are. Just because we're not dealing guns, we won't come off as weak to the other clubs out there."

"And you intend to keep your stake in the gym?" Rambo asked.

"Yes," Rev replied.

"Will there still be gambling?"

Rev and Deacon exchanged a glance. I knew this was a sore spot between the two of them, as well as many of the other guys. Since guns brought the most heat from the feds, it was only logical to give them up. The gym, on the other hand, was able to fly under the radar. Deacon had argued that we needed to keep the gambling going to pad our bank accounts in case we needed protection money. Rev, however, wanted to be completely squeaky clean. It was an issue that had yet to be decided, but if I were to put money on it, I would wager Deacon would win. You couldn't go legit overnight. It took time, but most of all, it took money.

"For now we will be keeping the gym," Rev said.

"Then you won't be completely legit," south Georgia's vice president said. His tone implied that he was glad we were still going to have some dirty dealings. I was sure what we were doing was rattling a lot of the old guard—the ones who had no idea how to make a living if it wasn't illegal.

"That is true. But where it counts the most, with guns, we will be legit."

While many of the men were nodding in agreement, a lone voice of dissent spoke up. "I have an issue with the way you disposed of your gun trade."

All eyes turned toward a scraggly looking man with a wiry salt-and-pepper beard. Although I had never met him, I knew who he was. Easy Eddy Catcherside was the east Louisiana president. Throughout the years, he'd spent more time on the inside of a prison cell than he had on the outside. His club could be considered ragtag at best, with many choosing to patch over to the Diablos when they started sweeping through the Southeast on a forceful membership drive.

After taking a sip of water, Rev calmly questioned, "What is your issue, Eddy?"

"Before riding off into the legitimate sunset, you boys made a pretty sweet deal with the Rodriguez cartel."

My breath hitched as I cut my eyes over to Rev's profile. He clenched and unclenched his jaw several times before replying. I knew he was thinking about the reasons behind aligning ourselves with one of the Mexican drug cartels. It had ensured Annabel's safety from Mendoza, the psychopath who had held her as a sex slave.

Rev stared Eddy down for a few seconds to collect himself. "Yeah, Rodriguez and I made a deal. Considering the parameters, I wouldn't exactly call it a sweet one. It's not like we pocketed any money from it."

"You want to explain why you didn't offer your gun business to your brothers first?"

"I don't see how the deals we make are any of your business," Deacon growled before Rev could respond.

Eddy smirked at Deacon. "I wasn't addressing you."

"I'm a patch-wearing member and officer, cocksucker, so anytime you question my chapter's judgment, I have the right to answer."

Rev put a hand on Deacon's shoulder to both calm and quiet him. He then turned his attention to Eddy. "I haven't tried to hide the reasons behind why I made the deal with Rodriguez. Nor do I think anyone could in good faith try to say that I have." Rev narrowed his eyes. "Perhaps if you spent less time trying to ingratiate yourself with the Diablos and more time on the business of your Raider brothers, you would know that."

Eddy's face turned purple as the veins in his neck bulged. He slammed his hand down on the table, the crack echoing through the room. "Don't you dare fucking accuse me of being disloyal to the Raiders! I was a patch member before you were even born!"

With a calm, level stare, Rev said, "While that is true, I don't believe there is a brother around this table who doesn't know about your *friendship* with them."

Eddy shot so fast out of his chair that it went slamming back against the wall. "This isn't about me and the Diablos. This is about you running guns to wetbacks across *my* territory without giving me and my boys any compensation."

"We're not running guns. The Rodriguez cartel is," Deacon said with a smirk.

"But you let it happen."

Rambo banged his gavel on the table. "Enough! Pipe the fuck down, Eddy."

"But I—"

Jabbing his finger in the air, Rambo growled, "I don't give two shits about what else you have to say! Take a fucking seat and respect the members of this table, or you'll be going home without a patch!"

Eddy's beady eyes widened at the suggestion of his cut being taken. After heaving out several frustrated breaths and shooting a death glare at us, he finally retrieved his chair and had a seat.

Rambo reached into his patch for a pack of cigarettes. After lighting one up and taking a drag, he said, "I would caution all of you to remember that what is done in your territory is your business. When it affects the territory of other brothers, then it becomes an issue. Right now I see nothing wrong with the Rodriguez cartel running guns across Louisiana. At the very least, other clubs will assume all of the Raiders chapters have an alliance with the cartel, which makes us look powerful."

Rev and Deacon exchanged a glance. I was sure neither of them had thought that the Rodriguez deal would actually have some benefit for the other Raiders.

Mississippi's president nodded. "I agree with Rambo. I also don't see any reason for Rev to owe anything to Eddy. We're along the same route, and he don't owe me a damn thing."

Rev grinned as the other states chimed in their agreement. "I appreciate that sentiment, boys."

"Total bullshit," Eddy muttered under his breath.

If Rambo heard him, he chose to ignore him. "Since we're in agreement on that, I make a motion to vote on whether to recognize the legitimacy of the north Georgia chapter."

When I found myself leaning forward on my feet, I couldn't help holding my breath in anticipation. One by one, the men around the table began to vote. Once the "yeas" started ringing out, the breath I'd been holding whooshed out of me.

Not too surprisingly, the only nay came from Eddy and his vice president. "Motion carried. Meeting adjourned until next year," Rambo said. He brought his gavel down hard to make it official.

As the men rose to their feet, we started shaking hands and thumping backs. When we were the only ones left in the room, we did some hugging of our own. "After all that fucking worry, I can't believe it all went down so easy," Deacon remarked as he lit up a cigarette.

"Considering what happened with Eddy, I wouldn't say it went down easy," Rev argued.

Deacon rolled his eyes. "Screw Eddy. His days as a Raider are numbered after he pulled that stunt."

Boone nodded. "Deacon's right. You don't go after your brothers or run your mouth like a fucking fool, especially not in a closed-door meeting with all the chapters present. You might as well be signing your fucking death warrant in the club."

"I don't know about you guys, but I'm hungry as hell. Let's head down to the dining hall and get some grub," Deacon suggested.

"Sounds like a plan," I said.

After Rev nodded, we fell in line with him down the hallway. Just as we rounded the corner to the dining room, Eddy stepped out in front of us. He gave Rev a menacing glare. "This ain't over."

Rev held up his hand. "Look, Eddy, I don't want any trouble—"

"It's too late for all that. I ain't gonna sit by and let this pass. I don't care what Rambo and the others think."

Standing toe-to-toe with Eddy, Rev towered over him. "Are you threatening me?"

Eddy's lips curled into a smirk. "And what if I am? You gonna sic your cartel boys on me?"

"Take your threats and get out of my fucking face before I hunt down Rambo and have him drag your ass in to take your patch."

"Pussy," Eddy taunted.

Rev shook his head. "I won't fight you, old man. No matter what bullshit you throw at me." After giving Eddy one final "fuck you" look, he sidestepped away from him and started down the hall.

"What a prick," Deacon muttered as we entered the dining room.

"Has he always been that way at meetings?" I asked as I grabbed a tray.

Rev shrugged. "I'm not sure, since I've only been president at the last two. I can't remember if Preacher Man or Case ever mentioned him."

"He probably had someone proxy for him at the meetings when he was in jail," Deacon said.

"They should have voted his ass out a long time ago," Mac remarked.

Deacon grinned. "Amen to that one."

Rev exhaled a long, somewhat troubled breath. "All right. Enough about that fucker. Let's focus on the positives."

"Yes, sir," Deacon replied, with a mock salute.

"Ass," Rev grumbled.

After lunch, we headed down the hill to where the party was gearing up around a towering bonfire. Now that the business aspect was over, the rest of the day would be another free-for-all into the early-morning hours. Then after breakfast on Sunday, everyone would pack up to head home.

I was hoping that Eddy and his assholes would leave early so they didn't kill anyone else's buzz. Although Rev had tried changing the subject off Eddy, it was all anyone could talk about in the dining room. Apparently, all the others had heard about Eddy's threat, and no one seemed to be taking it as lightly as we had initially. We soon learned from some of the older men that Eddy always carried through on a threat. It left a dark cloud hanging over what should have been a banner fucking day for us.

While I'd managed to avoid Samantha for the better part of the weekend, I couldn't help searching her out now. She and Kim were working the kegs and getting beer for a long line of thirsty Raiders. When she looked up to see me staring, she waved. After I waved back, she grabbed a cup and headed over to me.

"Need a beer?" Samantha asked.

"While I'd prefer some Jack or Patrón, it'll have to do."

She smiled as she handed me the red Solo cup. "Did your meeting not go so well?"

"Meeting went good. It's more about the bullshit that happened afterward," I replied as I gulped down some of the foamy liquid.

"The mood must be catching, because the other guys seem a little edgy."

"Edgy is a good way to put it." I looked up from my cup to find her staring intently at me. "Look, it's nothing you need to worry about."

"That might be true, but if you're upset, I want you to have someone to talk to. Especially since it doesn't seem like you can with the rest of your brothers. You know, since they're feeling the same way."

I sucked down the rest of the beer before shaking my head at her. "It's nice of you to offer, but I'm going to decline."

"Still having trouble with the emotional stuff?" she questioned with a smile.

"No. It's more the fact that the meeting dealt with club business, and you, sweetheart, ain't a member."

"Ah, so it's all part of the secret society stuff, huh?"

"Pretty much."

"Fine. Keep your secrets."

"Pity there's not a pool table for you to hustle some answers out of me, huh?"

Samantha laughed. "Yep. Where's a pool table when you need one?"

As I craned my neck around the bonfire, I asked, "How's Marley?"

"Running his ass off. I don't think he was in the tent two hours last night before his phone was blowing up with requests."

I chuckled. "Nothing fucking blows quite as bad as the prospect period."

"Yeah, but Marley is working himself to death, and he's just a hang-around."

"I wouldn't worry too much about that one. If he keeps working as hard as he's done this weekend, I don't see any reason why we can't fast-track part of his prospect period."

Samantha's eyes widened. "Really?"

With a shrug, I replied, "Sure, why not? He's obviously proving himself to be a real asset, and I'm not the only one who thinks so."

"That's awesome. He'll be glad to hear it."

"So we don't jinx anything, why don't we just keep it between you and me?"

Sam gave me a suspicious look. "I hope that doesn't mean if I don't tell him, then it'll be easier for you to bullshit me."

Holding up my free hand, I said, "Easy there. I'm not trying to pull one over on you. I just didn't want Marley to hear that and start slacking or something. You know, like he had it in the bag."

The fierce expression on Samantha's face lightened. "Oh, I see."

"Why do I have the feeling you wouldn't hesitate to bring out your claws?"

Samantha laughed. "You probably have that one right. But only when I think that I—or someone I care about—am being taken advantage of."

"I can promise you right here and right now that I'm not going to take advantage of you or Marley—and neither are any of my brothers."

She slowly nodded, and I could tell she didn't entirely believe me. "Okay."

"Hey, Sam!" Kim called.

Glancing over her shoulder, Sam replied, "Yeah?"

"Quit flirting with Bishop and get your ass over here and help me!"

Instead of being embarrassed by Kim's claims, Samantha grinned. "Yes, Captain. I'll be right there." She turned back to me. "Since I'm being paged, I better get back to work."

"You're a good woman to help out. The fact that Marley will have you for an old lady can only benefit him."

Her smile seemed to stay frozen in place. "Yeah, we'll see." She then hurried back over to Kim and the keg.

Not wanting to dwell on Sam's reaction to what I had said, I ambled around the bonfire, talking to brothers from different chapters. As the afternoon heat began to wane a bit, I took a seat in one of the folding chairs next to Rev and Deacon.

Both of them had their phones out and were texting frantically. "Pussies," I muttered under my breath.

"Yeah, well, if I ever want to get any pussy again, I know to check in with Alex to see how she's doing." Deacon peered up from the phone to give me a look. "Being stuck with the kids all weekend is rough, especially since Mama Beth is gone on that retreat."

I slowly shook my head at him. "Jesus, you're not just a pussy—you've grown a vagina."

"Fuck you," he muttered as he went back to texting.

Just as I was debating getting a beer or having Joe or Marley get me one, a surge of electricity crackled and popped its way through the air, causing the hairs on the back of my neck and on my arms to stand up. It was a sixth sense sort of feeling I got from time to time when something bad was about to happen. Since bad shit often went down in my world, I had learned to roll with it. The last time I had felt this way was on the way home from our meeting with Rodriguez's men. I had ended up shot, and Rev had been kidnapped by Mendoza.

I swallowed hard as I rose out of my chair. My gaze spun frantically around the field as I searched for an imminent threat. While my heart pounded out of my chest, I saw nothing out of the ordinary—just people laughing, talking, drinking, and eating. No one was arguing or fighting; no one had any weapons drawn. Realizing all seemed well, I exhaled the breath I had been holding. I brought my hand to my chest and rubbed my shirt over where my heart still beat erratically. Maybe it was all just a false alarm. Maybe what had gone down with Eddy had made me paranoid, which was the last fucking thing I needed.

"You okay?" Rev asked.

When I looked over my shoulder, his expression was grave. He had seen firsthand when I got the heebie-jeebies, as he and Deacon called them. "Just a false alarm."

But when I turned to sit back down, the sound of tires screeching caused me to freeze. I jerked my gaze from the people laughing and talking in the crowd to the hillside. When a black-paneled van crested the top of the hill, my stomach lurched into my throat. "Get down! Get down!" I screamed.

Just as the words left my lips, the sound of machine-gun fire echoed through the air. I didn't stop to think about Deacon and Rev—I knew they could take care of themselves. Instead, I searched through the crowd for her. I could barely believe what I saw. Instead of falling to the ground to protect herself like some of the others around me, she was shoving children under the food tables. A scream tore from my throat when the man helping her was hit in the back and fell to the ground.

Breaking into a sprint, I closed the short gap between us. I had no other thought in my mind but making sure she was safe, even if it meant sacrificing my life for hers. I dove on top of her, toppling her to the ground. As the gunfire and screams continued going off around me, I shielded her with my body.

She once again surprised the hell out of me by pounding her fists against my chest. "Let me up! We need ambulances in here. Stat!"

I figured she was going into shock from the way she was talking. I hoped and prayed that it wasn't from her being shot and losing blood. I had taken her down so fast I hadn't had the chance to see if she had been wounded.

When the gunfire finally ceased and the tires squealed off, I slowly rose to look at her. "Are you okay?"

"I'm fine. But I need—"

Before I could think better of it, I leaned down and bestowed a quick kiss on the top of her forehead. When I pulled back, she stared at me wide-eyed. "Sorry. I'm just so fucking glad you weren't shot or hurt."

Unblinking and unmoving, Sam continued staring at me. "You saved me."

"Yeah."

Sam started to say something else, and then her eyes went wide. "Marley!" she cried. After she pushed me off her, she jumped to her feet. Before I could grab her, she became lost in the chaos around me.

As I stood there frozen like a statue, it felt as if I had been dropped into the middle of a war zone. In that moment, I knew I would never forget the sounds of the screams. They would haunt me and my sleep for years to come. They were screams of agonized pain, screams of crippling fear, and screams of life-altering grief. Over the years, I had been in a lot of fights and fought a lot of battles as one of the Raiders, but nothing compared to the full-scale carnage around me. I didn't think there was a chapter that hadn't lost somebody.

At my side, Deacon was on his cell phone talking to a 911 operator. Rev pushed ahead of us to go to a hysterical woman whose husband or boyfriend lay in a pool of blood. I don't know how long I stood frozen as I surveyed the horror around me. Finally, I began to animate again.

Slowly, I put one foot in front of the other. It felt as if I were trudging through thick mud. Although I should have been searching for my fellow Raiders, I could think only of Samantha. While I continued walking, moments of relief came as I saw my brothers. Breakneck barked out orders to those around him to help some of the wounded. Kim and several of the women gathered a group of kids to take back to the motel. Boone limped along with his arm over Mac's shoulder. When I met his gaze, he gave me a nod to let me know that while he might've been hit, he was okay.

One by one I saw each of my Raiders brothers, and I heaved a sigh of relief that besides a few minor gunshots, we hadn't lost anyone.

Or so I thought.

At the far end of the clearing, I finally found Samantha crumpled on the ground. I broke into a run to get to her. But when I grew closer,

I skidded to a stop. She wasn't alone. She was huddled over Marley's blood-soaked body. From where he had fallen, he had borne the brunt of the gunfire coming over the hill.

"Sam?" I questioned.

Her cries momentarily ceased. She jerked her head up from Marley's chest to whirl around. Just as I would never forget those screams, I would never, ever forget the look of icy hatred that burned in her eyes. I didn't have to ask her how Marley was. I knew right then and there that he was dead, and in Samantha's eyes, I might as well have killed him myself.

EIGHT

SAMANTHA

Life changes in the blink of an eye. One minute you have the world resting precariously in the palm of your hand, and then the next you're scrambling to pick up the shattered pieces of what once was. Although I had been forced to learn that lesson when I was just eight years old, nothing could have prepared me for when I had to experience it again. The wound of losing Gavin might have cut into my soul over scar tissue, but it did nothing to dull the excruciating pain. It was as fresh as if it were the first time I had to lose someone who meant the world to me.

No matter how hard I tried to push the memory away, the night's agonizing events played on a macabre loop in my head.

"Gavin!" I screamed over the roar of the crowd. From the instant the shots rang out, pandemonium had ensued. I pushed and shoved strangers out of the way, not giving a damn about their well-being. I was no longer in hero mode like in the beginning when all I could think of was shielding those kids. Now all I cared about was getting

to Gavin, and I didn't give a fuck about anyone else. The longer I couldn't find him, the more the rising panic in my chest grew. It became so intense that I began to wheeze from being unable to breathe.

Normally, in a crisis like this, we would be wired, and I would know within seconds his location and status. But I was stripped of all the devices that I'd come to rely on when I was in the field.

And then through all the chaos I saw him. I would have known his form anywhere. At the sight of him lying in the grass at the edge of the clearing, tears stung my eyes. I began shoving people harder and harder in order to get to Gavin.

When I finally reached his side, I dropped down beside him. "Gavin? Can you hear me?" Quickly, I scanned his body to assess his wounds. My eyes clamped shut in pain when I saw he had been hit in both the chest and the abdomen. Any other day, those wounds wouldn't have been an issue, because he would have been wearing his bullet-proof vest.

Tears streaked down my cheeks, dripping onto Gavin's blood-stained face. I pulled my cell phone out of my pocket and dialed Peterson's emergency number. Before he picked up, I shook Gavin's shoulders. "Don't you dare die on me, Gavin!" I shrieked. Not caring about who was around me or might overhear me, I shouted, "That's an order, dammit!"

His eyelids fluttered, and my heart jumped in my chest. "Gavin? Gavin, please look at me!"

Slowly his eyes opened, and he gazed up at me.

"There you are. Stay with me. Okay?"

"Hello? Vargas, is that you?" Peterson's voice echoed from the phone.

Quickly, I related to him what had happened. Then I hung up before he could say anything else. I didn't have time to talk to him. I needed to devote all my attention to Gavin.

"Peterson knows what happened, so once the ambulance gets here, they'll radio in to take us to the best hospital around here. They might even airlift you, if you need it."

Gavin wheezed out an agonized breath. "Love you. Always have . . . always will."

My body shook as violent sobs racked me. "I love you, too. So fucking much. That's why I want you to stay with me. Please, please stay with me."

A beautiful smile lit up Gavin's face. Without another word to me, he closed his eyes. When he went limp in my arms, a scream tore through me. "No! Sweet Jesus, no!" I buried my head in his chest, sobbing as hard as I had done the day my dad was taken from me. And once again it was at the hands of a biker.

In my warped sense of reality, it seemed that one moment I had cradled Gavin's lifeless body in my arms, and then the next I found myself in a room off the ER at a hospital somewhere in Virginia. A scratchy blanket provided by an EMT was draped around my shoulders to fend off the rising chill spreading through my body. I blinked a few times to try to clear my eyes of the gritty feel from crying.

Someone had set a cup of black coffee on the table in front of me. Steam rose off the liquid. I reached out and took the cup in my trembling hands. As I brought the cup to my lips, I saw the rust-colored blood staining my hands.

Gavin's blood.

My throat clenched, and I found I couldn't take a sip. Instead, I felt like throwing up. With shaky fingers, I put the cup back down on the table. Once again, I found myself staring at my hands.

Twenty-two years ago I had done the same thing as I sat in a private holding room at the police station. No matter how many officers came inside that room with kind offers of sodas or candies, I ignored them and continued staring down at my hands covered in my father's blood. The only person I finally acknowledged was my mother after she burst into the room. She took one look at me and my bloodied hands and clothes and collapsed into hysterics at my feet. I had had to offer her comfort in those first minutes before she got ahold of herself. It had been a hell of a lot for an eight-year-old kid to endure.

Just like then, time seemed to stand agonizingly still. I didn't know how long I sat lost in my own world. I drifted in and out of a weird consciousness that was almost like sleeping, but I was fully awake. I paid no attention to the clicking hands on the wall clock. Time really had no meaning for me anymore. As with my father, it would be measured in the time before Gavin's death and then the time after.

When the door opened, I glanced up to see Peterson, his face ashen. He stepped inside and closed the door behind him. He didn't bother taking one of the chairs across from me. Instead, he sat down beside me. Eyeing the coffee cup in front of me, he reached into his jacket pocket and took out a silver-plated flask. He poured a dark amber-colored liquid into the foam cup.

Staring at me, he brought the flask to his lips. After he took a long swig, I snaked one of my arms out of the blanket to take my cup. Although I should have sipped slowly, I sucked it down in one long, fiery, bitter gulp. The alcohol hit my stomach with a searing jolt, and I shuddered.

"I don't know what the fuck to say to you right now," Peterson said, his voice hoarse. After I gave a brief nod, he eased back in his chair. "I'd ask how you're holding up, but it seems pretty evident. I'm sure you don't need any of my psychobabble bullshit that you're in shock or what a good agent and man Gavin was or that time heals all wounds, blah, blah."

I gave him a weak smile. "I appreciate you nixing all the bullshit words of alleged comfort." I held out my cup for a refill of the alcohol. He happily obliged me. After taking another long sip, I shifted in my chair. "Where the hell are we?"

"We backtracked you guys south to Richmond, since it had the closest field office."

I nodded. "What happens now with Gavin?"

"The bureau contacted his parents, and we're flying them out of Concord on the next plane. As his next of kin, they'll be taking care of him from here."

As I stared down into my once-again-empty cup, I couldn't imagine the grief the McTavishes were experiencing. I might've lost my partner and best friend, but Gavin was their only son—their baby boy after two girls. They'd always been so supportive of him, from when he became an agent to when he came out.

Not wanting to think about them or my grief, I met Peterson's gaze. "I guess we need to start working on what kind of story we're going to spin to Bishop and the other Raiders."

Peterson eased forward, taking my hand in his. "Samantha, there's no easy way to say this, nor is there a right time to say it."

I knew the shit was about to hit the fan when he didn't call me Vargas like always. I glanced up at him. "What is it?"

He exhaled a painful sigh. "Look, I'm just going to cut to the chase. We don't need to worry about a story for the Raiders, because without Gavin, there is no undercover case."

Blinking several times, I tried to process his words. "You're shutting down the mission?"

"Just the undercover aspect. We're still going to monitor the Raiders and do the best we can with what we have on the outside, as well as the work you two have done so far."

I jerked my hand away from his. "Are you fucking kidding me? Gavin hasn't been dead twenty-four hours, and you and the bureau are already shutting down the case!"

"It's nothing personal against Gavin. This is just how things are done. Undercover operations cost us money every second, and money talks." After crossing his arms over his chest, he added, "Deep down, you know that."

Even though what Peterson said was the truth, rage still boiled within me. It wasn't as if the bureau had nine-to-five hours, and that meant that cases were decided on in the midnight hour just the same as they were in the light of day. Of course, when you lost an agent in the field, it often meant things were expedited.

"There's still work to be done on the inside with the Raiders, especially after what happened tonight," I countered.

"While I might agree, there is no way to get another agent trained and inside, least of all to find one who could gain the Raiders' trust like Gavin."

"*I'm* on the inside."

Peterson's eyes widened before he ran his hand over his five o'clock shadow. "Look, you've been through a devastating trauma tonight. There's no reason why we need to be discussing this now. Take a week or two off to get your head on straight. Go back to Massachusetts with Gavin's parents for the funeral."

I gave an angry shake of my head. "Don't dismiss me as incapable of taking down the Raiders just because I don't have a dick."

A low growl came from Peterson. "You need to step back, get your head out of your ass, and really think for a moment."

"I *am* thinking. I'm wondering how you and the bureau can let all of Gavin's hard work for the last two months go to waste when I can do this."

"Pardon me for saying that it's not us who is dismissing you for not having a dick; it would be the Raiders. You won't get shit from any of them, even Bishop. You weren't some patched member's old lady. You were just a hang-around's girlfriend. It's a big fucking difference." When I started to argue, he held up his hand. "Don't think for a minute we would risk your life for what information it *might* bring. Especially not after losing Gavin."

I controlled the volatile anger pulsing through me by sucking in a few deep breaths and exhaling them. Peterson eyed me as if he knew I was doing everything within my power not to go off on him. When I was finally able to speak again without losing my shit, I said, "I know Bishop better than you do—he will talk to me. It can still work."

Peterson shook his head. "It doesn't matter, Vargas. The case is closed."

"You're the lead agent. You could reopen it."

"How quickly you forget that we all answer to somebody. The higher-ups would have my ass if I tried to reopen the case by sending you in."

With my anger rising again, I flicked the empty coffee cup with the back of my hand. It went sailing over the edge of the table. After it landed on the floor, I looked Peterson in the eye again. "I won't give this up. I can't. I have to find justice for Gavin." When Peterson opened his mouth to argue, I shook my head. "It's not just about Gavin. This case with the Raiders isn't so black-and-white anymore. They were attacked today after an important meeting this morning. I have to find out the truth."

Crossing his arms over his chest, Peterson sighed. "You're a grown woman with your own mind, and after living with my wife and two daughters, I know I can't tell you what to do. But hear me when I say that whatever craziness you have running through your mind right now isn't going to work. No matter how much you want to honor Gavin's life, you won't do it if you end up blowing your career, or worse, if you end up dead."

"What I do off the record is of no concern to the bureau," I countered.

"It is if it interferes with a mission."

"The case is closed—you said so yourself."

"No, the undercover aspect is closed. We will still be monitoring and collecting evidence on the Raiders." Peterson leaned forward to place his hand on my shoulder. "Once again, I have to ask you to forget whatever plans you're concocting in your head. You have a bright future at the ATF, Vargas. I want to be able to promote you in a year or two. The last thing I want to do is stand beside you as you clean out your desk because you've been fired." He grimaced painfully. "Or worse, to stand beside your casket."

With a roll of my eyes, I demanded, "How many times are you going to give me the fired-or-dead scenario?"

"As many as it takes to get it through your thick skull," Peterson growled.

I had opened my mouth to argue some more when the door opened. An agent I'd never seen before poked his head in. "The McTavishes' flight is about thirty minutes out. We have a car waiting to take you to meet them."

"Thank you, Agent Sunderland."

After nodding, Agent Sunderland closed the door.

"Would you like to come with me?"

Seeing Gavin's grief-stricken parents was the last thing I wanted to do. On the other hand, my only other option was to sit alone in the room with my thoughts. With a humorless smile, I asked, "You got anything left in that flask to help fortify me for the trip?"

"If I don't, we can make a pit stop."

My eyebrows rose in surprise. "What would the bureau think about that one?"

Peterson rose out of his chair and offered me his hand. "On this one occasion, I would tell them to fuck off."

I couldn't help being surprised when a laugh escaped my lips. "I never imagined you to be a rebel."

"Desperate times call for desperate measures."

After momentarily weighing his words, I slipped my hand into his. "Yes. I do believe they do."

NINE

BISHOP

Hours turned into days and then the days into a week. It was as if all record of Marley vanished the night he was killed. All the contact numbers the garage had on file were disconnected. The apartment complex where he was supposed to live had no idea who I was talking about when I went by there. There was no obituary in the paper, nor was he listed at any of the local funeral homes. I didn't know Samantha's number, or I would have tried her. It was the strangest fucking thing I had ever seen or heard of.

It was hell not being able to be a part of his funeral. Of course, as a hang-around, he wouldn't have been afforded any Raiders' burial rites. But at the same time, I wanted my chance to say goodbye. More than anything, I wanted to be able to tell him that I was sorry.

That was the God's honest truth—the feeling of dread kept me up at night. I was really fucking sorry. I was sorry that I invited him on the run when I should have known it could be dangerous. I was sorry that I hadn't been able to protect him better that day. More than anything, I was sorry I ever mentioned anything to him about the Raiders. It wasn't just that Marley would have been a whole lot fucking better off if he had never met me—he would have been alive.

Besides searching for Marley, that first week after the funeral was spent in mourning for the fallen Raiders. Funerals were spread out so all the chapters could attend. East Tennessee had lost two guys; North Carolina had lost a guy and another member's old lady. The funeral that haunted me the most and sent me into a drunken stupor was Alabama's, where we attended one for a member's twelve-year-old son.

Among the grief and guilt, the need for revenge plagued us. While Rev wanted to put together the pieces for a legitimate case to send the murdering fuckers to rot in prison, the other chapters wouldn't hear of it. They set out to take care of it with the old vigilante justice that we had once taken part in as well. Part of me wanted to get involved, thinking that if I could have the killers' blood on my hands, then I could somehow atone for what had happened with Marley.

Oh yeah, I felt nothing but guilt twenty-four/seven, and it was fucking eating me alive. To make matters worse, the usual methods of coping weren't helping. I'd banged two new girls who had been hanging around the clubhouse, but it still didn't get Marley off my mind. Even after I knocked out my opponent in the third round, the usual Friday-night fight did nothing for me, either. Finally, I'd turned my attention to working nonstop. As if by keeping my mind on transmissions and carburetors, I would somehow not go crazy.

I was lying on a creeper underneath a classic Impala when I felt someone nudge my leg. I slid out to see my boss standing over me with a concerned frown. "Something wrong, Rick?"

He scratched the back of his neck and shifted the wad of chewing tobacco in his mouth. "I think you need to shove off for today."

"I was gonna finish this one up."

Rick shook his head. "I usually don't complain when one of my workers is busting his ass, but in this case, I think you need to head home. Have a beer and get some tail."

After fighting the urge to throw my wrench at Rick in frustration, I hopped to my feet. "I just wanted to help. We're short now because of . . ." I couldn't bring myself to say Marley's name.

"That may be true, but if you keep overworking yourself, my ass will really be in a bind when you're laid in up in bed with a torn muscle or the flu."

I knew when I was beat, so I dropped my wrench in the toolbox. "Fine. But I'm still coming in at seven in the morning."

Rick grinned. "Stubborn ass."

I gave him a pat on the back before starting down the hallway to the bathroom. From my fingers to my elbows, my arms looked like a typical grease monkey's. Taking the already-blackened bar of soap, I began scrubbing my hands and arms. The more I thought of Marley, the more furious my movements became, to where I was practically clawing marks on my skin.

I whirled around at the sound of a voice behind me. My heart stopped and restarted at the sight of Sam standing in the bathroom doorway. Seeing her sent my mind on a trippy flashback of the night Marley was killed. I remembered her tears, the way she had cradled Marley's body, the way his blood stained her clothes. But the image that stayed with me the most was the look of undiluted hate she had given me when cradling Marley's body. I had to blink to clear my mind of the image.

There was so much to say, but instead, I could only stare at her.

Part of me expected her to vanish into thin air just as Marley had. It had been only a week since I saw her last, but everything was different about her. Her dark eyes, which were usually so expressive, were dull and hollow and ringed with circles. The jeans she usually filled out were visibly looser—another sign of how her emotional pain was wrecking her physically.

Finally, she broke the tense silence. "Hey," she said softly.

"Hey," I grunted. Although part of me was glad as hell to see her, I couldn't hide the animosity that was boiling within me.

She took a step back. "Sorry to interrupt. Rick said I would find you back here."

"Where the hell have you been?" I demanded.

Her dark eyes widened in surprise at both my tone and my question. "Yeah, about that. Look, I'm sorry that I didn't call. It's been—"

I sliced one of my hands in the air, silencing her. "You're *sorry*? Marley's been dead over a week, and during that time, you didn't think one fucking time that you might oughta call and let me know how things were going?"

Sam's remorseful expression darkened. "What the fuck, Bishop? I just lost my boyfriend."

With a mirthless laugh, I said, "I mean, I get that you're pissed at me for what happened, but it seems to me it's pretty cut-and-dried to reach out to a man's friend when he dies." I shrugged. "But I guess it's only complicated to a coldhearted bitch."

Anger replaced the sadness in Sam's eyes as she stalked toward me. "How dare you say that to me!"

"Just calling it as I see it, darlin'."

"You ignorant bastard. Do you have any idea what I've been through in the last week?"

"No, actually, I don't, but I'm sure I might've had a clue if you. Had. Fucking. Called me!"

She shook her head so fast I was sure she was going to get whiplash. "And just how the fuck was I supposed to do that when I didn't have your number? I came here to try to explain things to you, but you're too pigheaded to see anything beyond yourself. Poor pitiful Bishop!"

When she started to turn away, I reached out and grabbed her arm. "Oh no, you're not leaving. Not until you explain what the hell happened to Marley after the ambulance left."

She jerked her chin at the sink. "Finish cleaning up and then meet me at the bar across the street."

Standing toe-to-toe with her, I growled, "Woman, you gotta lot of fucking nerve ordering me around."

Sam rolled her eyes. "Just do it." She then tossed her dark hair over her shoulder and walked out of the bathroom.

"What the fuck?" I muttered.

After rinsing off my hands with record speed, I hustled out of the garage. As I climbed onto my bike, I couldn't believe Sam had just told me to meet her at Tucker's. I didn't know if Marley had ever told her that was where we went sometimes after work to unwind.

Just before I entered Tucker's, I slid on my cut. Although I didn't want any club affiliation at work, I didn't know what I might find inside. While I might've thrown back a beer or two with Marley, I was hardly a regular, so I wanted to set the tone just in case.

When I entered the room, I searched for Samantha. Part of me had worried that my grief and guilt had driven me so insane that I had hallucinated seeing her back at the garage. But thankfully, I spotted her sitting at a table with a pitcher of beer and two glasses.

I eased down in the chair across from her. While her eyes flared slightly at the sight of my cut, she didn't say anything about it. "Hope Bud on tap is okay," she said.

With a nod, I said, "That's what Marley and I always had when we came here."

Her expression turned sad. "Yeah, he told me." She slid her mug of beer back and forth between her hands. "I really am sorry that I haven't called you, Bishop. The only excuse I can give you is it has been a really hard week for me."

Although I was still pissed about what had gone down, I found that I couldn't look her in the eye. I felt like too much of an asshole for the way I had acted at the garage. For fuck's sake, who did I think I was? Hell, Marley was just a friend I'd known for a few months. He was her boyfriend.

After downing a few sips of beer, I said, "No, I'm the one who should be sorry. I acted like a real bastard."

When I dared to look up, Sam gave me a small smile. "While I won't argue with you about that, I do appreciate the apology."

"You're welcome."

Sam took a sip a beer. "The truth is that while I might've been Marley's girlfriend, I wasn't his blood family or next of kin. That was made really clear to me when we got to the hospital. I had no say over what happened to him. The next morning his parents came down and took his body back home."

"Where was home?"

"Michigan or Milwaukee." She shrugged. "Marley never really said. He didn't care for his family that much."

I realized that he'd never told me exactly where he was from, either. I think his answer had been a cryptic "around."

"You didn't go back for the funeral?"

"As much as I wanted to be able to say good-bye, I really couldn't afford to travel or be away from work." With a sheepish expression, she added, "Besides, I really wasn't welcome. His parents never liked me."

"That fucking blows."

"Yeah, it does," she said, and then gulped down several sips of beer. "In the end, I know how I felt about him and how he felt about me. Standing over his grave and throwing roses onto his casket wouldn't change that. You know?"

Although I nodded, I still wanted that closure. Even if there was no way in hell he could hear me, I wanted to be able to say the things to Marley that would clear my conscience. But as I glanced across the table, I realized that I still had a chance to make things right. "There's something I really need to say to you."

"Oh?"

I nodded and then proceeded to drain the rest of my beer. After swiping the back of my mouth with my hand, I stared into Sam's dark eyes. All the guilt over Marley that I had been feeling the last week bubbled to the surface, and I began speaking it out loud. I talked about Preacher Man's murder and then Case's. When I finished, I rubbed the stubble on my chin and shook my head. "Jesus, I can't believe I'm telling you this."

"Because I'm a woman or because you're not used to talking about your feelings to anyone outside the MC?"

"Both really. As a hang-around, Marley wasn't supposed to know shit about club business, and as a woman, you're sure as hell not supposed to know."

"But how can I understand what you're talking about unless you're honest with me?"

I held my hands up. "Look, all you need to understand is at the end of the day, I'm so fucking sorry for what happened to Marley."

She stared at me for a moment, unblinking and unmoving, as if she was shocked that something so sincere could have come from me. "It wasn't your fault."

"That day . . . the way you looked at me after you found Marley. I know you blamed me, too."

"But I was in shock, Bishop. I might've thought the Raiders

were at fault that day, but not you. And I still don't think it was your fault."

"In some ways, no, it wasn't my fault. I wasn't the one who shot him, but at the same time, it was because of bad blood between my club and another. If he'd never met up with me, he would still be alive today."

"It was an accident, Bishop. He was in the wrong place at the wrong time," she argued.

"Once again, you're being naive."

Anger flashed in her eyes. "Then explain it to me."

"I should have realized with the direction our club was taking, things could get dangerous at the run. I should never have let him come."

Sam's brow lined in confusion. "What do you mean, 'the direction of your club'?"

At that point, I didn't see how it could hurt to explain a few things to her. "You know what a one-percent MC is, right?"

"Yeah. A little bit. Like from TV."

I laughed at where her limited view came from. "So you know that while ninety-nine percent of the clubs out there are full of decent, law-abiding citizens, the other one percent aren't?" When she nodded, I added, "Well, since the time it was started back in 'sixty-seven, the Raiders have been a one-percent club."

"Your club does illegal stuff?"

"You could say that." I motioned the waitress over for another pitcher of beer. "You could also say that because of a lot of bad shit that has gone down in the last couple of years, we're moving to be legitimate."

Surprise flashed in Sam's eyes at my admission. "You are?"

I nodded. "We had it approved by the original chapter when we were in Virginia."

Samantha appeared almost dumbfounded by my admission. "Just how are you doing that?"

"Can't tell you that, sugar. I'm already overstepping my bounds enough as it is."

Sam nibbled her lip before asking, "Did Marley know about you guys going legit?"

I shook my head. "As I said, he was just a hang-around. My brothers could have had me by the balls for telling him club business." I gave her a pointed stare. "Just like they could for me telling you what I have."

A nervous laugh escaped her. "Like I'm going to tell anyone."

"You sure as hell better not. I'd hate to have to kill you." As soon as I said the words, I grimaced. "Sorry. That was a badly timed joke."

"It's okay." The waitress appeared with a new pitcher and refilled our beers. When we were once again alone, Sam leaned closer to me. "I know I shouldn't ask, but I need to know for my sake . . . and for Marley's. What were the reasons behind why he was in the wrong place at the wrong time?"

I exhaled slowly before chugging half of my beer. "Once again, I can't tell you all the reasons behind why it happened. All I can say is people within our organization—the Raiders—aren't happy that we don't want to live as gangbangers anymore, and they took that out on us."

"I see," she murmured.

Reaching across the table, I took her hand in mine. "I wish I could be more honest with you, and tell you everything you want to know. But I can't."

"I get it—I understand." At what must've been my doubtful expression, she added, "I swear."

"I'm glad." I squeezed her hand before releasing it. "And I'm really glad you came to see me, Sam."

"Me, too."

"You know, you don't have to be as alone as you think you are."

Her eyes widened.

"Even though Marley wasn't a patched member or even a prospect, the Raiders look out for their own, especially wives and girlfriends. You don't have to go through Marley's loss . . . the grief . . . all on your own."

"Who said I was?"

I shrugged. "No one. It's just a feeling I have." When she continued looking skeptically at me, I sighed. "Deep down, I think we're a lot alike. So I just thought if you were handling things like I was, then you could use a friend to talk to."

A confused look came over her face. "Why?"

"Because."

"You're right about me feeling alone . . . even isolated." Sam dropped her head to stare at the rim of her beer. "Guess it just wigged me out to hear you offering me a shoulder to cry on, because I just didn't imagine bikers could ever be so honorable."

"After what you've experienced, I can't say I blame you for thinking we're all soulless bastards."

Her dark eyes jerked up to gaze into mine. "Excuse me?"

"You know, with Marley being killed by bikers."

She exhaled a long breath. "Right. Yeah, I guess it is easy to paint you all as being bad."

"The truth is we're really not, especially not my chapter brothers."

"I'll try to keep that in mind."

"Good. And no more being a stranger, okay?"

She nodded. "Okay."

"First way to remedy that is to give me your cell number."

I wasn't too surprised when she was a little hesitant. Besides hiding her emotions like me, Sam had this whole aura about her that was like a feral cat—skittish and untrusting. Finally, she took a pen out of her purse and grabbed one of the napkins on the table. After she scribbled down her number , she handed it to me. "I hope that doesn't end up on some MC bathroom wall to call for a good time," she teased.

Chuckling, I shook my head at her. "You can rest assured that won't happen."

"Glad to hear it," she said as she rose out of her chair. I think we were both shocked as hell at her next move. As she leaned over me, her long black hair covered me like a shroud, filling my nose with the sweet smell of her perfume. The moment her lips touched my cheek, it felt like an electric shock through my body. Samantha quickly jerked away. "Good-bye, Bishop."

"Bye, Sam."

While she practically sprinted out the door, I remained dumb-founded in my chair by both her reaction and mine to the kiss. I didn't think I could ever remember a time when a woman had given me a chaste kiss. Racking my brain came up with no one outside my family.

A small voice within me railed at me to toss Samantha's number in the trash. It reasoned that there was something about her that was trouble . . . even dangerous. But as with so many times in my life, I chose to ignore that voice.

TEN

SAMANTHA

I initially thought Bishop was bullshitting me about the Raiders watching out for their own. Frankly, I didn't want anything they could offer me unless it came in the form of justice for Gavin. But Bishop was constantly surprising me, and I learned very quickly that he was truly a man of his word. Over the next week, he called or texted me every day. At first, it was just to ask how I was and if I needed anything. Then we started talking on the phone for an hour or two a night. We never really discussed anything of substance because in the end, we both had too much to hide. Most of the time, we talked about movies we had enjoyed, or the music we liked to listen to. Sometimes there were stories from our childhood—stories that didn't reveal too much of who we really were. We seemed to spend a lot of the time laughing, which was something I desperately needed.

Regardless of the subject matter, I started to look forward to our calls more than I should have. When I tried telling myself it was for the case I was building on my own, I knew I was the one doing the bullshitting. Although it went against every fiber of my being, I enjoyed talking with Bishop. He was so much more than the guy I had originally thought he was. He was so much more than a lot of the men I had dated in the past, although I didn't like admitting that to myself.

After two weeks of texts, phone calls, and two dinners, I was growing antsy for more MC information. More than anything, I was intrigued about what he had told me at the bar about the club going legitimate. I couldn't imagine how a deal with a drug cartel fit into that picture, but I knew I had to find out. I had even more time at work to stew about it because Peterson kept me chained to a desk. Each time I broached the subject of going back out in the field, he would shake his head sadly. "Not until you get your head on straight, Vargas."

A month after Gavin's death found me in totally uncharted territory as I made my way into the gym run by the Raiders. We had just finished dinner out together on Tuesday when Bishop asked, "Remember how you said you wanted to see me box sometime?"

My mind immediately went back to the night I'd met him and one of our first conversations. "Yeah. I sure do."

"Well, I have a fight scheduled on Saturday night, if you'd like to come."

Considering where Bishop would be boxing, I figured it might be a great way to get some more information on the club. I also couldn't ignore the part of me that wanted to spend as much time as I could with Bishop before our time together came to an end. "Sure. I'd love to."

Bishop gave me his signature cocky grin. "Awesome."

Tonight was about trying to piece together the truth about the Raiders, whether it was good or bad. At least that was what I told myself. When I got to the door, I found a hulking man guarding it. I couldn't help being reminded of the first time I had gone to the Raiders' compound. Before I could tell him who I was, he asked, "You Samantha?"

"Yeah. I am."

He grinned. "B's just inside."

"Thanks."

After he held the door open for me, I ducked inside. The hallway was relatively quiet, with only a few men milling around. Down the hallway past the double doors, I could hear the roar of the growing crowd.

Unsure of what to do or where to go, I called out tentatively, "Bishop?"

Within seconds, he popped out of one of the rooms. At the sight of me, his face lit up. "Hey, Sam." He waved me over, and I hurried down the hallway.

"I'm so glad you came," he said as he gave me a friendly hug. Although the physical contact was brief, I couldn't ignore the solid way his arms felt around me. His embrace sparked a desire of intimate longing and a feeling of comfort. I wasn't used to having a man make me feel that way with just the slightest touch. It was completely unnerving.

I smiled at him when I pulled away. "Me, too." Glancing around the room, I saw we weren't alone. Another man stood by the massage table, reading over a notebook. I could only imagine that it included gambling figures, which made me question Bishop's claim of the Raiders going legitimate. I recognized the man as Boone Michaels, the club treasurer, from his file. He glanced up and gave me a quick wave.

For a moment, all I could do was stare at Bishop. He had on the typical shorts that boxers wore. Of course, it wasn't the shorts that had me mesmerized. It was the first time I had seen him shirtless, so I couldn't help staring at all the intricately designed tattoos on his broad chest and muscular arms.

When I met Bishop's gaze, there was an impish gleam in his eyes. "Were you just checking me out?"

Knowing he wanted to get a rise out of me, I casually replied, "Maybe. You're on display, so I might as well enjoy the view."

Bishop threw back his head and laughed heartily. "Oh man, I love when you're sassy with me."

"And I love being sassy with you." And it was the truth. I always had fun bantering with him.

As sexual tension crackled in the air between us, I decided I'd better change the subject. "Will your brothers be there tonight?"

While Bishop appeared surprised by my question, he quickly recovered. "Some of the guys from the club might be, but Deacon and Rev are busy tonight."

"I see." Some of the hope I had on gathering information on the case faded.

A tall, dark-haired man stuck his head in the door. "It's time, B."

"Thanks, Vinnie. Do me a favor and walk Samantha out."

"Sure."

Bishop winked at me. "Make sure she gets one of the best seats in the house to see me win."

Vinnie nodded. "Will do."

I stood awkwardly for a moment, unsure of what to do. "I guess I shouldn't say break a leg or something like that."

With a laugh, Bishop said, "I think 'good luck' would be fine. If I needed it."

I shook my head and smiled. "You're pretty cocky, aren't you?"

"Just sure of myself and my abilities."

Vinnie coughed behind us, and I knew it was time to go. Acting on an impulse, I leaned in and kissed Bishop's cheek. When I pulled back, he stared at me in surprise. "For luck."

A genuine smile appeared on his face. "Thanks."

"You're welcome."

I then turned and followed Vinnie down the hallway. With the fight about to start, the crowd had gotten even louder. When we entered the gym, the roar was deafening. For a relatively small gym, there was a huge gathering of people. They filled the stands on both sides of the ring.

Vinnie led me down front to where I felt as if I was practically in the ring. Years ago, I'd gone to a fight once with my dad. Although the arena in Miami was ten times the size of this gym, we hadn't had seats anywhere near as good as where I now sat.

The music pumping over the loudspeakers ceased, and a wiry-looking man entered the ring with a microphone. "Good evening, ladies and gentlemen. Welcome to tonight's fight, between Alex Fuentes and Bishop Malloy."

When the announcer called Bishop's name, the crowd erupted in cheers and catcalls. He came into the gym with a beaming smile. He was obviously a crowd favorite. I noticed that several young boys jumped in front of his path with autograph books in their hands. Bishop not only graciously signed them but took the time to talk to each boy. It warmed my heart seeing his compassionate and caring side and added to my growing sense of awareness that he was so much more than just an outlaw biker.

Bishop and his opponent entered the ring and went to their opposite corners. Boone appeared to be giving Bishop a pep talk as he massaged his shoulders. Bishop would nod from time to time.

The moment the match started, I couldn't take my eyes off Bishop. He really was a force to be reckoned with. While some women might've ducked their heads at the punches and jabs, I was used to both seeing them and delivering them in my line of work.

In the eighth round, Bishop delivered a punch to the side of Alex's head that sent him reeling back. He collapsed onto the mat. While the ref smacked the floor of the ring, Alex struggled to get up, but he couldn't. The ref grabbed Bishop's arm and raised it over his head, which sent me and the crowd onto our feet.

Bishop didn't stay too long in the ring to enjoy his victory. Instead, he ducked under the ropes and came bounding over to me. Even though he was a sweaty mess, I happily dove into his arms. "Congratulations!"

Instead of replying, he just gave me a cocky grin that shot desire straight through me.

I grinned back at him. "What? You're not going to say I told you so?"

"No need to rub it in."

I gave him a playful smack on the arm. As we started out of the gym to the back rooms, Bishop draped a sweaty arm across my shoulder. "Did ya like it?"

I bobbed my head enthusiastically. "Although I probably shouldn't like guys beating each other up, I loved it."

Bishop laughed. "I'm glad to hear it. Of course, I don't want you to get used to it."

"Oh?"

"I'm only fighting now for the money for my bike shop. I would have quit a long time ago if it wasn't for the money."

My chest tightened a bit. "From the gambling?"

"Yeah."

"I see."

Lowering his voice, Bishop said, "We're working on going legit. It isn't an overnight process. It's going to take time in some areas." When I didn't immediately respond, Bishop took my hand and squeezed it. "I need you to believe me, Sam. You have my word that I'm telling the truth about this."

Since I desperately wanted to believe him, I nodded. I knew I would need to dig deeper to see just what areas had been legitimized if I was going to make a case for the Raiders' innocence.

"We okay?" Bishop asked.

I smiled reassuringly at him. "Yeah. We're fine."

When we entered the training room where we'd been before, Boone took a towel and started wiping the sweat from Bishop's chest and arms. I had to fight the urge to snatch the towel away from him and do it myself.

"You really nailed that one tonight, B. No stitches needed, no busted lip." He winked at Bishop. "Nothing that will keep the ladies away."

"I'm not worried about any of that."

Boone glanced in my direction. "Yeah, I guess you don't have to worry about that, since she looks at you like she wouldn't care one way or the other if your face was busted up. Kinda a lovey-dovey look like you've been giving her."

I could have sworn Bishop's cheeks reddened a little. "It ain't like that with Sam," he quickly protested. "How about working on this shoulder?" Bishop asked as he plopped down on the massage table.

Boone took the hint and shut his mouth. As he focused his energy on massaging Bishop's shoulder, the silence in the room was broken by Boone's phone ringing. When he glanced down at it, he grimaced. "Shit. It's Annie."

With a grin, Bishop said, "You better take it, or your ass will be in hot water."

"Shut up," Boone grumbled before he ducked outside into the hallway.

After Bishop rolled his shoulder, he winced in pain.

"Want me to do it?" I asked.

Bishop's eyes flared at my suggestion. "Sure. If you don't mind."

"It's the least I can do for the man of the hour," I teased as I walked over to the massage table.

My fingers tingled when they connected with Bishop's warm flesh. Working my hands, I kneaded his taut muscles. Bishop groaned and let his head fall back, which caused a tightening between my legs. Simply touching him and giving him relief from the pain was making me hot.

When I glanced at him, he was looking at me through hooded eyes. "That feels amazing."

"I'm glad."

He had started to say something when Boone came back into the room. He glanced at the two of us and grinned. "I see I've been replaced by a newer and more attractive model."

Bishop snorted. "Whatever."

"Listen, I gotta get home. Crisis with the plumbing. You okay?"

"Fine," Bishop replied.

"See ya later, then. Bye, Samantha."

"Bye, Boone."

After he was gone, Bishop and I stood in an awkward silence. "Guess I better get going, too," I said. The truth was I wanted to stay there with him in that room until we recaptured what we'd had when we were interrupted.

"Let me walk you out," Bishop said as he hopped down off the table.

"The rough-and-tumble boxer is a gentleman at heart, huh?"

He winked at me before pulling a T-shirt over his head. "We all have our secrets."

As we started out the door, Bishop nodded at the beefy bouncer. "Listen, there's something I wanted to ask you," he said to me.

"What is it?"

"Next Saturday night we're having a birthday party for my brother, Rev. Since he's our president, it's going to be a pretty big party—one that lasts all weekend. Members are coming in from all over the state. I wondered if you might like to come."

I drew in a breath as I carefully weighed my next words. This was exactly what I had been hoping for—a chance to be with the full Raiders MC again to see what I could overhear. While I wanted to give a hurried response, I had to temper myself. I knew I couldn't look overeager, which in turn could make me look suspicious.

Misreading my hesitation, Bishop said, "Fuck, I'm sorry. That was a real stupid thing of me to do."

"Excuse me?"

"After what happened to Marley, I guess the last thing you want is to be around a group of bikers."

Once again, I found myself speechless, but this time it was over Bishop's thoughtfulness. Then I felt like a complete bitch by using it to my advantage. "I would be lying if I said your offer didn't surprise me . . . and unnerve me a little. But at the same time, I think it might be good for me to be around the club again."

"Really?"

"Yeah. I mean, you say you guys are going legit, so I guess I can't help giving you a second chance, right?"

Bishop grunted. "Yeah, just remember you don't know shit about any of that. Got it?"

"I promise."

"So can I pick you up at seven?"

Just as I was about to agree, an image of my house flashed before my eyes. I quickly clamped my mouth shut. There was no way in hell I could let Bishop see where I was living. None of it matched the Samantha Vargas he knew. "Why don't I meet you there?"

"Are you sure?"

"Yeah, since I flaked out a few days after Marley's death, I've been working late to make up the time and get the boss off my ass," I replied. My mind felt as if it were treading water in the deep end to keep up with all the lies I was spewing.

"Oh, okay, then yeah, just come here." Bishop cleared his throat. "Guess if I picked you up, it would seem like a date, huh?"

Shaking my head, I stared down at my shoes. I realized I didn't have to worry about Bishop suspecting anything about me and the club. Instead, his worry came in the form of concern that we were overstepping some sacred bounds because of Gavin. He would have given any FBI profiler a run for the money with his being so honorable and considerate. The fact that he had a conscience wasn't something I had ever bet on, and in turn, it made things even more difficult. I needed him to be a Neanderthal who didn't give a shit about what Marley would have felt about him making a move on me.

"I guess it could be seen that way," I said.

"I, uh, well, I just didn't want you to think I was some bastard for hitting on you so soon after Marley died."

I knew I had to choose my next words carefully—I could either drive him away or reel him in. "Regardless of what's in your head, any woman would be flattered to be asked on a date by you."

"Is that right?" he questioned.

"Yeah, it is."

Bishop coughed. "That's good to know."

"I'm glad I could help," I said. And it was the truth. I did want Bishop to see he was more than he thought he was.

"So I'll see you Saturday night, then."

"See you then."

ELEVEN

BISHOP

I glanced down at my watch and grimaced. It was half past six, and I had only thirty minutes before Samantha was supposed to arrive for Rev's party. At the moment, grease stains blackened my hands all the way up to my elbows, not to mention that I was wearing the rattiest pair of jeans I owned. All day, I had fought a fucking nervous energy at the thought of being close to Samantha. I didn't know where the hell it was coming from. It wasn't as if she and I hadn't had dinner a couple of days ago or talked on the phone the night before. Maybe it had something to do with the fact that I had invited her to Rev's party. I had never invited a woman, even as just a friend, to the clubhouse, least of all to a family party. Although she had been around with Marley, she was still an outsider when it came to the club.

I felt like a fucking pussy for being nervous. I had never spent a day of my life worrying about women. Now Samantha had me spinning twenty-four/seven. Part of me was nervous about what my brothers were going to say when they saw me with her. Of course, I didn't know why I gave two shits about what anyone in the club had to say about my inviting her. It wasn't any of their damn business. But even though I tried telling myself that, I knew it was still going to be an issue.

Since I had needed an outlet for my restless energy, I thought it would be a good idea to put the finishing touches on the bike Deacon and I were giving Rev for his birthday. But my dumb-ass self didn't keep a good eye on the time, and the last thing I wanted was for Samantha to see me looking like the grease monkey I was.

Although tonight wasn't a date, I still wanted to look good. Sam was a real catch—the kind of woman a man went above and beyond to impress. Since we had reconnected after Marley's death, I felt I had been busting my ass whenever it came to her. Every fucking day I thought about her, and I couldn't wait to talk to her on the phone. She was the first woman I had really enjoyed spending time with outside the bedroom. She was so easy to talk to, and she seemed generally interested in me as a person, not as a Raider. Most of the women I came in contact with were all about the sex or being an old lady in the club.

Of course, the way I felt about Sam did little to ease the guilt that still resided within me about Marley. No matter how good things seemed between us, it was as if Marley were always a silent specter. I didn't know how to get past the guilt. It wasn't something I felt comfortable talking to Samantha about. I was afraid that if she felt the same way, I might scare her off, and that was the last thing I wanted to do. I wanted to be with her, even if it had to be just as friends.

After tossing my wrench into the toolbox, I wiped off my hands and then headed out of the garage. Instead of taking the time to go home, I hustled over to the clubhouse. I could take a quick shower and shave and then grab some clothes from my room.

The moment I swept in the door, I was bombarded with party

central. Streamers and balloons hung from the ceiling, while a giant HAPPY BIRTHDAY sign took up one of the walls. Out-of-town brothers called out my name and raised their beers. I threw up my hand as I headed to the bedrooms.

Just as I stripped off my jeans and shirt, a knock came at the door. "Yeah?" I questioned as I turned on the water in the shower.

Rev's voice came from the other side. "Emergency club meeting in five."

"Are you fucking with me?"

With a grunt of frustration, Rev replied, "No. I'm not fucking with you, although that seems to be everyone's consensus about this meeting."

I eyed the stream of water longingly before I reached over and turned off the shower. "Fine. I'll be right there."

"Good."

Without time to shower, I cleaned off my greasy arms as best I could in the sink. I sure as hell hoped the meeting wouldn't take long, and I could grab a shower just before Sam arrived. After drying off, I pulled on a fresh pair of jeans and a T-shirt. As I opened the door, I threw on my cut.

Out in the hallway, I ran into Willow taking an armload of towels into Deacon's room. "Hey, rug rat," I called.

She threw a look at me over her shoulder. "What, Uncle B?"

"I need you to do me a favor."

"Will it get me out of helping Grandma get ready for the out-of-town visitors?" she asked with a hopeful gleam in her eyes.

"Not exactly."

Her face fell. "Oh, well, what do you want me to do?"

"I've got a friend coming to the party tonight. I'm supposed to meet her at seven, but Uncle Rev's called an emergency club meeting. Can you be on the lookout for her?"

"Her?" Willow asked suspiciously.

Jesus, I wasn't going to be able to catch a fucking break with anyone. "Yes. It's a girl. Her name is Samantha, and she has dark hair."

"Okay. I'll find her."

I reached over to plant a kiss on her cheek. "Thanks, rug rat."

She huffed out a frustrated breath at the nickname she hated before heading into the bedroom. I went down the hall and then to the meeting room. When I slid into my usual seat at the table, I knew it had to be something heavy or Rev wouldn't have interrupted his birthday weekend with it.

Deacon echoed my thoughts when he said, "What is so fucking important that it called me away from a quickie with Alex?"

Boone snorted. "Yeah, this better be pretty important, Rev. You're still a newlywed, so you don't know what it's like to be a married man and have sex be limited."

"Amen to that," Mac said as he lit a cigarette.

Rev stared gravely around the table. "I just got some information from Rambo that I thought you needed to know."

At the mention of Rambo, we all sat a little straighter in our chairs. "After all this time, he's heard from Eddy?" Mac questioned. Just the mention of Eddy's name caused me to tense in my seat, my fists tightening in anger.

Rev nodded. "Rambo now has full confirmation that he was behind the shooting in Virginia." We all leaned forward with heavy looks on our faces. "There's this dude who owns a truck stop about five miles from headquarters. He's on good terms with the Raiders. He said that two guys with devils on their cuts came in to pay for gas about thirty minutes before the shooting. Since he knew the guys were in Raiders territory, he eyeballed them and saw them get into a black-paneled van."

"Holy shit," Boone murmured.

"Did he have it on tape?" Deacon asked.

"He sure as hell did. Once Rambo looked at the tapes, he realized it was a Diablos cut."

Deacon cocked his eyebrows at Rev. "But Eddy wasn't on the tape, right?"

"No. He wasn't," Rev replied.

"Is he still gone underground?" I asked. After the suspicions about Eddy's involvement grew, he had disappeared. No one could find him to question him about how it was possible the Diablos knew where we were. Club meetings were kept secret, so while they might have known where headquarters was, they had no idea when we would be there. Considering his friendship with them and his anger about what went down with us, it was the only likely answer for the shooting.

"He's finally emerged from whatever hellhole he's been hiding in," Rev replied.

"And now the Raiders are going to formally deal with the fucker?" Deacon asked.

"That won't be happening," Rev replied.

"Why the fuck not?" Boone demanded.

"Because he's now a patch-wearing member of the Diablos."

The table erupted in angry shouts and strings of profanity. That was the evidence we needed to solidify Eddy's guilt.

Rev held up his hand. "Truth be told, we should have seen this coming. He's been in fucking bed with those bastards for far too long. It makes sense he would finally join up with them. After the shooting, there was no going back."

Mac stubbed out his cigarette. "Yeah, but I can't see it being so easy for an ego-tripper like Eddy to give up his president's patch and be just another Diablo."

Deacon nodded. "They must've made him a pretty good offer to patch over."

"That's what really concerns me." Rev's expression was grave. "Who knows what kind of inside information he gave them?"

"Damn. Shit could get ugly," Boone remarked.

Silence fell around the table as the news sank in. I leaned forward in my chair. "So, what do we do? Just sit around until the Diablos make a move?"

Rev sighed. "Unfortunately, that's exactly what we do. Rambo and the other chapters are sending out feelers to their contacts to see what they can find out. But you guys know as well as I do that contacts expect to be paid, and usually it's in ways that we no longer deal with."

"So we end up like lame fucking ducks," Deacon muttered.

"Not entirely. We do have our protection from both the Raiders and the Rodriguez cartel. Eddy and the Diablos would have to be stupid to pull anything on us," Rev said.

Deacon motioned for Mac to hand him a cigarette. "Yeah, but let's not forget that Eddy is one stupid fuck who lives for revenge." After lighting up, he smiled grimly. "Sure puts a hell of a downer on your birthday weekend, bro."

Rev chuckled. "True. But it's nothing we haven't faced before. We just have to be diligent, like our other brothers. Hopefully, after what happened in Virginia, Eddy has gotten enough revenge. But if I get wind of the least bit of danger, I'll put us on lockdown."

I nodded along with the others. After I glanced down at my watch, I grimaced. As the conversation left the subject of Eddy and some of the others had risen out of their chairs, I asked, "So we're done here?"

Rev grinned at me. "What's your hurry? Don't tell me that you also have a hot piece of ass waiting on you for a quickie?"

Before I could answer, Deacon leaned over and put me in a headlock. "What are you talking about? When it comes to Bishop, it's always a quickie."

"Fuck you," I muttered as the others roared with laughter. After shoving Deacon off me, I rose out of my chair.

"Seriously, B. Where's the fire?" Deacon asked.

"There's no fire. I just wanted a chance to clean up before the party."

Deacon and Rev exchanged a look. "Since when do you need to 'clean up'?" Rev questioned.

I rolled my eyes. I knew once they got wind that I was meeting Samantha, I would never hear the end of it. "Fine. If you must know, I've asked Samantha to the party tonight."

Deacon's forehead furrowed with confusion. "Who the hell is Samantha?"

Before I could answer, Rev said, "You're dating Marley's girlfriend?"

Deacon chimed in with "The hang-around who got killed in Virginia?"

Making a time-out sign with my hands, I said, "Hold the fuck up. I'm not dating anyone. We've gotten to be really good friends, so I thought I would ask her to the party." Turning to Rev, I said, "Yeah, it's Marley's girlfriend. You got a problem with that?"

Rev's eyes widened in surprise. "No. But from your tone, I gotta wonder if you do."

Groaning, I rubbed my hand over my face. "I'm such a fucking bastard to be scamming on my dead friend's woman."

"If you're not dating her, then you're not scamming. There's nothing wrong with being friends with her," Rev said diplomatically.

Deacon snorted. "Sorry, man, but there's no way in hell Bishop is just friends with this chick."

I crossed my arms over my chest. "Is that so?"

Deacon nodded. "I might not be your blood brother, but we have one thing in common. We are incapable of being friends with a woman."

"I'm friends with Annabel and Alexandra," I countered.

He rolled his eyes. "That's different. They're both taken. This Sam chick doesn't have a man anymore, does she?"

"No."

"Then you do want more with her," Deacon said.

Rev and the others leaned forward in anticipation of my response. I sighed. "Fine. I do want more with her. And by more, I mean more than just fucking her."

You could have heard a pin drop in the room after my declaration. Glancing around at my brothers, I demanded, "Jesus Christ, would you stop staring at me and say something!"

A huge grin spread on Deacon's face. "I'll be damned. Our little brother is all grown up now."

When Rev nodded in agreement, a growl erupted from me. "Seriously? I'm twenty-fucking-five."

"Maybe you're that old in years, but until you're ready to open yourself up to another person, then you're just a kid," Rev said.

"You two are full of shit." I looked to Boone and Mac. "What about you?"

Boone smacked me on the back. "I gotta agree with them. Being a man ain't about fucking every piece of ass that moves. A real man has opened his heart up at least once to be shredded by some bitch. Some of us luck out more than others and have the first woman we open up to be the only one for us. But then others have to suffer through heartache." He winked at me. "Now it's your turn."

I furiously rubbed my face as I let their words sink in. "I'm so screwed," I muttered.

"Yep. But don't worry. It's a good screwed," Rev said.

After bringing my hands away from my face, I asked, "But what about Marley?"

"What about him?" Deacon questioned.

With a grunt, I said, "You can't be such an unfeeling asshole that you wouldn't have an issue dating one of your dead brothers' girlfriends."

Deacon placed his hand on my shoulder. "I think you're missing the vital point here."

"And just what would that be, Mr. Know-it-all?"

"The fact that Marley is dead."

"Uh, I think I'm aware of that one," I snapped.

Rev sighed. "I think what Deacon was trying to say is that even though Marley is dead, you and Samantha are still alive. As hard as it is, life goes on, and people move on. Look at Kim and Breakneck. Case was Breakneck's brother, and he's okay with dating his widow. And as far as the Raiders are concerned, we know that they weren't sneaking around together, because Kim was so committed to Case."

Cocking his head, Deacon eyed me suspiciously. "You two weren't hooking up behind his back, were you?"

"Fuck no!"

"Were you scamming her while he was alive?"

Avoiding his stare, I said, "No."

"You're lying," Deacon countered.

Throwing up my hands, I replied, "Fine. Before Marley got killed, I thought about her more than I should. Anyone who looks at her would want to fuck her, but I actually liked her, too."

"Did you hit on her or make a pass?" Rev questioned softly.

"Fuck no!" I again replied.

Rev nodded. "I believe you. Since you remained loyal to Marley by not hitting on Samantha, I don't think there was anything wrong while Marley was alive."

"Me, either," Deacon chimed in.

"Really?" I questioned more to Rev than Deacon. After all, Rev was known for his moral compass.

"Hell yeah. And I say go for it with her." At what must've been my skeptical look, he added, "If you're still having issues with the guilt, talk to Breakneck. See how he handled the situation with Kim."

"Good suggestion," I murmured. I wasn't sure if anything would take away the guilt that I had, but I guessed the only thing I could do was give it a try.

Rev grinned. "Come on, lover boy. We'd better get going. You don't need to keep Samantha waiting one minute longer."

With a roll of my eyes, I followed him out the door.

TWELVE

SAMANTHA

At five until seven, I pulled my car into the clubhouse parking lot. Well, the late-model Honda Accord wasn't actually my car. I had borrowed it from a buddy, since it better suited the lifestyle Bishop would expect than the usual Mercedes convertible I drove.

After killing the engine, I remained seated, twirling the keys on my finger while staring ahead. My mind whirled with thoughts from the past. Most of all, I thought of the last time I had been here with Gavin—the night I had first laid eyes on Bishop Malloy. I couldn't help marveling how much had changed in so little time. Since getting to know Bishop better, I thought of him in an entirely different light than I had at our first meeting. But when my thoughts went to Gavin, I had the usual searing pain of agony go through my heart. It was just the focus I needed to keep my eye on the prize, which was finding out the truth about the Raiders.

A knock on the car window sent me jumping out of my skin.

When I composed myself enough to glance over, a small dark-haired girl stared curiously at me. "Samantha?" she asked through the glass.

"Yeah," I croaked.

A grin spread across her cheeks. "Uncle B sent me to get you."

"Willow?" When she nodded, I smiled. Bishop had spoken many times about his niece. The love he had for her was evident from the way he talked about her. I turned in my seat and grabbed the gift bag for Rev. Then I cracked the door. After Willow backed up, I opened it and stepped out of the car.

"I didn't mean to scare you. Uncle B told me to be looking out for you."

"Where is he?"

"He said he had an emergency club meeting with Daddy, Uncle Rev, and some of the other guys."

The hairs on the back of my neck stood up. "I see."

Taking my free hand, Willow tugged me along. "Come on."

I followed behind her. This time there were two bouncers at the front door, which I figured was because they needed more crowd control tonight. The two men didn't give me a moment's glance, considering that I was with Willow. She waved to them before pushing on through the front door.

Just like the time before, I was met with thumping music, loud conversation, and hazy smoke rings. "Do you come to a lot of the parties here?" I asked. I couldn't help asking the question.

"Mommy and Daddy only let me come to some of them."

"I see."

"I get to come tonight, since it's Uncle Rev's birthday." She crooked her finger to beckon me closer. When I leaned down, she added in a low voice, "I think people act naughty after my bedtime.

Mommy gets mad if Daddy stays too late. She says there's nothing he can be doing but getting into trouble when he stays."

I had to bite back a smile at her words. "She's probably right."

Willow smiled happily as she swung my hand back and forth in her own. "Uncle B said to take you over to Mommy and the other women."

"Okay. That sounds good."

After Willow led me through the wall-to-wall crowd inside the roadhouse, we went out the back door. As soon as we got outside, we entered what could only be classified as birthday party overload. Clear and multicolored Christmas lights were strung up all around the clearing, along with Chinese lanterns. My nose picked up the delicious smell of hamburgers and hot dogs cooking. When I looked to where the aromas were coming from, I saw several bikers, with beers in their hands, stationed at three commercial-sized grills.

Willow then steered us over to where a multitude of picnic tables had been set up. Some of the tables, with their red-and-white-checked tablecloths, were overflowing with food and drinks, while others were set with plates and plastic forks. In the middle of all the tables, there was a towering, three-tiered birthday cake with a motorcycle on top. "Wow," I murmured.

"Pretty cool, huh?" Willow questioned.

"That's the biggest birthday cake I've ever seen."

"Uncle Rev promised me I could have the motorcycle on top."

"Do you like playing with toy motorcycles?" Considering that she was outfitted all in pink, I hadn't pegged her for a fan of cars.

"No. I wanted it because it's made of chocolate."

I grinned down at her. "Now, that sounds like my kind of motorcycle."

A feeling of apprehension came over me when I glanced down

the grouping of tables to where several of the Raiders women were setting up some of the food. Once again, I recoiled slightly at the sight of some of the ladies wearing cuts with "Property of" patches on the back. But I knew from my research that a lot of the women considered the patches a badge of honor, just as their husbands or boyfriends did their patches.

When Willow and I walked up to the group, all conversation silenced at the sight of me. Although I had met several of the women when I went on the run, all of these faces were new. "This is Uncle B's girlfriend, Samantha," Willow introduced.

At the mention of the word "girlfriend," several of the women gasped in surprise while a few narrowed their eyes at me. Almost instinctively, my hands flew up in front of me. "Friend, not girlfriend. Bishop and I are just friends." My explanation did little to lighten the animosity flowing through the air.

A busty brunette, who was outfitted from head to toe in black, stepped almost toe-to-toe with me. "Willow, will you run to the kitchen and get us some more ketchup?"

"Sure, Miss Annie. Be right back," Willow replied before sprinting off toward the house.

I felt like a real chickenshit after Willow left me alone with the women. I glanced nervously around the group. Where the hell was Kim or Alexandra and Annabel? The better question, though, since most of these women were new to me, was whether the Raiders had a revolving door of women. A large part of me didn't really want to know the answer.

When I remembered the gift bag in my hand, I thrust it out lamely. "This is for Rev."

Annie's eyebrows shot up. "You got Rev a present?"

I nodded. "It's his birthday, isn't it?"

Annie pursed her lips. "That's not the point."

"I'm sorry. I don't get what you mean."

After sweeping her hands to her hips, Annie questioned, "Do you often buy presents for other women's husbands?"

Annie's tone had me swallowing hard as I glanced at the other women. "Um, well, I didn't think—"

"I don't know where you come from, but around here, we don't take too kindly to floozies trying to flirt with our husbands."

Once again, I held my hands out in front of me. "I swear, I wasn't trying to flirt with Rev. I just—"

I was interrupted by a familiar voice behind me. "Okay, Annie, that's enough yanking Samantha's chain."

Relief flooded me when I realized it was Kim. With a friendly grin, she threw her arm around my shoulder. "If anyone gets to give her shit, it's me."

I laughed. "Thanks a lot."

"You both better cool it. If you keep up the ragging, she'll be running for the hills the first chance she gets, which I'm pretty sure would have Bishop on your ass."

When I whirled around, I saw Alexandra Malloy standing behind me. This time she was without her adorable son. Instead, she held a platter of cheese in her hands. She gave me a warm smile. "It's good to see you again."

I glanced over my shoulder at Annie, who winked at me. I exhaled a long breath. "So all that jazz about the present was just you fucking with me?"

Annie laughed. "Consider it a little initiation rite into the Raiders women."

"Jesus, you scared the hell out of me."

"Need a clean pair of panties?" Kim asked teasingly.

"Yeah, I do. I was just waiting for you all to jump me."

Annie laughed. "Sorry about that. We like to see what a girl is made out of before we invite her into our circle."

"They just didn't know you had passed the most important test already," Kim said.

"And what would that be?"

"Why, the Kim test, of course!"

"I see. Glad I managed to pass it with flying colors." Nodding at Alexandra, I asked, "Did she do the same thing to you?"

"My situation was a little different, since I was coming here as Willow's teacher, rather than just a hookup with one of the guys." When my eyebrows shot up at her summation, she quickly added, "Not that you're just a hookup."

"No. She's far more than that," Kim said knowingly.

"I am?"

Kim grinned. "Bishop has never, ever invited a woman to a Raiders party before."

"Isn't that because he usually gets his pieces of ass from the pool of women here?" I countered.

While the other women snickered, Kim's blue eyes widened. "Damn, girl, I can't believe you went there."

"Truth hurts, right?"

She shook her head. "It might've been true six months ago, but it sure as hell isn't true now." Reaching over, she cupped my chin. "I've known Bishop since he was a little kid, and I've seen a change in him since he's been seeing you."

"Well, we're not really seeing each other," I argued.

"Then whatever it is you're doing." Kim turned to Alexandra. "Aren't I right?"

Alexandra smiled. "I haven't known Bishop as long as Kim has, but he is certainly different."

At that moment, Rev's wife, Annabel, joined the group. "I would say he's positively smitten."

Kim snorted. "As much as a man like Bishop can be."

Annabel crossed her arms over her chest. "Just what would you call it, then?"

"I don't know, but I sure as hell wouldn't call it smitten." Kim tapped her chin. "Maybe pussy-whipped?"

"Uh, that's not the case, I can assure you."

"Don't worry, Sam. Bishop's and your sex life is strictly your business," Kim said.

Before I could argue that we didn't have a sex life, Alexandra said, "That's utter and total bullshit."

"It is not," Kim countered.

Alexandra wagged a finger at Kim. "You know as well as I do that nothing is sacred, especially when it comes to sex. Everyone has their nose stuck in everyone else's business."

Kim sighed. "Maybe you're right."

"After we caught Annabel and Rev screwing in the pantry, you had to tell them all about seeing Deacon's ass when he and I had done the same," Alexandra said, her eyes twinkling.

Annabel groaned. "Thank you for that commentary, Alex. Now anyone who didn't know about Rev and me does."

"That must be one hell of a pantry," I mused.

Kim winked. "Maybe you and Bishop can take a turn in there."

"Once again, we're *just* friends." I knew regardless of how many times I said that, the women were not going to believe me. I tried ignoring the voice inside me that couldn't help wondering what it would be like if Bishop and I were more than friends. At the same time, my libido, which was limping along after an extreme dry spell, couldn't help getting hot and bothered about the thought of having sex with Bishop in the infamous pantry.

"And there's nothing wrong with them being just friends. Right, ladies?" Annabel said.

"Of course," Alexandra replied.

When I looked at Kim, she wore a surprisingly somber expression. "I know it's probably hard for you to think of more with Bishop after what happened with Marley."

I sucked in a harsh breath as her words took me off guard. "Yes. It is."

She cupped my cheek tenderly. "Your Marley was a good man, and I know you miss him bad. But just don't forget that life is for the living. I lost a lot of time I could have had with Breakneck by hiding in my grief for my Case. I finally had to realize that Case wouldn't want me to be unhappy the rest of my life. He would want me to have a good life, and to make his brother, who had been through a rough patch, happy."

"Thank you. That means a lot."

Kim smiled. "Just know that we're all here for you and want you to be happy . . . especially if it's with Bishop."

I laughed along with the others. "Okay." Realizing I was still holding the present, I handed it to Annabel. "I hope you know I didn't mean anything by getting Rev something. Bishop said he loved nonfiction books on history."

She smiled. "It's fine. In fact, it would be pretty rude to show up at someone's party without a gift."

Kim snickered. "Of course you would say that, Miss Manners."

Waving her hand dismissively, Annabel replied, "Whatever. Besides, Rev loves gifts. I swear he acts just like a little boy again on his birthdays."

"So, what did you get him?" I asked.

"Eggs," Annabel replied, with a dreamy smile.

I furrowed my brow in confusion. "Does he like to eat them or something?"

Alexandra and Kim busted out laughing at my remark, which earned them a disapproving look from Annabel. "They're not chicken eggs to eat. They're *my* eggs," Annabel replied.

With a shake of my head, I said, "You guys like to give some strange gifts around here. I'm not sure he's going to enjoy the book I got him."

"Trust me, Rev's a major history nerd."

"That makes me feel a little better."

Annabel smiled. "You want to hear why I'm giving my husband eggs for his birthday?"

Although I knew a lot about Annabel, this was certainly something that hadn't been recorded. Teasingly, I said, "I'm not sure I want to, but I really need to get the whole story."

After drawing in a deep breath, Annabel proceeded to tell me things that brought tears to my eyes. While I had known from the file that she had been kidnapped and sold into human trafficking, I had no idea the full extent of what had happened to her. The miscarriage that led to an emergency hysterectomy had been left out of the file, as well as the emotional toll it had taken on her.

When she finally finished, all I could say was "Wow." Although I wasn't a crier, especially when I was around others, I found moisture blurring my vision.

"Annabel is the strongest woman I know," Alex said as tears sparkled in her eyes.

"All the credit for my strength goes to Rev. If it wasn't for him . . ." She forced a tight smile to her face. "Well, if it wasn't for him, I wouldn't be here in more ways than one."

"That's really sweet," I murmured. It was hard imagining how the version of Rev that Annabel painted could also serve as the president of an MC. He seemed more like a college professor than a gun-toting vigilante. Once again, I realized that my preconceived notions were far off the mark.

"He's the most amazing man I've ever known. That's why I didn't want to wait anymore. Rev thinks we're waiting two more years for me to finish vet school and start a practice before I have my eggs harvested. But since I'm not carrying the baby and we have tons of helpers around, I see no reason to keep him waiting any longer."

"Well, I have to say that my gift certainly pales in comparison to that," I teased.

Annabel laughed. "Don't worry. He doesn't get to know about the eggs until later tonight when we're alone. He has a simple gift from me in the pile."

"That's good to know."

Willow returned with her arms laden with ketchup bottles. "Is this enough?" she asked as she started setting them down on the table.

"Yep. I think we're good," Annie said.

Once she was free of the ketchup, Willow turned her attention to Annabel. "Has Poe come by today?"

Annabel grimaced. "Shoot. I totally forgot to feed him today."

Willow's face lit up. "I'll go feed him."

"Thanks, sweetie."

The next thing I knew, Willow had grabbed my hand. "Come on, Sam. I want you to meet Poe."

"Okay," I replied. Considering all the stories that Bishop had told me about Poe, I was pretty anxious to meet him. "See you guys later," I called over my shoulder.

"We'll let Bishop know where you are," Alex said.

"Thanks."

Willow dragged me down the hill at almost warp speed. I barely got a chance to take in the compound that I had read so much about. Of course, I had seen pictures in the files, but it wasn't the same as seeing it for myself. It made everything so much more real to see it in person. It once again emphasized the fact that the Raiders were people.

When we reached the cul-de-sac, we veered off to a house on the left. Instead of going up the stairs to the front porch, Willow took me around the side of the house. The backyard ended where the woods began.

In a singsong voice, Willow called, "Poe! Come out, come out, wherever you are, Poe!"

I watched in amazement as some of the bushes at the edge of the woods began to rustle. Within a few seconds, the large rack of a deer became visible through the foliage. Willow clapped her hands. "Come on, Poe. Come and get your corn."

She then abandoned my side to go up on the back porch. When she reappeared, she had a cupful of dried corn in her hand. "He loves this stuff."

"He does?"

Willow nodded. "It's funny to listen to him eat it, too. He chomps it so loud," she said with a giggle.

I couldn't help laughing at both her enthusiasm and the fact that I was about to meet the pet deer of hardened bikers. It was all just too bizarre. It was sure as hell not something I would've found in any of the files on the Raiders, nor would anyone at the bureau have believed me if I told them.

Poe started slowly out of the woods, putting one long leg in front of the other. But then, as if he sensed a stranger, he momentarily faltered. Willow shook the cup at him. "Come on, Poe. Samantha won't hurt you."

His love of corn overrode any remaining fear. He quickly made his way across the backyard. When he was in front of us, Willow reached over and scratched along the ridge of his nose, which he appeared to enjoy. Then she poured out the cup's contents onto the grass in front of her. Poe immediately dipped his head and began to eat. At the loud crunching, Willow laughed. "See?"

I smiled. "Pretty funny."

As Poe continued to chomp on the corn, Willow asked, "Wanna pet him?"

"You think he'll let me?" I questioned.

"You won't know unless you try."

"True." I reached out my hand and brushed it down Poe's flank. "Interesting."

"What is it?"

"He feels different than I thought he would. He's soft but not as furry."

"His coat is pretty thin now that it's summertime. It'll thicken up again in the fall," Willow said matter-of-factly.

I grinned down at her. "My, my, aren't you the deer expert?"

"After Aunt Annabel rescued Poe, she and Uncle Rev bought me lots of books on deer."

"I hear Uncle Rev loves to read."

Willow nodded. "Yeah, he loves books almost as much as my mommy and I do." She ran her hand down Poe's spine. "Aunt Annabel knows the most about animals because she's in vet school, but she likes all kinds of books, too."

"I'm glad to hear you say that. I got Uncle Rev a book for his birthday."

"He'll love it."

"But I didn't tell you what it was about."

Willow gave me a little huff. "You don't have to. He loves all books."

"Yeah, well, what if it's a book about doll collecting?" I countered with a smile.

Wrinkling her nose, Willow said, "No. He wouldn't like that one very much. He would probably end up giving it to me."

I laughed. "You don't have to worry. I skipped the one about doll collecting and got him one about military strategies in the Revolutionary War."

"It sounds boring, but I know Uncle Rev will love it."

"Thank you. While I would like to take all the credit for picking it out, your uncle Bishop gave me some suggestions."

"Hello there," a voice called behind us.

I whirled around to come face-to-face with Bishop's mother, Elizabeth Malloy. After reading about her in the bureau's files, I couldn't help being intrigued by her. As a child and teenager, she had been the epitome of a Goody Two-shoes. Just as she graduated with honors from high school, she had met John Malloy at church. It was an unlikely match, considering that she was one of the deacons' daughters, and John was fresh out of prison for armed robbery. Of course, by the time they met, John had rehabilitated himself from a former biker hood to become a born-again Christian. Later he would become a preacher and start his own church, Soul Harbor. But then, thirteen years into their marriage, John seemed to snap one day. He went from loving husband, father, and minister back to outlaw biker. While they had never officially divorced, he and Elizabeth, or Beth as she was known, never lived together again.

I had learned most of the information from the files, but Bishop had also talked to me some about his parents. We both could commiserate on the loss of our fathers. While I had to fudge some of the details about my dad, I was pretty honest with Bishop. After I'd kept my feelings buried for many years, it felt good to talk about my dad to someone outside my family.

In her arms, Beth held baby Wyatt. Beth glanced from Willow

to me. Without missing a beat, she extended her hand to me. "I'm Beth Malloy."

"Samantha Vargas," I said as I shook her hand.

"Samantha is Uncle B's girlfriend," Willow added.

Beth's blue eyes, the ones Bishop had inherited, widened to the size of dinner plates. "Oh, is that right?"

"Actually, we're just friends."

Like the other women, Beth appeared tempted to call bullshit on the "just friends" argument. But instead, she plastered on a welcoming smile. "It's very nice to meet you, Samantha. I'm glad you've come out to celebrate Nathaniel's birthday with us."

"Me, too. I can tell how much Bishop loves his brothers from the way he talks about them."

A loving expression came over Beth's face. "Although they have their fights and arguments, it's such a blessing how much they love each other."

"You must be very proud of them," I said.

Beth laughed. "I am. They've given me far too many gray hairs trying to be the death of me, but I love them with all my heart and soul."

I tried for a moment to imagine what it must be like to be the mother of three MC men. I was sure they did give her gray hair from worrying with the type of shit they were involved in. I wondered just how much she knew about their illegal dealings. A part of me figured she wasn't the type to turn a blind eye, but rather just not to ask too many questions.

"Hey there," Bishop called as he jogged up to us. I could barely hide my surprise when he gave me a quick hug. Although we often exchanged hugs at the end of our dinners, it felt different here on his home turf, so to speak. Not to mention that it happened in front of his mother.

"Sorry I wasn't able to meet you," he said.

"That's okay. Willow has been a wonderful hostess."

Bishop grinned. "I figured as much."

"Your meeting go okay?" I asked.

A dark look flashed in his eyes before he quickly covered it up. "Yep. And now we're ready to have some fun." He bent down to tickle Willow. "Are you ready to party?"

Bouncing up and down, Willow replied, "Yes!"

"Good. I'm glad to hear it." Turning to me, he asked, "Sam?"

I laughed. "Yeah, I'm ready."

He nodded and then turned to his mother. "Mama Beth, are you ready to put on your party hat and dancing shoes?"

She swatted his arm playfully. "I don't know about dancing, but yes, I'm ready to celebrate Nathaniel's birthday."

Bishop groaned good-naturedly. "Don't be an old party pooper. You can break it down with the best of them."

Beth chuckled. "If I tried to 'break it down,' as you say, I would end up with a broken hip at best."

Bishop and I laughed along with her. It was nice seeing the easy rapport between the two. After my father had died, my relationship with my mother became stronger, but it wasn't the same as it had been. I couldn't help wondering if Bishop and Beth's relationship had changed after his father's death.

"Will you carry me up the hill, Uncle B?" Willow requested.

"Don't you think you're getting too big for that?" Bishop asked teasingly.

She huffed out a frustrated breath. "No, I'm not!"

"Fine, fine." He turned around to where his back was facing her. "Okay, rug rat, jump up."

Willow jumped onto Bishop's back, wrapping her legs around his waist and her arms around his shoulders. "Come on, let's go! I'm hungry!" she exclaimed.

"You're so bossy," Bishop grumbled as he started up the hillside.

Beth and I fell in step beside him. "What do you want to eat, Willow?" Beth asked.

"I want a giant piece of cake with lots of icing."

"Not until you eat your dinner."

"Okay, then, I want a hot dog."

"What else?"

"Just a hot dog."

"Not some of your mom's delicious chili?" Bishop asked. He then cut his eyes over to me. "You need to make sure you try some. It's amazing."

"I certainly will," I replied with a smile.

"I just want a hot dog . . . and some cake and ice cream."

"Ah, just the sweets, huh?" Bishop asked.

"Yep."

"No cake until you've eaten a good dinner, Willow," Beth instructed.

When Willow began to pout, Bishop leaned back to whisper in her ear, "Don't worry, rug rat. I'll hook you up with some cake and ice cream."

She giggled. "Thanks, Uncle B!"

As Bishop and Willow started ahead of us to make a beeline for the food table, Beth grunted next to me. "Willow's uncles love to spoil her."

I laughed. "I can see that."

"And it's not just them. Most of the men in the club and even their wives are complete pushovers when it comes to her. By the way they act, you would think she's the only little girl running around."

"It doesn't seem to be going to her head. She seems like such a sweet child."

"She is. In spite of all the spoiling, she is still well-mannered.

Sometimes I think the spoiling doesn't affect her because of the hard start she had in life."

I knew all about Willow's "hard start" from reading her file. Her former life with a drug-addicted mother had been hard to read about, especially the part where her mother had been murdered in front of Willow by the now-deceased leader of the Nordic Knights.

Bishop brought me out of my thoughts. He had put Willow down, and now he beckoned us with his hand. "I wouldn't be a gentleman if I started before you two."

Beth gave him a sly smile. "My, you must really be someone special, Samantha, if Bishop is letting us go first. Usually, he's elbowing people out of the way to eat."

I couldn't help laughing, especially when Bishop scowled at his mother. "Well, if it is a side he's showing just for me, I guess I'll appreciate it."

"Women," Bishop grumbled before thrusting a plate into my hands.

THIRTEEN

BISHOP

I had to admit it felt pretty fucking surreal sitting next to Samantha surrounded by my family. Even though we were only eating hamburgers and hot dogs and drinking cheap beer, it felt significant. Of course, I couldn't help thinking that the last time she had been here at the compound, it had been with Marley, and now she was here with me.

As my date. Well, sort of.

No matter how many times I repeated that in my mind, I couldn't seem to wrap my head around it. Sure, there were still too many gray areas between us to think of this as a date. I had even said as much to Sam on the phone. But deep down, I couldn't help feeling as though we had finally turned a corner in whatever it was that we were doing. I wanted more with her, and I was willing to wait as long as I had to. As though maybe if enough time went by, I wouldn't feel so bad about her being Marley's girlfriend.

Even though my brothers had given me shit about Samantha, I

was glad I had talked to them. It was good to know I had their blessing. From the way she was getting along with Mama Beth and Alexandra and Annabel, I knew she would get their stamp of approval as well. Although in the end, I wouldn't have let their opinion change my mind about her.

The screech of a microphone sounded, followed by Kim's earsplitting whistle. I turned around to see Breakneck was taking the stage with his guitar. Immediately, it felt as if I'd been punched in the chest by the memories flickering through my mind.

"Are you okay?" Sam asked.

With a nod, I replied, "Just kinda overwhelmed at the moment. Breakneck hasn't sung or played the guitar at a party since my dad died."

Sam gave me a sympathetic look. "Oh. I'm so sorry."

"It's okay. I'm glad to see him back up there. We used to have some crazy times singing along with him."

"I would've liked to see that."

I chuckled. "No. You probably wouldn't have. None of us Malloy boys can really sing. We just think we can when we've had too much alcohol."

Throwing her head back with a laugh, Samantha said, "I think the same thing happens to me. I pity anyone within a mile radius of me at a karaoke bar. I never would have stepped foot in one if Gavin hadn't liked them. I used to tell him the things he could get me to do for love."

My brow furrowed in confusion. "Who's Gavin?"

Samantha's face flushed. "Oh, just an old boyfriend."

The mention of Samantha's old loves had my fists clenching at my sides and I wanted to punch the wall. I hated that just the mention of an old boyfriend could turn me into a raging idiot. Samantha's past was none of my business, and I sure as hell wouldn't want to have to discuss mine with her.

Breakneck's tapping on the mic interrupted me. "Evening, everybody. I wanted to come up here and do a song for Rev's birthday. It's been a while since I've done this song. Haven't done it since I lost two of the best friends I've ever had, Preacher Man and Case. But I think it's time to bring this one out of retirement, since it was both men's favorite song." The crowd erupted into whistles and clapping, which caused Breakneck to grin. "Before I get started, I'm going to ask Deacon, Rev, and Bishop to come up here and help me like they used to."

While Deacon shot off the bench, Rev furiously shook his head back and forth. "Oh, hell no," he said.

"Oh, go on, honey," Annabel urged beside him.

Rev opened his mouth to argue, but Deacon interrupted him by grabbing his arm and dragging him up off his seat. "Come on, B. Help me get his ass up there."

With a chuckle, I got up and took Rev's free arm. "Asshole," Rev muttered as we pulled him through the crowd and onto the stage riser. Breakneck motioned to the microphone stand beside him so we could do the harmony on the chorus.

Once we were assembled, Breakneck lifted his gaze to the sky. "This one's for you guys—Preacher Man and Case." He then gazed back out into the crowd. "Here's 'The Weight.'"

Breakneck started strumming the opening of the song I knew so well. Closing my eyes for a moment, I could see myself riding on the back of Preacher Man's bike, my arms wrapped tight around him as "The Weight" blared out of the radio speakers. I could always feel him humming along when I rested my head on his back.

"'I pulled into Nazareth, was feeling 'bout half past dead,'"

Breakneck began in his smooth voice. So much had happened since the last time I heard him sing. We'd all faced our own personal tragedies. We'd lost a father, Kim lost a husband, and Breakneck lost a daughter, all to the violence of the MC world. It was then that I was first able to really feel thankful that we were changing the vision of the club. Even with the threat of Eddy and the Diablos hanging over us, I knew we had made the right decision. I couldn't help thinking that my old man and Case would approve of what we were doing.

When it came time for the chorus, Deacon, Rev, and I leaned in around the microphone and sang our hearts out. Once the song ended, we received thunderous applause and whistles. I smacked Deacon and Rev on the back. "Felt good to do that again."

Deacon grinned. "It sure as hell did."

"Yeah. It did," Rev said, smiling.

After I hopped down off the stage, I headed straight for Samantha. She jumped up off the bench and threw her arms around my neck to give me a hug. "That was awesome!"

I chuckled at her enthusiasm. "I think you're just a little bit prejudiced," I said as she pulled away.

"Nope. I just call it as I see it."

Deacon and Rev appeared beside us then. "We still got it, huh?" Deacon asked with a smirk.

Alex grinned at him. "Oh yeah. You do." As she rose off the bench, she handed Wyatt to Beth. "Now I think you owe me a dance or two."

"I think I can oblige you with that one," Deacon said.

As they headed over to the dance floor, Rev went over to Annabel and pulled her up. "Will you honor me with a dance, Mrs. Malloy?"

A dreamy expression filled Annabel's face. "Of course I will. But they're not playing a slow song."

"I'll make them play one. It is my birthday," Rev said.

Once they left, Samantha and I were all alone. With an awkward silence hanging around us, I wondered what I should do. Was asking her to dance coming on too strong, or would she be offended if I didn't? The whole gray area of friendship was a real pain in the ass.

Just as I was about to man up and ask her, I felt a tug on the back of my shirt. I turned around to see Willow staring up at me. "Will you dance with me, Uncle B?"

Since I was incapable of ever telling Willow no, I held out my hand to her. "Of course I will." Once she slipped her hand in mine, I glanced over my shoulder at Sam. To my surprise, she didn't seem pissed at my picking a six-year-old over her. "I'll be right back."

She gave me a warm smile. "Have fun out there."

Willow jerked me along until we were in the middle of the couples. Rev hadn't yet asked for a song change, so it was still a fast one. I started making goofy moves that rewarded me with giggles from Willow. She then started copying what I was doing. With her love of ballet, she was a pretty natural dancer, even when doing the sprinkler. When I looked back at the table, Sam and Mama Beth were both laughing at our antics.

As soon as the song was done, I squatted down beside Willow. "Would it hurt your feelings if I asked Samantha to dance with me now?"

Her face lit up. "No. It wouldn't." She patted my shoulder. "Samantha is really, really nice. I think it would be good if you made her your girlfriend."

"Oh, you do, huh?"

Willow nodded. "Poe really liked her, too, and you know he doesn't like just anyone."

I refrained from arguing with her that I couldn't base a potential relationship on the fact that a deer—who had probably been after the corn—approved of the woman in question. "It's good to know that Poe liked her."

"All the family likes her, so you should, too."

Once again I had to remember that Willow was just a kid. She was such an old soul sometimes. "Thanks for the dance, rug rat."

"But I'm the one who asked you."

I grinned. "Yeah, but that doesn't mean I didn't enjoy it." Pulling her closer, I said, "Now give your favorite uncle a hug."

"But, Uncle B, I love you and Uncle Rev the same. I promise," she argued as she threw her arms around me.

As I rubbed her back, I said, "I know. I'm just teasing you." When I pulled away, I winked at her. "Now if you still want to dance, go over to Joe and tell him as a prospect, he has to dance with you."

Willow wrinkled her nose. "That's okay. I don't want to dance with him."

"Why not?"

She shrugged. "Just because."

Although I could have pressed her, I already knew the response. He wasn't Archer, whom she had a crush on. Back when he was a prospect, she would have loved to make him dance with her. Of course, Archer was twenty-one and totally wigged out by Willow's crush. He worried at any moment one of us Malloy men was going to kick his ass for being a pervert. We loved to give him shit about that.

"All right, then. I'm going to ask Samantha to dance."

"And I'm going to get more cake."

"You do that. But just don't let your mom and dad know it's your third piece."

Bringing her finger to her lips, she shushed me. "They'll never know unless you tell them."

I raised my hand. "Scout's honor."

She giggled as she ran off in the direction of the food table. With more confidence in my step than I felt, I made my way over to Samantha. She and Mama Beth were chatting like old friends, which was really nice to see.

As I stood in front of her, I cleared my throat. "You wanna dance?"

"Sure." She climbed off the bench and turned to Mama Beth. "Don't go anywhere, because I want to hear more embarrassing stories about Bishop when he was little."

With a groan, I swept my hand across my face. "Seriously, Mama? That's what you two were over here talking about?"

"I thought you liked having beautiful women talking about you," Samantha countered with a smile.

"Not when it includes stories that make me look bad."

"But they were sweet stories . . . and funny ones. Like the time you sat on Santa Claus's lap and asked for a wiener as big as your dad's."

I rolled my eyes. "Seriously, Mama. You've known Samantha barely an hour, and you break out the wiener story?"

Mama Beth grinned at me. "But you were so cute and so serious about it. If only we'd had a video camera then, I would have sent it to *America's Funniest Home Videos*."

"Okay, that's enough. You two are not allowed to talk to each other ever again."

Mama Beth and Samantha only laughed at me. "Isn't he cute when he's mad?" Mama Beth asked with a grin.

"He's adorable," Samantha teased.

"No matter how old you get, you'll always be my baby," Mama Beth said as she cupped my cheek.

As Samantha said, "Aw," I threw up my hands. "That's it. Let's go dance. Now."

Sam grinned. "Now you're a caveman barking out commands, huh?"

Taking her by the hand, I led her over to where the other couples were. When I found a good place for us that wasn't too close to the band or too crowded, I let her hand go. I then slid my hands around her waist and drew her close to me. Samantha wrapped her arms around my neck. At the feel of her curves against me, I couldn't help the shiver of desire that ran through me.

"Are you okay?" she asked.

"Just a little chill. I'm fine," I muttered.

We swayed in awkward silence. "So, I have a question."

"Shoot."

Fighting a smile, Samantha asked, "Did Santa finally bring you a wiener as big as your dad's?"

I threw my head back with a laugh. "Yeah, he did. I could argue it was the best present he ever got me."

With a giggle, Samantha said, "You're terrible."

"You're the one who brought it up."

"After that story, how could I not?"

I scowled at her. "Did she tell you anything else embarrassing, like how I used to strip down and run naked through the streets?"

"Nope. But I'm glad that you did," she mused.

"For the record, I stopped that shit when I was five. It's not like I'm still doing it."

Sam waggled her eyebrows at me. "That certainly would be interesting."

"I don't think Mama Beth would find it as cute and funny if I did it now."

"I wouldn't think so."

"It's safe to say I'd probably scar Willow for life if I did something like that."

Sam laughed. "I imagine so." Tilting her head back, she stared up at me. "Speaking of Willow, I think she wants everyone to think I'm your girlfriend."

With a grimace, I replied, "Yeah. Sorry about that."

"You don't need to be sorry. She's just looking out for you and wanting you to be happy."

I chuckled. "She's a mess."

"You're so good with her."

"She's pretty easy now. I don't like to think about when she gets to be a teenager."

Samantha laughed. "I'll admit teenage girls are pretty scary with all the hormones. I know I gave my mom fits."

"With the hormones come the boys, and I'll have to beat the hell out of any guy who hurts her . . . or puts the moves on her."

"Poor girl. Between her uncles and her father, she'll maybe get to date when she's thirty."

I grinned. "Damn straight." Cocking my head at her, I said, "As beautiful and sexy as you are, I bet you had half the men in your family keeping tabs on you and guys."

She laughed. "Yeah, I did. They would have been protective anyway, but when you throw in the fact that my dad had died, they were extremely protective."

"So you didn't get to raise too much hell as a teenager?"

"Not really. But the truth is, I really didn't want to get into too much trouble." At what must have been my surprised expression, Samantha grinned. "Sorry to disappoint you. I guess it's safe to say I'm not exactly a rebel."

I shook my head. "Oh no. I disagree on that one. You're interesting. Mysterious . . ."

"And exotic. Remember you called me exotic the first time you met me?"

I stared at her in surprise. "You remember that?"

She nodded. "You were the first person besides my mom to call me that."

"You're kidding."

"Nope. She always said I looked exotic like Olivia Hussey—the girl who played Juliet in the 1968 movie version of *Romeo and Juliet*." At what must've been my blank expression, she added, "Sorry, I must be the only one to remember the play and the movie from high school."

With a sheepish look, I said, "I dropped out in ninth grade." Before Samantha could say anything, I quickly added, "But I got my GED last year."

"Good for you."

"Thanks. I was tired of being a loser."

"You could never be a loser, Bishop. You have too much drive and ambition."

"I didn't always. I was pretty much a lazy drunk when I was a teenager," I admitted.

"It's hard for me to imagine you like that."

"Trust me, it wasn't pretty. I gave my poor parents hell with all the trouble I got in."

"What turned you around?"

"My old man. He had me start prospecting at eighteen so that I could have some direction." Shaking my head with a smile, I said, "In some ways being in an MC is like going into the military, and the prospecting period is like boot camp. Being disciplined by all the men I knew and admired really helped to put me in my place."

Samantha's expression turned serious. "Can you ever imagine not being part of the MC?"

I shook my head. "Nope. It's not only in my blood, but it's the only world I've known. Plus, it's how I met you."

She gave me a small smile. "That's true."

"Don't worry, Sam. The MC world isn't going to bury me until I'm an old man."

"How can you be so sure?"

"We won't be living by violence anymore, so we can't die that way."

"That's a very interesting concept. One that I hope is true."

"You just have to trust me."

Something flared in her eyes. After staring at me for a few seconds, she finally replied, "I'll try."

I smiled at her. "Forget about your feelings for the MC world and just enjoy tonight. Enjoy dancing with me."

"I am. I really am."

"I'm glad, because I am, too."

A teasing smile played on Samantha's lips. "The first time I ever laid eyes on you was when you were dancing."

My eyebrows shot up in surprise. "Really?"

She bobbed her head. "I say dancing—but it was really more like humping on the dance floor."

I barked out a laugh. "Yeah, I guess that's the only real dancing I know how to do."

"You're not so bad with the slow, non-humping kind."

"Thanks."

"You're welcome."

As I stared intently at Samantha, I said, "I really like dancing with you."

"You said that already," she murmured, gazing into my eyes.

"I wanted to say it again because I really meant it—it wasn't just some bullshit line."

"Is that right?"

"Yeah. More than just dancing, I like being with you. I like the way you laugh at my stupid jokes, how you don't take any of my bullshit, and how you keep me on my toes. Most of all, I like how I feel I can tell you anything."

Samantha's tongue darted out to lick her lips. Although it seemed like a nervous gesture, it caused my dick to jump in my pants. "I feel the same way about you."

"I'm glad to hear it."

As the song came to an end, Samantha kept herself flush against me. Neither one of us seemed to want to move. We wanted to stay right there in the moment.

And I knew then there was no turning back.

FOURTEEN

SAMANTHA

As Bishop and I finished our slow dance, we headed back to the picnic tables. No matter how hard I tried, I couldn't fight the overwhelming feelings swelling in my chest. It had been such an eye-opening evening—meeting his mom, hanging out with the other Raiders women, and then seeing him interact with his brothers. I had come to see him in an entirely different light than before. It made the line I had tried to draw between us even more difficult to maintain.

"Thirsty?" Bishop asked as I took a seat.

"Yes. I'd love a beer."

He grinned. "Give me two seconds." He then trotted off to the drink table. After grabbing a few beers, he hurried back. "Here you go."

"What excellent service. Should I tip you?"

"I could think of several ways you could pay me back," he replied as he took a few long swigs.

"Are you alluding to what I think you are?"

He shrugged. "Maybe . . . Maybe not." When I cocked my head at him, he winked at me and then launched into a conversation with Boone about the latest fights down at the gym. It gave me ample time to do a little thinking about what my next move should be, which was both good and bad.

Gavin's words came back to me, as if he were sitting right beside me. *Even though it's frowned upon, I see nothing wrong with getting a good fuck or two out of him to gain information.* The problem was, I wasn't sure it was just for information. I had developed a need for Bishop. After sucking down the beer, I made up my mind to stop with the teasing and innuendo. It was time to act. Would he want me, though?

I rose off the picnic bench. As I set my longneck down, I could feel Bishop's eyes burning into my back. When I glanced at him over my shoulder, his eyebrows rose questioningly. Slowly, I turned around. As I met his blazing baby blues, I held out my hand. His body shuddered slightly before he leaned up to put his hand in mine. I tugged him up off the bench, pulling him close to me. His warm breath against my cheek caused me to shiver with building anticipation. "What are you doing, Sam?"

Without a moment's hesitation, I replied, "Getting you to take me somewhere we can be alone."

He pulled back to look at me. Both longing and regret flickered on his handsome face. "You gotta know that nothing good is gonna come with me being alone with you right now."

"I know."

"And you're okay with that?"

It was the same question raging through my mind. Did I want to fuck Bishop to get in even deeper with him because of the case, or was it because I was starting to feel more for him than I should? In the end, I tuned out the voices in my head. "Yeah, I am," I responded, my voice resonating with certainty.

With a brief nod, Bishop tugged on my hand and started leading me away from the others. We went around the back of the clubhouse and then passed the pawnshop. As we continued walking, the lights grew dimmer and dimmer until we found ourselves in shadowy darkness. Bishop stopped us in front a tall chain-link fence that ran the length of the property.

After gazing around, I swallowed hard. I'd never had sex out in the open before, and I could feel my once-firm resolve slowly fading. "Here?"

"It's really the only place we can be alone, with all the brothers being in from out of town. I gave up my room in the clubhouse." A lustful gleam burned in Bishop's eyes as he pulled me against him. I could feel the hardened length of him through his jeans. "But if you want, I'll put you on the back of my bike and take you anywhere you want to go."

Deep down, I knew it was right here and right now, or I was going to lose both my nerve and my buzz. I brought my arms up to wrap around his neck. "I just want to be with you."

I drew his head down to where our lips were almost touching. We stayed like that for a few seconds, both of our chests heaving and our bodies trembling. This was our figurative cliff, and we were just inches from free-falling off it. Before we could think any more about it, Bishop crushed his lips against mine. For such a hardened tough guy, his lips were so very smooth. They felt as soft as velvet as they moved against mine.

I tightened my arms around his neck, drawing him as close to me as I could. My breasts strained against the bulging muscles of his chest. I couldn't seem to get close enough to him. I had to fight the urge to jump up and wrap my legs around his waist and grind myself against him. As his warm tongue entered my mouth, I moaned.

He proved within seconds he was one hell of a kisser. He was also one for multitasking, because as his tongue caressed mine, his hand palmed my breast through the fabric of my dress. My nipple pebbled under his fingertips, and I gasped when he pinched it between his thumb and forefinger.

While one hand continued to knead my breast, the other dipped below the hem of my dress. I sucked in a breath when it skimmed against my thigh before journeying farther upward. It had been too damn long since a man had touched me, and as Bishop's hand cupped me, my head fell back, banging against the fence.

"Fucking hell. You're drenched," Bishop said in a ragged voice.

"I know," I groaned. Gazing up at him, I said, "Please don't stop touching me."

"Hmm, I like the sound of you begging." His fingers began to work me over my panties, but I wanted more. I wantonly kicked my legs apart, spreading them as far as I could for him. Bishop read my mind by jerking my panties to the side and thrusting two fingers deep inside me.

"Oh yes!" I cried, moving my hips against his hand. At that point, I didn't give two shits if anyone at the party could see or hear us. I just wanted to come.

Bishop's hot breath singed my neck. "I love the way you feel on my fingers. Tight. Wet. Hot. I can't wait until it's my dick pumping inside you."

The combination of his words and what his talented fingers were doing sent me soaring. I cried out his name along with a string of expletives while my walls convulsed again and again.

Before I had a chance to recover, Bishop had dropped to his knees before me. Both of his hands reached beneath the hem of my dress to tear my soaked panties down my thighs. After I stepped out of them, he pushed my dress up to my waist, his fingers digging into my ass. The cool night air danced along the heat between my legs. He tilted his head to the side as he gazed up at me. "Damn me to hell, but I've wanted to taste you since the first night I saw you."

His words and expression caused me to shudder. "I've wanted you for a long time, too," I said as I cupped one of his cheeks tenderly. My fingers then brushed into his hair, and I guided him closer to my core. "Taste me, Bishop. Make me come on your tongue like I did on your fingers," I instructed.

He responded by burying his face between my legs. I groaned, gripping the strands of his hair tighter. He was just as good with his tongue as he was with his fingers, which he also started to use on me again. As his crooked fingers worked inside me, his tongue danced and teased along my clit. My hips rose and fell to give even more friction to the way he was touching and sucking me.

"Bishop!" I cried, my fingers clenching his sweat-soaked hair. I tugged and jerked at the strands as he sent me closer and closer to the edge with his mouth and fingers. When I came, I saw stars, but not the ones over our heads. As I tried to still my erratic breathing, Bishop rose off his knees.

"That was . . . amazing," I murmured when I could form coherent thoughts again.

His signature cocky grin stretched across his face. "Thanks, babe. But we're just getting started."

My hands reached out to loosen his belt. I unbuttoned and unzipped his pants, freeing his straining erection. When I started to stroke it, Bishop shook his head as one of his hands fumbled in his pocket. "You can repay the favor next time. I need to be inside you. Now."

After he took out a condom, he tore into the wrapper. In the dim light, I watched as he slid it down his length. He shoved his jeans down his thighs to where they pooled around his ankles. Turning me around, Bishop pushed me into the fence. He took my arms and put them over my head. My fingers clutched the chain links.

"Hold on tight, babe," he murmured into my ear. One hand gripped my waist while the other went to guide his cock into me. Since I was more than ready for him, he entered me with one harsh thrust that filled me up completely. I cried out as Bishop grunted. With both hands now gripping my waist, he set up a punishing rhythm. The air around us was filled with the sounds of our moans and heavy breathing, along with sweat-soaked skin slapping together.

One of his hands left my waist to roam my body. It cupped my breast, tweaking the hardened nipple, along with stroking my clit as he continued pounding in and out of me. I couldn't do anything but focus on the pleasure of what was probably the best sexual experience of my life.

I had never had three orgasms in one night, but Bishop delivered another blinding one. I could do nothing but cling to the fence as the shudders and spasms rolled through my body. I began to wonder if my trembling legs would keep me upright.

Bishop quickened his pace, his thrusts becoming even more harsh and unforgiving before I felt him tense up. His head fell forward, and he buried it in my neck. Hearing my name come off his lips as he jerked and twitched within me caused a pleasurable shiver to run up my spine.

His heavy breathing was warm against my skin. After picking his head up, he gently eased out of my body. For a few seconds, I still clung to the fence, trying to gain my bearings. There was a flurry of activity behind me as Bishop discarded the condom and then pulled up his jeans. Taking me by the shoulders, he slowly turned me around.

Without a word, he went about pulling up my panties and then straightening my dress. When he was finished, I gave him a sheepish grin. "Aren't you the gentleman?"

He winked. "I try."

Tilting my head, I couldn't help voicing the question that was running through my head. "Is this when you say 'Thanks, babe' and send me on my way?"

Bishop's brow crinkled in confusion. "Why would I do that?"

I shrugged. "Most men aren't up for cuddling or pillow talk, and once they've gotten what they want or need, they're done with you." I bit my tongue to keep from saying, *At least that's what I'm used to.* While I might've partly been using Bishop for the case, I still had to contend with the fact that I didn't want to be used. There were also those feelings for him that ran deeper than I wanted to admit.

Crossing his arms across his chest, Bishop eyed me intently. "After a fuck like that, a man would have to be a dumb-ass to be done with you."

His compliment sent heat both to my cheeks and between my legs. "It was pretty amazing," I murmured.

"Just 'pretty amazing'? I'll have to try harder next time," Bishop countered, a pleased twinkle in his eyes.

"I look forward to your efforts."

Bishop laughed as he took my hand. "Come on." Instead of leading us back to the party, he took us down the hill toward the houses.

"Where are we going?"

"It's hot as hell, and I want to cool off." He cut his eyes over to me. "You in the mood for a swim?"

"Sure. I didn't realize you had a pool."

With a grin, Bishop replied, "I don't."

"Then how—"

"You'll see."

He stopped at one of the houses on the left. Bishop dropped my hand to dig in his jeans pocket. "Is this yours?" I asked, unable to hide the surprise in my voice.

"Yeah."

As I took in the modest but well-kept house, I thought about how often I continued to underestimate Bishop. My own MC prejudices caused me to underestimate him. "Twenty-five years old and you have your own house, a steady job, and a dream of owning your own bike shop."

A smirk curved across his full lips. "Don't forget that I'm also a master at fucking who generously gives ladies multiple orgasms."

I snorted. "How could I forget?"

"Beats the hell out of me."

"All joking aside, it is impressive, Bishop."

His lighthearted expression became serious. "You really think so?"

"Yeah, I do."

"Thanks," he murmured before ducking inside the house. I took a tentative step inside, since he hadn't actually asked me to come in. I bit back a smile because the décor was exactly as I had imagined. Posters of half-naked women on the walls, leather furniture strewn with clothes, and beer cans littering the tables.

When I caught his eye, he said, "I do have one fault."

"Your taste in decorating?"

He snickered. "That and I'm a fucking slob."

I laughed. "Perfection can be annoying. Stay a slob."

"Yes, ma'am," he replied with a mock salute.

After grabbing two large flashlights off the mantel and then a blanket off the back of the couch, he paused, his expression growing serious. "I'm surprised you're not pissed off and giving me shit about why I didn't bring you here." At what must've been my confused expression, he added, "You know, to fuck."

"Oh," I murmured. The truth was the thought hadn't even crossed my mind. When he'd said all the rooms at the clubhouse were full, I had believed him. Besides, considering that I was using him, I really didn't have any room to be judgmental.

With a sheepish look, he said, "Most women would be pretty pissed that I didn't have the decency to bring them here."

Although it stung to think of him with other women, I gave an apathetic shrug. "Most women might, but I'm not most women. We're not in a relationship, so you don't owe me jack shit, except maybe a good time." I crossed the room to stand beside him. "And trust me, I had a really good time out there."

"Me, too," he murmured. "It's just that I haven't ever brought a woman here."

"To have sex with?"

He shook his head. "To do anything with. My house has always been off-limits to women. Now, my room at the clubhouse—I've made good use of it."

Pursing my lips, I said tersely, "I see."

Bishop grimaced. "Sorry. That was a douche move to mention my past."

"It's okay." Knowing that we needed a subject change, I motioned to the flashlights. "You know, I can't help being a little concerned that you're taking me somewhere that needs flashlights."

Sweeping a hand to my hip, I countered teasingly, "I will be coming back, won't I?"

"Maybe . . . maybe not," Bishop replied, with a wicked gleam in his eyes.

I would've been lying to myself if I hadn't admitted there was a small part of me that was slightly anxious. Everything that had transpired tonight could have been a setup working toward an ending where Bishop took me out to the middle of nowhere to unmask me and then kill me. I had to stay on alert and not let my amorous feelings for him screw me over.

When Bishop laughed, I realized I hadn't hid my fears well enough. "I'm only joking, Sam. Since I'd kick anyone's ass who tried to hurt you, I'm sure as hell not going to do anything to you myself." He threw an arm around my shoulder and started leading me to the front door.

I momentarily faltered when we started into the woods. Bishop turned around to smile at me. "Still thinking I'm going to Jack the Ripper you or something?"

"You *are* dragging me into the woods. At night."

"We can't go swimming if we don't." At what must've been my skeptical expression, he said, "There's a stream about a mile through here. My brothers and I go swimming there all the time. It has the coolest and clearest water you'll ever see."

"At this point, couldn't I just turn the hose on you to cool you off?"

Bishop threw his head back and laughed. After he'd had a hearty chuckle, he leaned in to brush his lips against my cheek. "I promise if you come with me, I'll make you come a few more times."

"You sure as hell better," I replied defiantly, which earned me an impish grin from Bishop.

The bouncing beams of the two large flashlights lit the way as we started into the woods. We hadn't been walking long when we came to an ATV parked to the side of the pathway. Bishop motioned to it. "Your chariot."

"And here I thought we would be walking the whole way."

"That wouldn't be very gentlemanly of me, would it?"

"No, I guess not." I slid onto the back of the seat, leaving room for Bishop. After he turned on the ATV's lights, he took my flashlight and his and put them in the back. Then he got on in front of me.

"Hold on tight. It gets bumpy."

Without any hesitation, I slid my arms around his waist and tightened my thighs around his. I tried to ignore how comforting it felt being so close to him—how the muscles of his strong body made me feel safe and secure. The next thing I knew, the ATV was lunging forward into the dark night. Bishop drove it the same way he drove his motorcycle, which made me want to piss my pants. But I managed to hide my fear while also clinging to him for dear life.

When we reached a clearing, we drove on through what would have been waist-high grass if we had been walking. I didn't even want to think about what could have been lurking in the grass. Bishop drove us right down to the water's edge.

Even though I only had the sole beam of the ATV's light to illuminate things, I could still make out why this place held an allure for Bishop. "It's beautiful," I said.

Bishop rose off the seat. "Give me a second, and you'll really get to see it."

Curiously, I watched as he took one of the flashlights and disappeared off to the side of the bank. After a few seconds, a sound like a lawn mower filled the air. Then light flickered on all around me. Gazing around, I took in the beaming torches and trees lined with twinkling bulbs.

When Bishop reappeared, I asked, "You guys have a generator all the way out here?"

He nodded. "We set it up a few weeks ago when Rev and Annabel got married and had their reception out here." He motioned to the water and the clearing. "So, what do you think now that you can see it better?"

"It's breathtaking. I can see why your brother wanted to get married out here."

Bishop smiled. "Besides being beautiful, this place has a lot of meaning."

"For your family?"

"Yes. And historically." After scratching the back of his neck, Bishop said, "If Mr. History Nerd Rev were here, he could tell you all about the place."

"It wasn't the site of some bloody battle back in the day, was it?" I teased.

Bishop laughed. "Nah, nothing creepy like that. More like Cherokee Indians, who once lived around here, thought the water had healing powers. They would come here when they were physically sick." He gave me a pointed look. "Or emotionally sick."

My eyebrows shot up in surprise. "Really?"

Bishop made a cross over his heart. "Scout's honor."

"Who knew you were bringing me to a place that had such meaning? I just thought you wanted to go swimming to get me naked."

With a waggle of his eyebrows, Bishop said, "I sure as hell did."

I laughed. "I can't say I'm too surprised, or that I'm disappointed."

"I'm glad to hear that."

When he started to reach for me, I shook my head. "I'm thinking after coming so far, you owe me a little."

"Like what?"

I jerked my chin up. "I think you should be the one to get naked first."

He grinned. "Sounds good to me." After he kicked his boots off, he jerked his shirt over his head and tossed it on the ground. He didn't take his eyes off mine as his hand went to the button of his jeans. I held his gaze as he slowly unbuttoned and unzipped the denim.

When he first started to pull off his jeans, I hadn't realized I had been holding my breath. But as he slid them down his muscled thighs, I exhaled in a long whoosh. I knew what he had felt like both in my hands and inside me, but there was something to be said for seeing his dick in the flesh.

"Like what you see?" he asked as he stood proudly before me.

"The front view is good," I replied, with a smile.

Holding out his arms, he turned slowly in the light, letting me take him in. His chest, back, and arms were covered in multicolored tattoos that ended around the bottom of his abs and the top of his ass. And his ass . . . it was perfect as well. Rounded with hardened muscles that I could imagine gripping tight as he pumped in and out of me.

Once he had made a full turn, he rested his hands on his hips and cocked his head at me. "Now it's your turn."

I eased off the back of the ATV and came to stand in front of him. As I blocked the light, Bishop's face became a little shadowy. After working a few buttons, I pulled the dress over my head. Bishop's steamy gaze lit my skin on fire. My hands came around my back to take off my bra. Once it was on the ground with my other clothes, I slid my panties down my thighs.

When I was fully naked before him, Bishop's expression was one of pure admiration. "You're fucking stunning."

I couldn't help smiling like a lovesick schoolgirl at his summation. "Thank you."

He took a few steps forward to where we were almost touching. I jumped with surprise when he reached out to tenderly cup my face in his hands. "I remember the first night I ever laid eyes on you. I thought you were the most exotically beautiful woman I'd ever seen."

"Really?"

His expression darkened slightly. "Marley would've kicked my ass if he knew what I was thinking about you in my head that night." He gave a slight shake of his head. "I would have deserved every hit for how much I wanted to take you to my room and fuck you senseless."

Sensing he was heading to an emotional place that wouldn't be good for either of us, I decided to change the subject, and I did it in a big way. I reached between us to take his half-mast cock in my hands. He gasped at the touch while his dick jumped, swelling appreciatively in my hand. As my hand slid up and down, Bishop's chest rose and fell in the same pattern. When he dipped his head to kiss me, I jerked back and then dropped his throbbing erection. With a teasing laugh, I swept past him and started to run into the stream.

"Oh, I'm going to get you for that!" Bishop shouted behind me.

"Come and get me, then," I challenged as I started splashing into the shallow water. I sucked in a harsh breath when the chilly water hit my naked skin. It took a few moments to get used to it.

By the time I was waist-deep in the water, Bishop was at my side. His strong hands grabbed me by the waist, causing me to gasp at the contact. He held me tight with my back against his chest for a moment before hoisting me up out of the water. "Put me down," I demanded.

When I glanced over my shoulder, Bishop flashed me a wicked grin. "With pleasure." Then he tossed me into the deeper water. I had thought the water had been cold before, but there was nothing like being enveloped by it. I shot to the surface, coughing and sputtering.

"You're an asshole!" I spat as I pushed my wet hair out of my face.

"You deserved it, cock tease," Bishop replied as he swam over to me.

I laughed. "Okay. Maybe I did." With all the strength I could muster, I lunged at him, dunking his head into the water. When he came back to the surface, I smirked at him. "And you deserved that."

"Okay, I'll give you that one," he agreed as he scrubbed his face.

Lying back in the water, I floated for a moment, gazing up at the sky. "I still can't believe a place so beautiful is out here in the middle of nowhere."

"I forget how amazing it is sometimes. It usually takes someone else seeing it to make me realize," Bishop said as he floated beside me.

Turning my head to look at him, I couldn't stop myself from asking, "So, you bring a lot of the girls you fuck out here?"

My question was met with a scowl from Bishop. "No. Actually, I don't."

I glanced back up at the sky, regretting the fact that I had let myself ask such a question, like some insecure shrew. I couldn't believe that just a few short weeks with him, and I was acting completely out of my character. I had never been the needy female in relationships. In the end, Bishop's love life, both past and present, wasn't any of my business. Regardless of what I was beginning to feel for him, I had to continue focusing on the task before me. "Sorry," I murmured.

When Bishop stood up in the water, I followed his lead. His serious expression caused my stomach to twist anxiously. I expected at any moment for him to stalk out of the water and take me back to the roadhouse. But just as he always did, Bishop surprised me.

"Look, Sam, there's no denying the kind of man I am—a man whore, a slut, a womanizer." He drew in a deep breath. "But maybe I'm looking to not always be considered that. Just like I have professional dreams, I have personal ones, too."

My chest tightened, and I fought to breathe. "You do?"

He nodded. "I've never wanted to be like some of the older men in this club who are fifty and sixty years old and still fucking every piece of ass that moves. I want a home . . . a family. I want what my old man had with my mom before he threw it all away, only to regret it until the day he died. I want what Deacon and Rev have."

I didn't know what to say. At that point, I wasn't sure I could've said anything even if I wanted to. I just stared at him in utter awe. What must've been my bewildered look caused Bishop to laugh. "Guess I shocked you, huh?"

After bobbing my head, I licked my lips. "It's a good shock, though."

"Really?"

I smiled. "Yeah, it is. I would have to be a bitter shrew not to be affected by what you just said." I brought my hands out of the water to cup his cheeks. "You deserve for all your dreams to come true, especially the one for a family."

"Thank you," Bishop murmured. He pulled me into his arms. Our wet skin fused us together, chest to chest and heart to heart. After staring into my eyes for a few seconds, Bishop brought his warm lips to mine. I moaned into his mouth. Damn, the man could kiss. It was like a lightning bolt of tingling electricity from the top of my head down to my toes. As his tongue thrust into my mouth, I ran my hands up his broad back, my fingertips trailing over the corded muscles.

In that moment, I abandoned all thoughts of Gavin and the case that had preoccupied me for so long. On a physical level, I wanted to be with Bishop for what he could give my body, not what I could do to him or to advance my career. But then I also wanted to be with him for who he was on the inside—the kindness, the tenderness, and the good heart he consistently revealed to me. The lines were once again blurring, but it felt too good being with him to give a shit about the consequences.

When Bishop's hand slid up my waist to cup my breast, I broke the kiss. "I thought we came out here to swim," I panted.

"Nah, that was just a ruse so I could get you out here to fuck again," Bishop replied as he started kissing down my neck and onto my chest.

With a laugh, I said, "At least you're honest."

Bishop grinned up at me. "I take fucking very seriously."

"Mmm, lucky me," I said as Bishop's mouth closed over my nipple. As his tongue swirled around and around the hardened tip, my head fell back. When he kissed and licked a trail over to the other nipple, I opened my eyes to take in the blackened sky scattered with shimmering stars. I couldn't imagine a more perfect setting to be with someone—it was beautiful and illicit and romantic all at once.

"I think it's time we took this to the shore," he said.

"But it feels so good in the water," I protested.

With a chuckle, Bishop replied, "Yeah, it does feel pretty fucking amazing, but I'm never going to hold any wood in this cold water."

I snorted at his honesty. "Then by all means get us out of here."

Bishop cupped my buttocks and hoisted me up to wrap my legs around his waist. He then started walking us out of the water. The cool night air rushed over my wet skin, raising goose bumps along my arms and legs. When we got to the edge of the bank, he started easing me down onto the blanket of grass. The long blades pricked the skin along my back.

"Have you ever fucked under the stars?" he asked as he loomed above me.

"No. I think it's safe to say you're taking my rustic sex virginity tonight with all the outdoor sex."

Bishop laughed. "I'm honored." When I reached to pull him down beside me, he gave a shake of his head. "One sec."

I moaned in protest when he rose off me. He went over to our pile of clothes and dug another condom out of his wallet. Rising onto my elbows, I cocked my head at him. "I'm glad to see you carry so much protection on you at all times."

He at least had the presence of mind to give me somewhat of a sheepish look. "Yeah, well, it never hurts to be prepared," he mumbled as he tore into the wrapper.

"I'm just glad I get to benefit from your preparation," I teased.

He sank down beside me on the grass before rising onto his knees. With both hands he shoved my legs wide apart. "Speaking of preparation, I think it's time I got you ready to take me."

With a giggle, I said, "What you meant to say was ready to take that giant cock of yours, right?"

A wicked grin flashed on his face. "Damn straight."

I winked at him. "Then do what you have to do."

Before I knew it, Bishop had buried his face between my legs, causing a loud shriek of pleasure to escape my lips. I pinched my eyes shut and let the feelings overtake me as he licked and sucked my clit. Not only could the man kiss, but he was a god when it came to going down on a woman. He didn't even need to add his fingers to have me writhing on the grass, cursing repeatedly and calling out his name. His mouth, and especially his tongue, was all he needed. Over and over, it lapped at my soaked center, darting in and out of me, sliding along my clit.

The pleasure seemed to go on and on because just as I would

get close to coming, Bishop would pull away, letting the high build over and over again to where I thought I would eventually pass out. Finally, when he felt I'd had enough, he let me come. Never had I let a man take over or let myself be controlled. Never. But how glad I was to let him do what he truly did best.

Just as the last aftershocks of the orgasm flowed through me, Bishop rose between my legs. He then thrust hard inside me, stretching and filling me. "Jesus, you feel amazing," he muttered as he set up a punishing rhythm. I wrapped my legs around his back, drawing him deeper inside me. My hips rose and fell with his thrusts. I was just about to come again when he stopped.

"What are you—" I started to ask, but Bishop silenced me by kissing me. His tongue darted into my mouth, and I tasted myself on him. Slowly, he pulled his hips back to thrust deeply back into me. "Jesus," I murmured. While the hard and fast fucking had been amazing, this was even better. I could feel every delicious inch of him as he worked in and out of me. But more than that, it was the way his mouth and tongue mirrored the actions of his hips and his dick. Although I didn't want to think about it, what we were doing now was more like making love than fucking or having sex. The fact that we were outside in a blanket of grass and under the stars made it all the more romantic.

He pulled away from kissing me to stare into my eyes. I couldn't remember a time I had felt more connected with a lover. It was so intense that I finally had to close my eyes and bury my face in the crook of his neck. Anything to not focus on the feelings ricocheting through me.

Bishop's breath warmed against my ear. "Open your eyes, Sam."

When I dared to look at him, he smiled. "I want to be looking in your eyes when you come."

"Did you really just say that?" I demanded before I could stop myself.

Bishop's movement within me stilled. "It wasn't some sort of line. I really meant it."

"I know you meant it, and that's the problem."

He dipped his head to nip my bottom lip with his teeth. "Woman, you're not making any sense."

"It wasn't supposed to be like this," I whispered.

Bishop's expression told me he understood exactly what I meant. "Stop overanalyzing it and just feel."

"Okay."

Without another word, Bishop started thrusting slowly inside me again. I kept my eyes on his. I even kept them open when he dipped his hand between us to stroke my clit to make me come. As my walls clenched around him, I still kept my eyes on his. I didn't know when I had ever felt something more, physically and emotionally.

A few more thrusts had Bishop groaning and coming inside me. He broke eye contact only when his head came down to kiss me. When he was finished, he eased out of me, took off the condom, and tossed it aside. Although there was so much I wanted to say and to ask him, there were no words between us. I just let the feelings of contentment and extreme satisfaction wash over me.

Instead, I allowed Bishop to roll me onto my side in the grass. I couldn't hide my surprise when he spooned up beside me. I had never imagined him being one for after-sex cuddling. He seemed way more like the wham-bam kinda guy. It was just another one of the many contradictions of his character. "Knew it would be incredible with you," Bishop whispered, which caused my heart to swell in my chest.

Lying there in the grass, I felt so safe and protected with his arms wrapped around me and our legs tangled together. I closed my eyes, a contented sigh escaping my lips as I let myself fall asleep beside the man who had started off as my enemy.

Sunlight streaked across my face, waking me from a deep sleep. As I started to stretch, I realized I wasn't alone. A man's arm was draped over me with his hand cupping my breast. It hit me like a ton of bricks that I wasn't in the warmth and safety of my bedroom at home. Instead, I was naked and waking in a bed of overgrown grass. I had slept with Bishop. Actually, I had slept with him twice if I was counting. The delicious soreness between my legs reminded me how good it had been with my well-endowed partner. I couldn't remember the last time I'd had such a memorable sexual experience, least of all with a guy whose dick was big enough to leave a reminder the day after.

Glancing over my shoulder, I eyed Bishop, who was still dead to the world. A smile teased my lips at the sight of him. He appeared almost baby-faced with a shock of hair falling across his forehead. I had to fight the urge to reach out and curl it around my finger. His broad chest rose and fell with his labored breaths. In the daylight, I got a better look at all his tattoos. Normally, I didn't find them too attractive on men, but there was something about the way they looked on Bishop that made all the difference.

My aching muscles moaned in agony as I pulled myself to a sitting position. Sleeping on the ground, coupled with an intense fuckfest, had left me feeling physically as if I had been run over by an eighteen-wheeler. Emotionally, I felt almost as beaten up. While I didn't regret sleeping with Bishop, I felt overwhelmed with emotional turmoil. The more time I spent with Bishop and the Raiders, the less I could paint them as the villains I once thought them to be. There had to be something I was missing—something that made them worthy of being a target of the bureau.

Lying back down, I brought my hand to Bishop's face. I ran my thumb over his full bottom lip. "Wake up, sleepyhead."

At my touch, Bishop began to stir. His eyelids fluttered, and then he stared up at me. His bright blue eyes widened in disbelief as they moved from me to the clearing and then back to me. "Oh fuck," he muttered, and then rolled away from me.

"Wow, that's not the reaction I expected," I mused aloud as I tried not to sound as hurt by his rebuff as I was.

Bishop groaned as he sat up. "I'm sorry. I'm so fucking sorry."

"What's wrong with you?" I asked.

"Everything," Bishop muttered.

I rose to sit beside him. "Would you please tell me what is going on in that head of yours besides morning-after remorse?"

Cutting his eyes over at me, Bishop exhaled painfully. "I'm a fucking bastard."

My eyebrows shot up in surprise. "What are you talking about?"

"Jesus, Sam, last night it all felt so right, but now in the light of day . . ." He ran a hand over his face. "I thought I was going to be able to handle it—to not let it bother me. But it does. Fucking hell, it does."

I reached out to tentatively touch his cheek. "Bishop, you're not making any sense."

His eyes closed in agony as he said, "Marley."

While I had expected Bishop to bring Gavin up, it was still hard to hear his name come off Bishop's lips. It took me back to another grassy clearing—the one where I had held Gavin as he died. Thinking about Gavin caused my heart to ache. I couldn't help the sharp intake of breath or the pain that hit between my ribs. I looked out at the lake before trying to find my voice.

Before I could, Bishop continued. "Even though Marley wasn't a patched brother, I broke a cardinal rule last night. You don't fuck a brother's girlfriend or old lady." He opened his eyes and stared at me. "That's why I'm a fucking bastard."

"No, you're not. You're too good a man to ever be a fucking bastard."

"Before Marley died, I wanted you. It wasn't just about wanting to fuck you—it was about wanting us to have what you had with Marley. After he died, I still wanted you, and I'm a heartless bastard for making a move on you."

"Bishop, it's okay. There was nothing wrong with what we did last night."

"Oh hell yes, there was. And as long as I still possess a small fucking bit of decency, it ain't ever happening again."

My heart shuddered in my chest. There were so many implications that went along with his declaration. "You don't mean that."

"I sure as hell do. I'm pissing on Marley's memory every time I think about fucking you or when I put my hands on you or my dick in you." He swallowed hard, and it looked as though he was trying to fight back the tears that threatened in his eyes. "I know you're sick with grief about losing him, and I took advantage of you. But I promise you don't have to worry about it happening ever again."

Sick with grief. Yes. Absolutely. But I had to stop this train of thought. "You're wrong. I knew exactly what I was consenting to last night," I argued.

"That's what you think right now. But what about later on when it sinks in what we did? You'll hate me for letting things go on."

"There's nothing to sink in. I *wanted* to have sex with you last night. I *want* to have sex with you again. But more than the sex, I like you, Bishop."

Bishop's forlorn expression lightened a little. "You do?"

"Yeah. I do."

He appeared momentarily happy at my admission, but then his face clouded with worry again. "But Marley—"

"Is gone, but we're both here."

Bishop shook his head. "He was my friend. I can't do that to him . . . or to his memory."

When he pulled himself up off the grass, I knew he was serious. At the crux of his being, Bishop was honorable, and even though he would hate to do it, he would cut me out of his life. I couldn't let him do that. I needed to stay a part of his world. While I had to admit that a part of it would be for the case, I knew more than anything I needed to stay for how I felt about Bishop. Which confused the hell out of me.

There was only one thing to do. It felt as dangerous as flinging myself off a cliff. But desperate times called for desperate measures.

As I glanced up at the sky, I could almost hear Gavin saying, *Ah, go on and out me, Vargas. I'm dead. What harm can it do?*

Taking a deep breath to steady my nerves, I stood up. "Look, I need to tell you something about Marley—something that might change everything you think about him."

"What do you mean?" Bishop asked as he jumped into his jeans.

"I was never Marley's girlfriend."

Bishop's brow furrowed in confusion. "What are you saying?"

"Marley was my friend, and I would do anything in the world to help him when he needed me. When he started hanging around with you and wanting to be a part of the MC world, he needed me to be his girlfriend."

An expression of disbelief came over Bishop's face. "You weren't his girlfriend?"

"No."

"You guys were never a real couple?"

"No. Just the very best of friends."

After I braced myself for Bishop's wrath, he merely shook his head. "Just tell me one thing."

"Okay."

"Why the hell would he ask you to do something like that?"

"Because Marley was gay."

FIFTEEN

Bishop

There are moments in life when you have the rug unceremoniously jerked out from under you, sending you crashing down onto your fucking ass. This moment felt like that feeling except hyped up on steroids. Dumbfounded, I just stood there, frozen in disbelief like a fucking statue or something. I guess Samantha realized the level of shock I was in, because she once again said, "Marley was gay."

I blinked as I tried processing what she had just repeated. "You're fucking with me, right?"

"No, Bishop. I'm not."

Throwing my hands up wildly, I said, "Then you're just telling me Marley was gay so I'll keep dating you."

Samantha rolled her eyes at me before she snatched her dress off the ground and jerked it over her head. "Wow, you have one hell of an inflated ego if you think I would do that, not to mention that I would have to be pretty fucking psychotic to make something like that up just to keep you."

"Okay, I'm sorry. That was stupid of me to think, least of all say out loud."

"Damn straight," she snapped as she slid on her panties.

Needing to say the words aloud, I said, "Marley was gay."

Samantha's reply of "Yes" came as an angry hiss.

"Fucking hell," I muttered as I began pacing around the clearing. Speaking those three little words was life-altering. If what Samantha said was true, it changed everything between the two of us. It erased everything I had been beating myself up over, except the guilt of Marley's death.

Holy shit.

Marley and Samantha had never been a real couple. All this time the guilt had been eating me alive, it had been for nothing. Thinking aloud, I muttered, "But . . . but how is it possible Marley was gay? He was a man's man—he rode a motorcycle and worked as a mechanic, for fuck's sake."

"Don't tell me you're ignorant enough to believe in stereotypes," Samantha said. When I looked at her, she had crossed her arms over her chest, and her expression had darkened.

"Look, I'm sorry. My mind is overloaded right now as I'm trying to process the fact that not only was my good buddy gay, but he lied to me about it." I stopped pacing for a second. "And just why in the hell did he lie to me?"

"He knew to fit in with you guys and truly be accepted that he couldn't be out."

"That's crazy. We wouldn't have given two shits if he was gay," I argued.

Samantha's eyebrows rose accusingly. "Oh really? You yourself just spouted a stereotype."

"I'm in shock, okay? I'm going to say bullshit I don't mean."

"Yeah, well, just how many openly gay members do you have

in the Raiders?" When I didn't immediately respond, she huffed out a breath. "Exactly."

Closing the gap between us, I put my hands on Sam's shoulders. "You're right that we don't have a lot of openly gay guys, and it probably would have been hard on him to make it if he was out. But gay or straight, he was still someone I cared about—a lot."

"He would've appreciated that."

"As his friend, you just decided to go along with his lies?"

"I would call it self-preservation more than lying. And yeah, because I loved him, I wanted to do whatever I could to help him out. If it was pretending to be his girlfriend, then I was happy to do that."

I ran a hand through my hair. "This is all so crazy, and it changes everything."

"It does?"

"It sure as hell does. I've been beating myself up for months now because I thought I had been wanting a brother's girlfriend when all along there was nothing romantic between you two."

"It didn't help that I was flirting with you."

"I thought you were just teasing me—like you were the older woman playing at being a cougar, and I was your little cub."

With a roll of her dark eyes, Samantha said, "You've really got to work on how you handle the age difference between us." She jabbed her finger into my bare chest. "While a woman may be able to handle being a cougar, she is never going to enjoy hearing the words 'older woman.'"

I winced. "Okay, okay. I'll work on that."

"You sure as hell better."

After brushing a strand of long dark hair out of Samantha's face, I said, "I promise I'll make it up to you the next time we're alone together."

The frown on her face disappeared and was replaced with a

smile. "I'll make sure that you do." She brought her lips to mine for a gentle kiss. When she pulled away, she stared intently at me. "Since you know the truth, are you willing to give us a chance?"

Now that I knew I hadn't been dishonorable to Marley, there was not a single reason why I shouldn't date Samantha. Pulling her flush against me, I smiled. "Hell yeah."

"Good." She jerked her chin at the ATV. "Are you ready to head back? I'm starving and in desperate need of a shower."

"Yep. Just let me turn the generator off." Once I completed that chore, I returned to find Samantha already seated on the back of the ATV. "Listen. I need to ask you something else."

"Okay."

"Is there anything else you need to tell me? Like you're really a man or something?"

Samantha snorted. "I would think after last night you wouldn't have any doubts about that one."

I waggled my eyebrows at her. "I don't. I just didn't want there to be any more secrets between us."

Her face fell slightly. "There's not."

"And the only thing Marley lied about to me was his sexuality, right?"

With a nod, Sam said, "The rest was all true . . . at least as far as I know."

"I guess we'll never know all of Marley's secrets, huh?"

"Guess not."

"Sometimes it's okay to be a little mysterious," I said, leaning over to kiss Samantha's full lips. Just as I thrust my tongue into her mouth, her stomach growled loudly. I pulled away to grin at her. "Guess you weren't kidding when you said you were hungry."

"Sorry."

"Don't apologize. I need to remember to feed my woman if I'm going to keep her out all night working up an appetite."

Samantha snorted contemptuously. " 'My woman'? You sound like a caveman."

I slid onto the seat in front of her before throwing a look at her over my shoulder. "Just remember you are my woman."

"Is that a fact, Caveman?" she asked teasingly.

"It sure as hell is."

She brought her arms around my waist. "I guess there are worse things I could be than a caveman's woman."

"I want to hear you say that you're my woman."

"Honestly, Bishop."

"Say it," I instructed as I revved the ATV's motor.

Samantha turned up her chin and stared at the sky. When she didn't respond, I said, "I'll stay right here until you say it—your growling stomach be damned."

"I don't take orders," she said as she continued eyeing the clouds.

Whirling around, I grabbed her by the waist and dragged her around to sit on my lap.

"Bishop, what are you—"

I silenced her by crushing my mouth against hers. At the same time, I brought my hand between her legs. She gasped when I began to stroke her over her panties. "Say it, Samantha."

"Mmm," she whimpered, her hips rising and falling in time with my hand.

"Say that you're my woman, or I won't let you come."

"You don't play fair," she panted.

"No, babe, I don't. And I always get what I want." As my fingers grazed against her stomach, she sucked in a breath, which she wheezed out the moment I slipped two fingers inside her. "Are you going to say it now?"

Staring me straight in the eye, Sam said, "I'm your woman, you fucking Neanderthal asshole."

I threw my head back with a laugh. "I guess that's one way to say it."

She ground her hips against my hand. "Now make me come."

"I'm the one to give the orders around here."

Samantha grabbed the hair at the nape of my neck and tugged it hard. "If you don't make me come now, I won't let you fuck me for at least a week. If not longer."

I groaned. "Man, you drive a hard bargain."

She grinned. "And you let your dick make all your decisions."

"I am a man, aren't I?"

"True. Very true."

I began to pump my fingers harder and faster inside Samantha. She pulled my head to hers, and we started kissing madly. Our tongues battled with the same intensity as my hand and her hips. As she started over the edge, she moaned into my mouth. I pulled back to watch as her eyes pinched shut with pleasure and she bit down on her lip. Damn, she was fucking hot when she came.

When her walls stopped clenching around my finger, I withdrew my hand. Samantha gave me a lazy smile. "Part of me wants to forgo breakfast and a shower to just stay out here and fuck all day."

"Sounds like a plan to me."

She placed her palm on my chest and pushed me back. "Feed me first and we'll talk about fucking the rest of the day."

"What if you ate some of the food off me?"

Samantha rolled her eyes. "You're impossible."

"But you love me anyway."

Her expression turned serious. "Not yet, but I have a feeling you're going to make me fall in love with you."

My heartbeat thundered loudly in my chest at her response. While I had jokingly mentioned love to Samantha, I had felt so drawn to her over the last few weeks. She was the first thing I thought of in the morning as well as when I went to sleep. Did that mean I *loved* her? I'd never been in love before, and now I couldn't imagine being with any other woman but her. With the smell of her on my fingers and on my tongue, along with her supremely gorgeous body tucked close against me, I revved the motor.

Thankfully, Samantha was behind me, because I knew there was a ridiculous smile on my face the entire way home.

Playing the part of a gentleman, I drove Samantha all the way out of the woods, rather than stopping where we'd found the ATV. When we pulled into my driveway, people were ambling around the compound as they slowly came back to life from last night's partying. Probably some of them hadn't gone to bed all night and had toasted the sunrise with stale beer. I had done that more than a few times myself.

I led Samantha up the front walk and onto the porch. When we got inside, Samantha headed to the kitchen.

"What are you doing?" I asked.

"Looking for something for breakfast."

"Sorry, babe, but you're not going to find anything edible in there."

She cocked her head at me. "You have a perfectly functional kitchen with no food?"

"I could lie and say I haven't been to the store, or I could tell the truth, which would be my mother spoils me by cooking all my meals."

Samantha's eyes widened. "You're joking."

"Sadly, no. She used to cook three meals a day for us Malloy boys, but with Rev and Deacon married off, it's just me."

After giving a low whistle, Samantha said, "Doesn't your mother know she's ruining you for any woman? Please tell me she doesn't do your laundry, too."

I scowled at her. "No, smart-ass, I manage to do my own laundry. Mama Beth just loves to cook, so it gives her something to do since she's retired."

Holding up her hands, Samantha said, "Okay. Eating breakfast at your house is out. Where else can I get some food around here?"

"After a party, there's usually a big breakfast up at the clubhouse." I also knew Mama Beth would be cooking her usual Sunday morning spread, but I figured the safer choice would be to take Samantha to the clubhouse. The last thing I needed was Rev and Deacon giving me shit in front of Sam.

"Thank God. Just let me grab a quick shower, and I'll be ready to go."

"You might have to wait on the shower. We'll need to hurry on up there before the herd makes a run on the food and there's nothing left."

"Then why don't you hop in one shower, and I'll hop in the other?" Samantha suggested.

"That sounds like a good plan except for the fact that I only have one bathroom."

She slunk over to me and wrapped her arms around my neck. "That could create a problem if I wasn't a generous person who would offer to share my water with you."

"Aren't you sweet?" I mused as I cupped her ass with my hands.

"I try."

When she rubbed her crotch against mine, I groaned. "If I get in that shower with you, we'll never get out in time for breakfast."

"Not even for a quickie?"

"You and quickies just don't go together. Me and my dick like to take our time with you."

Samantha laughed. "I see." She took a few steps away from me. Her hands went to the hem of her dress as she asked, "Is there anything I could do to change your mind?"

"No, I—"

Before I could finish, I was hit in the face with the dress. Once it fell to the floor, I got an eyeful of her fabulous rack. Being the incredible cock tease that she was, she cupped her breasts and tweaked her hardening nipples. Motioning to the growing bulge in my crotch, she said, "I think you both like what you see."

"You're evil."

"I like getting what I want. I think it's safe to say we both have that in common."

"That could be a real problem if we're both too stubborn to give in."

"Yeah, but I think I've got the upper hand with this one." Slowly she shimmied her panties over her hips and down her thighs. Once she was naked, she cocked her head at me. "Shall I go turn the water on?"

I wanted so badly to be strong, but there was no way in hell with a throbbing dick and a gorgeous naked woman I would be able to say no.

"Bishop, you didn't answer my question," Samantha said. When she slid her hand between her legs, I growled and charged at her. After I crushed her against me, Samantha giggled. "Guess that answers my question."

"Go turn the water on," I instructed.

Samantha pulled my shirt over my head. "Yes, sir." She then swished her hips provocatively as she made her way into the bedroom.

When I started to follow her, I heard a knock at the door. "Fuck," I grunted before turning around and going to the door. When I opened it, Mama Beth stood there.

"Hey, sweetheart, you didn't show up for breakfast, and I was worried."

Throwing an arm over my shoulder, I furiously scratched the back of my neck as I tried to come up with an excuse. Just as I opened my mouth, Samantha appeared in the living room wearing just my T-shirt. "Bishop, I'm getting cold without you," she called.

Mama Beth stared past me to take in Samantha. At the sight of Mama Beth, Samantha gasped and turned red. She tugged at the bottom of the T-shirt to cover herself better. "Now I can see you were busy," Mama Beth said.

"Yes, but I should've called you about breakfast. I know you always expect me."

"That's true, I do. And I'll expect you to come up to the house to eat as soon as you're finished cleaning up." She gave Samantha a pointed look. "The invitation includes you."

"Thank you, Mrs. Malloy. That's very kind of you," Samantha said meekly. I almost laughed at the humble way she was acting around Mama Beth.

"I guess I better head back to the house and warm up the food."

"You don't have to do that. We're perfectly capable of heating it up ourselves."

"I know that. But I don't mind." Embarrassment flooded me when she patted my cheek as if I were five years old. I was pretty sure she did it not out of affection but to tease. "See you in a few minutes."

"Bye, Mama."

"Bye, Mrs. Malloy."

When the door shut behind Mama Beth, Samantha groaned and covered her face with her hands. "Oh my God! I'm so mortified!"

I laughed as I closed the gap between us. "Babe, it's no big deal."

Jerking her hands away, she gave me an incredulous look. "Not only did your mother see me half-naked, but she heard me talking about sex. And let's not forget she knows we were fucking, and that's why you missed breakfast."

"She doesn't know we were fucking." When Samantha cocked her head at me, I added, "We could have been sleeping after we were fucking," I teased.

Samantha smacked my arm. "This isn't funny. I've never cared about what my boyfriend's parents thought about me, but for some reason, I care about your mother."

My chest tightened with her words. Not only was I stoked that she gave a shit what Mama Beth thought, but I'd never had someone call me her boyfriend before. I didn't expect it to mean as much to me as it did. "So I'm your boyfriend, huh?"

She swept her hands to her hips. "I thought we established that this morning. If you're not on board with us, I can always call you my fuck buddy or friend with benefits."

I grinned. "No, I like boyfriend better." I slid my arms around her waist. "And yeah, I'm on board with what we're doing. It was just nice hearing you call me that, since I've never really been someone's boyfriend before."

"There's a first time for everything, huh?"

"Yep."

Samantha groaned again. "God. I don't think I can face your mother."

"It'll be fine. She's a very understanding woman, I promise."

"Really?"

I nodded. "It means a lot that she invited you to breakfast. If she was really pissed, she would have ignored you."

"I hope you're right."

With a smack on her luscious ass, I said, "Come on. We're going to run out of hot water."

"Normally, I would say that you could figure a way to heat it up, but I'm going to pass on that so we can get to your mom's quicker."

"You're turning me down?"

"I'm not giving your mom one more reason not to like me. Now hurry up!"

I merely grinned as I let Samantha lead me into the bedroom.

After a lightning-fast shower, we made it to Mama Beth's in less than half an hour. The sounds of laughter filled the air as we swept through the front door. Although I was late, my brothers and sisters-in-law still sat around the oak table in the dining room while Willow and Wyatt played on the floor in the living room.

At the sight of us, Rev grinned. "Well, well, if it isn't the sleeping beauties."

"Yeah, what kept you guys?" Deacon asked.

I mouthed a *fuck you* at him before motioning for Samantha to take a seat next to Annabel. I took a seat at the end of the table.

Samantha gave Mama Beth and the others an apologetic look. "I'm sorry we're late. Bishop didn't tell me he was expected at breakfast, or I would have made sure we were here on time," Samantha said.

Mama Beth smiled. "It's okay. We're just glad to have you with us now." She set a heaping plate full of biscuits and gravy, grits, sausage, bacon, and eggs in front of Samantha. "I just fixed it all for you because I wasn't sure what you liked."

Samantha's eyes lit up. "Trust me, I like it all. Thank you."

"You're welcome." She then brought me my usual plate.

"Thanks, Mama."

"Ah, so we're Mr. Manners now that your girlfriend is here, huh?" Deacon asked, a wicked gleam burning in his dark eyes.

I should have realized that my brothers, especially Deacon, were going to love nothing better than to ride my ass about Samantha. Instead of once again mouthing for him to fuck off, I ignored him and dug into the heaping pile of food.

"Samantha, did you have a good time last night at the party?" Mama Beth asked.

"Yes, I did. Everyone has been so sweet to welcome me."

"Generally, the Raiders are a friendly bunch," Mama Beth mused.

"Does the party go on all day?" Sam asked.

Rev nodded. "Most people will start heading back later this afternoon, while some will stay and head out in the morning."

With a smile, Annabel said, "You can count me out for another late night. I have to leave to go back to school tomorrow."

"Don't worry, babe. I'll be turning in early myself. I've got that meeting in Chattanooga in the morning."

"Oh, that's right."

"You're still coming with me, aren't you, B?" Rev asked.

After gulping down some scorching coffee, I said, "Sure am. What time do we have to leave?"

"Five a.m."

I groaned. "Jesus, why does it have to be so early?"

Rev laughed. "Samantha, will you make sure he gets up on time in the morning?"

The insinuation that Sam would stay another night with me caused both of us to choke on our food. When we started to recover,

Rev gave us a sheepish look. "Sorry about that. I didn't realize it was such a touchy subject. I just figured things were settled between you guys."

I brought my gaze to Samantha's. "They are settled." When she smiled, I added, "We just have to work all the kinks out."

"I'm sure you both will do just fine," Mama Beth said.

"I agree," Alex chimed in.

Deacon rolled his eyes. "What's next? Having us toast to the happy couple?"

"Shut up," I muttered.

"Uh-oh, I think he's blushing," Rev said.

Glaring at the two of them, I growled. "I really hate you both right now."

When Deacon and Rev both burst out laughing at my response, I vowed to punch the hell out of them the moment I got them alone.

After breakfast, I took Samantha back to the clubhouse to hang out. We spent the rest of the day shooting pool, talking to the guys, and drinking. She seemed to like my MC brothers as well as she did my blood brothers. I was pumped that she was able to finally see us in a different light than she originally did. The way she thought of us got me thinking about the meeting I was going to in the morning.

"Hey," I said.

"Hey yourself," she replied with a smile.

"Why don't you come with me to Chattanooga?"

Her dark eyes widened. "But I thought you had a meeting to go to."

"I do. But it doesn't mean I can't have you along."

"Well, I would, but I have work in the morning."

I felt like a giant pussy for being disappointed. "That's okay. Another time."

Samantha leaned forward in her chair. "I could always call in sick."

"You would really do that?"

"Actually, my boss has been a little more lenient on me lately."

"Ah, I see." Sensing we needed a subject change away from Marley, I grabbed her by the waist and dragged her over to sit in my lap. "So you'll stay with me tonight?"

Her eyebrows shot up into her hairline. "I thought you didn't have women stay at your house."

"I didn't. Until you."

Dipping her head, she let her lips graze against mine. "Yes. I'll stay."

I slid my hands into her hair, letting the silky strands fall between my fingers. "I'm glad."

Just as I started to bring my lips to hers, she said, "But I'm going to need a change of clothes."

With a laugh, I said, "You sure as hell know how to kill a moment."

"I would really be killing a moment if I was in stinky clothes tomorrow."

"Fine. We'll throw your clothes in the wash."

"And just what am I supposed to wear until they're done?"

My mouth licked and nibbled across her jawline, causing her to shudder and tilt her head back to give me better access. "You'll need to be naked for what I have in mind for the rest of the night."

SIXTEEN

SAMANTHA

I woke the next morning to the bellowing sound of an unfamiliar alarm clock. When I shifted in bed and came up against a rock-hard body, the realization hit me that I wasn't at home. I had stayed the night at Bishop's. I had broken his rule not only of women not coming to his house but of not staying over.

Today we were rising early to go to Chattanooga on some club business. Yesterday when the secret meeting was broached by Rev, I had immediately felt divided. Part of me wanted to go to see what I could uncover, while the other part of me feared what I might find. I wanted more than anything to believe Bishop when he said his club was going legitimate. It was just incredibly hard to imagine the Raiders going clean after years of illegal dealings.

Bishop cursed as he slapped the alarm clock off. When I turned over to face him, he was furiously rubbing his face and eyes to wake up. "Good morning," I said.

After a wide yawn, Bishop grumbled, "Morning."

"I guess it's safe to say you aren't a morning person, huh?"

"Fuck no." He cocked his head at me. "Are you?"

I shrugged. "I'm okay with getting up early."

"Well, as long as you're with me, you better not be okay with it."

"What do you mean?"

"I mean, I don't want you throwing open the curtains at the crack of fucking dawn while whistling a happy tune."

I snorted at his summation. "You have nothing to worry about on that front, trust me."

Bishop grinned. "I'm glad to hear it." He stretched in bed and groaned again. "Fuck, I do not want to get up and get on the road."

Snuggling up to his side, I asked, "So, what's so important about this meeting that has you getting up early and missing work?"

"It's just something Rev and I need to do. . . . I guess you could say it's for Rev more than me, but I need to be there for support."

As I traced the ink lines of one of Bishop's tattoos with my finger, the irrational side of me couldn't help worrying about what Rev needed to do and why Bishop needed to be there for support. It didn't sound good at all, and that fact made my stomach churn. Of course, I couldn't imagine why Bishop would ask me along if it were something illegal. Maybe he planned to use me as a lookout or diversion. That thought made me feel like a paranoid fool. More than anything, I hoped that today would give me evidence to support the claim that the Raiders had gone legitimate in their business dealings. I hadn't yet broached the subject to Peterson because I wanted to make sure I had some concrete evidence to back me up. He had no idea that while I worked on the paper trails of other cases, I was secretly working on the Raiders.

"Are you sure about me going? It sounded kinda like a brothers' thing."

"Of course I'm sure. You heard Rev say that Annabel couldn't go."

"Yeah."

"And there will be some other women there."

"It's good to know I won't be the only vagina," I said teasingly.

Bishop laughed. "You'll be the only vagina that belongs to me."

"Yes, Caveman."

Bishop dipped his head to bring his lips to mine for a tender kiss. "I'm starting to dig you calling me Caveman. Kinda makes me hot."

I grinned. "Why am I not surprised?"

"Guess we better get up and get going. Rev will have my ass if we make him late."

"Where exactly is it we're going in Chattanooga?" I asked as I sat up in the bed.

"You'll see."

"You really expect me to just get on the back of your bike and let you take me wherever you want?"

He laughed. "I sure as hell do."

"You're such an egomaniac!" I huffed.

Pulling me against him, Bishop nuzzled my neck. "Yeah, but you like it."

I gave a resigned sigh. "God forgive me, but I do."

He gave my bottom a resounding smack. "Let's get this fine ass of yours in the shower."

We got on the road at a little after six in the morning. After stopping for a quick breakfast at seven, we continued on our way. Just before we reached Chattanooga, we pulled off at an exit.

I was wondering if it was for a pee break or gas until we topped the hill and I was momentarily blinded by the gleaming chrome coming off a multitude of bikes. They were parked in a rest stop for truckers.

After we turned in, I noticed that while the men and women were wearing cuts, they were all different. There wasn't a unified chapter like at the party in Virginia. Several of them had armbands that read BACA.

Instead of turning off the engines and getting off the bikes, Rev and Bishop just pulled into the back of the group. A man at the head of the line waved to them. He then did a count of the bikes and nodded. Once he got on his bike, the others around us started up their engines.

"What's going on?" I shouted over the roar of the pipes.

"You'll see," Bishop replied cryptically.

I didn't have a chance to try to get any more information out of him because we started out of the parking lot in a two-by-two formation. After getting back on the interstate, we traveled a few miles before taking another exit. I couldn't imagine what was going on. Was it some kind of hit to be staged on an MC, and all these men were unified together? If anything illegal went down, I was in deep shit with the bureau for not letting them know what I was doing. Even if they were aware, it was bad news for agents to be caught up in illegal action. At least I had my cell phone on me with a direct link to Peterson in case things went south.

As we roared into a residential neighborhood, both my curiosity and my worry reached a fever pitch. I was pretty sure the last thing the residents wanted at eight in the morning was a bunch of noisy Harleys. After winding around a few streets, we came to a stop outside a small frame house with a well-kept yard.

Bishop eased down his kickstand and then cut the engine.

Slowly I took off my helmet as I eyed Bishop's back. In a low voice, I asked, "Are you guys about to do a hit on some unknowing biker?"

Whirling around, Bishop stared wide-eyed at me. "What the fuck did you just say?"

"You didn't answer my question."

With a bark of a laugh, Bishop replied, "No, Sam, we're not here to kill anyone. For fuck's sake, I told you we were going legitimate. I'm not sure how a club could be legitimate one minute and then killing someone the next."

"Yeah, well, I didn't know what all these other guys were up to."

"I can promise you it isn't murder."

"Then what is really going on?"

"You'll see," he once again replied.

I grunted in frustration as I hopped off the bike. Rev motioned for us to follow him. He led us over to a walkway where some of the other men and women were forming a line. I wondered if it was some high-ranking biker we were waiting on, or the leader of a gang. It was obviously someone who garnered a lot of respect.

When the front door creaked open, I stood up on my tiptoes to get a good look at who was coming out. A young girl with flowing blond hair appeared in the doorway. Her black-and-white Converse sneakers carried her out onto the porch. When she raised her head to see all of us, she bit down on her lip and nervously tugged at her black-and-white-checked dress. When her parents appeared at her side, I looked from her to Bishop. "Okay, just what the hell is going on here?"

Before he could answer, Rev placed a hand on my shoulder. "The little girl's name is Ansley. She has to be in court this morning to testify against the man who raped her."

I widened my eyes in horror. "She can't be more than seven or eight."

"She's eight," Rev said.

"But she's just a baby to have been through something so horrible!"

"I agree. That's why we're all here. The men and women here belong to BACA, or Bikers Against Child Abuse. We come to lend moral support and physical strength to children who have suffered physical, emotional, and sexual abuse. Sometimes they need someone to walk them home from school, and other times they need someone to go along with them to court. That's why we're here today."

"That's . . . amazing." It was all I could murmur in response. After all, how could you put into words what these people were doing? It humbled me greatly just standing there with them.

"Well, a lot of us have experienced abuse in our past, and we want to somehow make it easier."

Staring intently into Rev's eyes, I couldn't help wondering what kind of abuse he had endured. It made me wonder if Bishop had suffered the same fate, and that was why he had also gotten involved. As if he could hear my internal thoughts, Rev lowered his voice and said, "I was raped when I was eleven by a member of my father's church."

I brought my hand to my mouth as I gasped in horror. "Oh, Rev . . . I'm so, so sorry. Did you have to testify against him in court like Ansley?"

Rev and Bishop exchanged a look before Rev shook his head. "He never went to court."

"You mean he got away with it."

A cold, unfeeling look entered Rev's usually friendly eyes. "I wouldn't say that."

"Then what . . ." I clamped my lips shut as realization of what had happened struck me. Rev's rapist had never stepped foot inside court because someone had killed him. I couldn't help wondering whether it was their father. Although I wasn't a parent, I could only imagine how agonizingly devastating it would be to see your child hurt like that. I would be tempted to put the person six feet under as well. Then it hit me. I had wondered what had driven Preacher Man from his church and back to a life as an outlaw biker. Now I knew the answer.

"Your father killed him. Didn't he?" I questioned in a low voice.

"Yeah. He did."

Staring Rev straight in the eye, I said, "Good for him."

Rev gave me a tight smile. "Thank you."

Sensing we needed a subject change, I asked, "Where does everyone come from?"

"All over the country," Bishop replied.

"Really?"

He nodded. "Most are from close by, but there's some people who ride fourteen or fifteen hours to get here."

"That's really impressive they would do something like that for a stranger."

With a teasing grin, Bishop said, "Yeah, it is hard to imagine us low-life bikers caring about anything other than booze and women, right?"

From the time I was eight years old, I had never felt anything other than disgust and utter hatred for bikers. *How could I not?* I had just lost my very best friend to a biker's gun, so surely Bishop would understand how hard it would be for me to think anything otherwise. But in his eyes, and in truth in mine, I hadn't seen bikers as men who could be trusted or capable of kindness. The Raiders were slowly proving there could be good men and women in an MC.

Heat rose in my cheeks. "I didn't mean it like that."

"One day I'm going to totally erase those thoughts from your mind."

I smiled at him. "You're doing a really good job. I promise."

He winked at me. "Thanks."

I watched as the leader of the group went over to speak to the girl and her parents, then began to introduce the bikers and the women. Each person went around and shook the girl's hand. While I felt somewhat apprehensive, Bishop barreled forward with a bright smile. "Hi, sweetheart, I'm Bishop." Motioning me forward, he said, "This is my girlfriend, Sam."

"Hi," she said.

"Hi," I replied. Feeling that I should say or do something more, I added, "I love your shoes. I had a pair just like them when I was your age."

Ansley's eyebrows shot up in surprise. "You did?"

"I sure did."

"Hard to believe they made them way back then, huh? Like the dinosaurs might've had a pair," Bishop teased.

When I playfully swatted his arm, Ansley giggled. I couldn't imagine a sweeter sound in the world at that moment. I had to wonder after what had happened to her how she was able to laugh at all. "Okay, it's time to load up and head out," the leader, whose name I learned was Bobby, said.

We waved good-bye to Ansley and headed back to Bishop's bike. "Surprised?" Bishop asked as he handed me my helmet.

"That this was the meeting you were going to, or that you partake in something like this?" I asked.

"Both, I guess."

"I would have to say I'm very surprised. But at the same time, I'm relieved to see that this is what you and Rev were up to and not something bad."

"There is no more bad stuff for us. I want you to understand that."

Deep down, I wanted nothing more than for that to be the absolute truth. I wanted to be able to take what I had learned to Peterson and have any outstanding interest on the Raiders shut down. But I had to have more concrete evidence than just Bishop's word. I had to know for sure they were no longer dealing in guns, and I wasn't sure how in the hell I was supposed to find that out.

"I do . . . or I will. I promise," I said as I climbed onto the back of his bike.

We left the neighborhood in a perfect formation, just the way we had come in. Except this time, Ansley's parents' car was in the middle of the pack, which gave it the perfect protection. After winding our way through the town, we reached the courthouse. The expressions on the bystanders' faces when we pulled up were priceless. I guessed it wasn't every day they saw a procession of bikers.

After the bikes were parked in a neat line, everyone started getting off. Ansley and her parents waited until we were all assembled outside the car. Then they got out, and we led them up the courthouse steps and into the building. It took a few minutes to get us all through security. Half of the guys had chains that set off the metal detector. It then took several elevator cars to get us all up to the fourth floor.

After we arrived in the courtroom, we settled in two rows close to the front. We were a somber group as we waited in reverent silence. As part of my job I had been in court too many times to count, but this was the first time I had seen this level of support and unified strength for a victim.

We hadn't been seated long when the bailiff asked us to rise for the judge. Once the judge was seated, he asked the prosecution to call their first witness.

"We call Ansley Marie Butler."

Ansley slowly rose out of her chair. Her legs shook violently like a newborn colt's. As she started down the row, everyone patted her on the back. Some bumped fists and some of the women reached out to hug her. When she got to me, I smiled and patted her back. Although words seemed totally inadequate in that moment, I bit back the tears as I whispered, "You've got this."

After giving me a weak smile, she started up the aisle to the witness box. As she took the stand, I suddenly became overwhelmed with a flashback so intense that I began shaking in my seat. When I stared ahead, it was no longer Ansley raising her right hand to swear to tell the truth and nothing but the truth on the Bible.

Instead, I saw my nine-year-old self as I testified at the trial of the man who killed my father.

Feeling the bile rising in my throat, I clamped my hand over my mouth and bolted out of my seat. I ran down the aisle and burst through the courtroom doors. My gaze spun wildly around to find a restroom. When I saw the sign, I broke into a run. I barely made it into a stall before I emptied the contents of my stomach. Over and over again, I heaved until there was nothing left within me.

When I finally finished, I flushed the toilet and staggered out of the stall. I placed my palms on the sink basin and stared into the mirror. As I was transported back to that horrible place, tears overran my eyes, sending mascara-blackened tears down my cheeks.

The morning I was due in court, my mother had come into my room to dress me. She had put me in a simple black dress that had scratchy material and made my skin itch. My protests about the fabric fell on deaf ears as my mother brushed my hair. She swept it back on the sides with black barrettes. She ignored me once again when I protested that I wanted to wear my usual ponytail. That morning she seemed to be in an almost trancelike state of going through the motions. She didn't talk to me or my brother or sister. We had exchanged looks among ourselves during the period of silence.

As I eased down onto the hard chair in the witness stand, I kept my head tucked to my chest. I didn't dare look across to the defendant's table. I knew if I did I would lose all my nerve, and I wouldn't be able to give the carefully rehearsed answers that the prosecutor had gone over with me. Earlier that week, I had spent several miserable afternoons reliving in horrific detail the night of my father's murder.

My stomach twisted tighter and tighter into knots as Mr. Greenly led me through the events of that night. I swallowed hard to keep down the bile rising in my throat. I didn't want to do anything wrong, least of all throwing up. I knew everyone was counting on me to put Willie away. Most of all, I felt I couldn't screw up because I owed it to my father to get him justice.

The questions seemed to go on and on. Finally, we got to the one I was dreading the most. Mr. Greenly approached the witness stand. He leaned on the railing and gave me a reassuring smile. "Samantha, is the man you saw shoot your father present in the courtroom today?"

When I stared into Mr. Greenly's dark blue eyes, he nodded encouragingly. Slowly, I began turning my head to the defense table. All the while, I kept my gaze on my lap, staring at the silk handkerchief my mother had slipped into my hand right after they called my name. "He's over there," I whispered.

"I'm sorry, but I need you to repeat that," Mr. Greenly said.

Raising a shaking hand, I pointed at the table. "He's there."

The defense attorney's voice caused me to jump. "Your Honor, the witness has not visually identified my client."

I pinched my eyes shut. My body trembled so hard my knee knocked the microphone stand, causing a loud screech to echo throughout the room.

"Samantha," Mr. Greenly's kind voice said.

"I can't," I murmured.

"Samantha, the court has to have you look at Mr. Bates in order for your testimony to be recorded."

Tears of agony overflowed from my eyes and spilled down my cheeks. With my eyes still shut, I pictured my father's smiling face in front of me—the way his strong arms felt when he drew me in for a tight hug. And it was then I felt my father's strength enveloping me.

I opened my eyes wide and stared at Willie. Sitting in a suit and tie, he looked much different from the way he had that night. But all I had to do was imagine him in the leather vest he had worn before, and there were no doubts.

As he sneered at me, I pulled my shoulders back and once again pointed at Willie. "Him. He's the man who killed my father."

I was jerked out of my flashback at the sound of the bathroom door flying open. "Sam?"

Lifting my head, I gazed at his reflection in the mirror. "Sorry. I just needed a minute."

Bishop's expression was filled with concern. He closed the gap between us and came to stand beside me. "What's wrong?"

"Nothing."

"Don't bullshit me, Sam. You just bolted from the courtroom, and I come in here and find you in tears." He put his hands on my waist and turned me around to face him. "Please tell me what's wrong."

I knew that I had two options. I could concoct an elaborate lie by saying that seeing Ansley had brought back memories of a young girl I had seen murdered. Or I could tell him the truth about my father—or at least the version that wouldn't out me as an agent.

In the end, it was a no-brainer. I chose the second. "You know how my father died when I was eight?"

"Yeah," Bishop replied.

"Well, he didn't just die. He was murdered by a biker named Willie Bates."

Bishop's blue eyes widened. "Go on."

Leaning back against the sink, I told him everything about that night. Then I told him about having to testify at the trial. "When Ansley took the stand, it sent me reeling with a flashback. I had to get out of there."

Bishop drew me into his strong arms. His hands ran along my back. "I'm so sorry, babe," he murmured into my ear.

It meant so much to have Bishop's sympathy, because he knew what it was like to lose a loved one to a violent death. A quiet "Thanks" left my lips, but no other words seemed adequate.

He pulled back to look me in the eye. "Now it all makes sense about the way you felt about bikers. It went deeper than just what happened to Marley."

"Yes. It does."

"No one should have to go through what you did as a kid." Bishop's hands came to cup my cheeks. "If I could take the pain and hurt away from you, I would."

Tears pooled in my eyes at his kind words, and I knew he was sincere about taking away my pain. Once again, he was such a paradox of appearing so tough outside and being so tender on the inside. Words seemed inadequate to express my gratitude. All I could murmur was "You really are the sweetest man I know."

When Bishop started to bring his lips to mine, I brought my hand up to stop him. "Trust me, you don't want to do that."

"You get sick or something?"

"Oh yeah. Big-time."

He gave me a sympathetic smile. "Come on. Let's get you out of here."

"What about Rev?"

"I'll tell him you need to get back."

"But then he'll have to ride by himself."

Bishop chuckled. "He's a big boy, Sam. He can make it home on his own. He rode all the way to Virginia in the middle of December by himself."

"What in the hell would possess him to do that?"

"He was going to tell Annabel he loved her."

"Damn, that's romantic," I mused.

"Yeah, Rev's a deep guy. He's a hell of a lot more romantic than I'll ever be."

"I don't think that's necessarily true."

He cocked his eyebrows at me. "You got some crazy feat in mind to make me prove myself?"

I shook my head. "It doesn't always have to be grand gestures. What you just did was pretty romantic."

Bishop gave me a skeptical look. "I just came to look for you. I'd hardly call that really exceptional."

"But you cared enough to be worried about me, and you came into the women's bathroom to make sure I was all right."

"Oh Jesus, I hadn't even thought of that. Let's get the hell out of here."

I laughed as I let him drag me by the hand out the door. "I hate that I didn't get to say good-bye to Ansley."

"Don't worry. She has plenty of support at the moment. Maybe I can get her address and you can send a card or something."

Once again, I was touched by his compassion. "Thanks. I would like that."

As we pushed through the plate-glass door, Bishop said, "I just can't wait for that piece of shit to go to prison. He'll get tortured in there for being a kiddie rapist."

"You and me both."

We spent the rest of the walk to the bikes in silence. When Bishop handed me my helmet, I said, "Thanks."

"It's just a helmet."

I smiled. "No. I mean, thanks for bringing me here today and letting me be a part of what you guys were doing."

"You're welcome. And I was glad to have you along." He planted a soft kiss on my lips. "I always like having you with me."

"And I like being with you," I replied. It was the truth. Regardless of the reasons why I had originally started hanging out with Bishop, I genuinely enjoyed his company. At first it had been more about friendship and now it was growing into something much more serious. Although I knew we were on dangerous ground, I didn't want to worry about it. I just wanted to enjoy the moment.

But in the back of my mind, I knew my secrets couldn't stay buried forever. You could live a double life of lies for only so long before it caught up with you and you had to pay the consequences.

I just never imagined how hard that would be.

When we got home, I was physically and emotionally wiped. On the ride home, I'd had too much time to relive painful memories from the past of my father and some of Gavin. While I knew I should head on home, I didn't want to spend the rest of the day alone. Part of me argued that I should go in to work. That at the very least I needed to talk to Peterson about what I had learned so far about the Raiders.

As if he sensed the way I was feeling low, Bishop said, "Why don't you hang around for a while? Stay the night. You can always get up early in the morning to go home before work."

Normally, I would have been determined to deal with my problems on my own and not to rely on anyone else to get me through. But I didn't do that. Instead, I kissed Bishop. "Thank you. I'd really like to stay."

He smiled. "Good."

"You'll let me know when you get sick of me, won't you?"

"I doubt that will ever happen, but if it does, I'll be sure to let you know." As he unlocked the front door, he asked, "Are you hungry?"

"I thought you didn't have anything in the house to eat?"

"I don't. But I'll see if Mama Beth does."

I laughed. "I think I'll pass for now. I really just want to take a hot shower and then go to bed." Bishop didn't argue with me that it was only one in the afternoon. Instead, he just nodded.

Without another word to him, I cut through the bedroom and into the bathroom. After turning on the water, I stripped out of my clothes and dipped inside. The emotions of the day soon overwhelmed me. Placing my arms on the tile, I buried my head in the backs of my hands and sobbed.

The sound of the shower curtain opening startled me, and I whirled around. Bishop stepped into the shower. Swiping the tears away, I asked, "What are you doing?"

"Getting clean. What does it look like I'm doing?" He picked up the bar of soap and started scrubbing himself for good measure.

"You don't have to do this."

"Do what?"

"Pretend so I can save face."

"I'm just here taking a shower." He stared pointedly at me. "Unless you want to talk."

Bringing my hands to my face, I moaned, "God, I hate myself

for feeling this way." As I peeked at him through my fingers, I added, "I hate letting you see me this way."

Bishop drew me against his chest. "Don't ever feel that way, Sam. I'm here for you no matter what. Today was a bad day for you. It triggered a lot of long-buried emotions. I totally get that, and I totally get you having some meltdowns today."

I rested my chin on his shoulder as I rubbed my hands along his broad back. "Even though I don't want to believe you, deep down I know that you mean every word you say."

"I do mean it." He dipped his head to where his breath warmed against my ear. "Now, why don't you let me take care of you for a little while?"

"Okay. I can try."

Bishop turned me around to face the showerhead. When he started sweeping the bar of soap over my skin, I glanced at him over my shoulder. "What are you doing?"

"Taking care of you, like I said."

"You really don't have to do this."

"I know. But I want to."

Instead of continuing to protest, I pinched my lips shut and just enjoyed what Bishop was doing. It felt so intimate having his hands over my body in not just a sexual way. There was tenderness and care in the way he soaped me up. He took the time to massage my shoulders, and he planted tender kisses along my neck before he washed me there. I'd never had a man take care of me before. Of course, I'd never really wanted or allowed one to. But something about Bishop made me want to give up a little control. He made it easy to want to give in to him, since he was so attentive to my needs both in and out of the bedroom.

Once he had finished soaping me up, he took the showerhead

off and rinsed me. When he stopped for a moment, I thought he was done, but he was lathering up his hands with shampoo. "Sorry that you're probably going to smell like a man with this soap and shampoo. I don't have anything feminine around here."

I laughed. "It's okay. I want to smell like you."

When he finished rinsing my hair, I placed my hands on his chest and pushed him against the shower wall. Looking him in the eyes, I slid down his body until I was on my knees before him.

"Sam, what are you doing?"

"Now it's my turn to take care of you." I took his cock in my hand and began to slowly pump up and down. It quickly came to life, growing and swelling in my hand. Darting my tongue out, I licked and teased along the head. Bishop watched me with hooded eyes.

When I sucked the head into my mouth, he groaned, and his head fell back against the tile. I sucked him harder and faster, taking him deeper and deeper each time. His hands came to tangle in the strands of my hair. "Oh fuck, Sam," he murmured.

As I continued working him with my mouth, I brought my free hand up to cup his balls. At my gentle tug, he hissed and banged his head against the wall. When I felt them tightening in my hands, I knew he was close to coming.

When he tried to pull me away, I shook my head.

"You gotta stop, or I'm going to come."

I let him momentarily fall free of my mouth, but I kept pumping him with my hand. "But I want you to come. I want to taste you."

"Fuck me," he muttered as his eyes flared.

He didn't argue with me anymore, which was good because I wouldn't have listened to him. I wanted to give him physically what he had given to me emotionally. Once again, I slid him into my mouth, my teeth slightly grazing him.

"Sam!" he cried as he found his release.

I lifted my eyes to watch him come. He was so beautiful and sexy when he did. When he was finished, I licked him clean.

Bishop leaned down and helped me up. "I really like the way you take care of me."

I grinned. "You're very welcome. I was glad to repay the favor."

"I'd like to pay some favors to you now," he said as his hand came between my legs.

I sucked in a breath. "But we were even," I protested.

"Do we really have to keep score?" he asked as his breath scorched the skin along my neck.

"I guess not."

He bent down to grab my calf before bringing my foot to rest on the faucet. "You should know by now I don't play fair." He then sank to his knees before me.

"No. You don't." When his mouth dipped between my legs, I gasped. "But you sure know how to play."

No man had ever gone down on me like Bishop. He had a true oral gift. This time he had me arching my hips and crying out his name without even using his fingers. His tongue was masterful in the way it was able to be soft and hard and gentle and forceful almost all at once.

After I came, I eased him up off the shower floor. I wanted him inside me as soon as possible, and I was glad to see his cock was already at half-mast again. "Take me now," I pleaded.

"Jesus, I love it when you beg." Bishop bent down to slide his arm behind my knees; then he swept me up into his arms.

"What are you doing?" I asked as I wrapped my arms around his neck.

"Taking you to my bed."

"That'll be a first for us," I mused. After the many times we had been together over the last few days, we had yet to have sex in a bed.

Last night, we had ended up on the floor of the living room after starting out on the couch. I had slept with him in his bed last night, but that was after we had already exhausted each other.

Bishop gently laid me out on top of the comforter. He stared down at me with both tenderness and obvious hunger. I spread my legs wide before him, urging him to take me. He groaned before turning to dig a condom out of the nightstand. Once he had it on, he covered me with his body.

His lips crushed against mine as our tongues battled frantically against each other. "Hurry, Bishop, I want you inside me," I panted against the corner of his mouth.

Bishop took me by surprise by rolling us over and bringing me up to straddle him. "You take me," he commanded.

When I took his cock in my hand, he groaned and bucked his hips. I quickly rose and guided him between my legs. Slowly I eased down on the length of him. I had to bite my lip to keep from crying out at how wonderful his filling me felt.

I began to ride him slowly at first. Rising off him and slowly coming back down. Bishop's hands fondled my breasts. He massaged and kneaded them until the nipples were hardened peaks. As I began to move faster, he rose to take one of my breasts in his mouth. He alternated between my breasts and teased and sucked the nipples as I bounced on and off him.

Changing our position, Bishop sat up in the bed, and I wrapped my legs around him. His hands came to cup under my buttocks, and he worked me on and off him. In this position, we could kiss, which made it all the more pleasurable to me. Sex seemed more intimate when his lips were on mine. It wasn't long before I was tensing up and crying out his name. He then flipped me onto my back and began pounding in and out of me. He came with a shout.

LAST MILE

Later, as we lay tangled in each other's arms, I knew there was no going back. I had to do whatever was in my power to make sure there were no charges brought against Bishop. Even if I lost my job, I couldn't risk a life without him. Regardless of how quickly it had happened, I had fallen in love for the very first time.

SEVENTEEN

BISHOP

After such a monumental three days together, I hated to see Samantha go back to work on Tuesday. I would have preferred to stay in bed with her for an entire week. But it wasn't just about the sex. No, it was so much more. It was our conversations, the way we could laugh together, the way she put me at ease. I also loved the fact that she got along so well with my family. I'd never thought about how important it would be to have a girlfriend who appreciated both my MC family and my blood family. Hell, I'd never thought about a girlfriend, period. Samantha fit right in with both of them.

Of course, I had to get back to work myself at the garage. I was sure that if I had asked for more time, Rick would have given it to me. But I hated to leave him when he was getting the new mechanic settled in. The new guy actually had twenty years of experience. Unlike Marley, he didn't have too much to say, which made me miss the guy even more.

After thinking about her all morning, I couldn't stop myself from calling Sam on my lunch break. When she answered on the third ring, I smiled into the phone. "Hey you."

"Hey yourself."

"Just wondered how you were doing."

"Good. How about you?"

"Good."

"Do you miss me? Is that why you called?" she questioned teasingly.

"Yeah, as a matter of fact, I do miss you, but I also had another reason to call."

"Mmm, that's so sweet. I miss you, too."

"I'm glad to hear it."

"What's the other reason why you called?"

"I wanted to see if we were still on for dinner."

"Of course. How could I say no to a home-cooked meal?" she replied.

"Ah, I see how it is. You're just using me for my mother's cooking."

"That and for your fabulous dick."

I barked out a laugh. "At least you're honest."

"You know there's more to you than your dick."

"Like my rock-hard body, handsome face, and killer smile?"

Samantha tsked at me. "My, my, aren't we cocky today?"

"Well, you said you liked honesty."

With a giggle, Sam said, "True. Very true." Someone called her name in the background, and her response was muffled as though she had put her hand over the mouthpiece. After a few seconds, she said, "Listen. I gotta go. But I'll see you at six, right?"

"Yeah, about that. I don't know if you've been paying attention to the weather, but we're under a tornado watch. It's supposed to blow in around five o'clock. You should cut out of work early and get here before it gets bad outside."

"Aw, that's really sweet of you to be worried about me."

"That's what boyfriends do, right?" After all, it had only been a couple of days, so it was really new to me how to act. I was completely fucking clueless.

"Yes, it is. And you're doing a really good job at the boyfriend thing."

"Thanks. So you'll head out early?"

"I really need to stay. There's something I need to talk to my boss about, and he's been hard to pin down the last two days."

"Can't it wait?"

The line was silent for a few seconds. "I suppose one more day wouldn't hurt."

"Good. So get your fine ass up here as early as you can."

"I will."

"Good. I'll see you then."

"Bye, Bishop."

"Bye."

I woke the next morning tangled in Samantha's arms. She had arrived just as the sky opened up and rain began to pelt down. As we sat around the table at Mama Beth's at dinner, the wind howled while thunder rattled the windows. Eventually, we all went down into the basement, which was a good thing because the tornado sirens started going off. We'd had to use flashlights to get home, since the power had gone out. Lighting candles made for a romantic rest of the night as the storm continued to rage outside.

Glancing over at Samantha, I couldn't help a huge grin as I watched her sleep. She had reeled me in hook, line, and sinker with her exotic beauty, her humor, and her intelligence. Most of the time I felt she was too good for me. Of course, she'd never made me feel that way. Sam always made me feel like her equal. She'd made sacrifices for me, considering her bad history with bikers. But she had shown strength and courage through it all. Although I didn't understand it, she was always able to see the good in me.

When Samantha stirred, I reached over and kissed a trail across her jawbone to her lips. A little moan escaped her when I covered her mouth with mine. When I pulled away, she smiled up at me. "Good morning," she said.

"Good morning to you."

"What time is it?" she asked as she stretched her arms above her head.

"Not sure. Power must've been out most of the night."

"That sure was some storm."

"Yeah, it was." I cupped her buttocks and squeezed one of the cheeks. "Of course, it was pretty nice riding it out with you riding me."

Sam grinned. "I would have to say it's the best way I've passed the time with the power out."

My phone rang on the nightstand, and I reached over to get it. It was Rev. "Hello?"

"I need you to come up to the clubhouse."

"What's shaking?"

"The storm knocked out the security system last night, and I'm a little worried about a security breach."

"You mean you're a little paranoid."

"Smart-ass. Just get up here."

"Fine. I'll be there in ten."

When I hung up, Samantha peered curiously up at me. "Something wrong?"

"Just Rev being a worrywart. He needs me up at the clubhouse," I replied as I flung off the sheet.

"I should probably get ready for work."

"The bathroom is all yours." I pulled a T-shirt over my head. "Come up and say good-bye."

Samantha smiled. "If I have time, I will."

"Make time," I said.

"Okay, Caveman. I will."

As I hopped into my jeans, I thought about how much I was starting to enjoy her little nickname for me. "See you in a little while."

She gave me a wave as she went into the bathroom. After heading out of the house, I pounded down the porch steps. Gazing left and right, I checked to see if there was any damage to the compound. Everything looked pretty good. There were only a few large tree limbs scattered around.

When I got inside the clubhouse, I found Deacon and Rev sitting at a table with Boone and Mac. "So you got all the officers out this morning, huh?" I asked as I slid into a chair.

"I got the alerts about the system being down last night, but there was nothing I could do about it in the storm," Boone said.

"What are we looking at?" I questioned.

"The wired fence along the perimeter was down for the night. It went out even before the power did. The cameras turned off around the time the storm blew in." Boone sighed. "We were pretty fucking vulnerable for most of the night."

"I think we each need to take a portion of the property and check for any breaches," Rev said.

Deacon nodded. "Sounds like a plan."

Just as we rose out of our chairs, the front door blew open, and agents poured into the room. I didn't have to see the backs of their jackets to know they were ATF. "All right, everyone freeze, and put your hands in the air!"

"What the fuck is this about?" Deacon demanded.

The agent trained his gun on Deacon. "I said put your hands in the air!"

"Okay, okay." He reluctantly threw his arms over his head.

The crowd parted, and an older agent with salt-and-pepper hair stepped forward. He flashed his badge at us. "I'm Agent Peterson with the ATF. We have a warrant to search the premises on suspicion of harboring illegal guns."

Rev shook his head. "I'm sorry to waste your time, but you won't find any guns here," he said politely.

Agent Peterson stepped forward to stand toe-to-toe with Rev. "Really? Then can you explain why we received a tip this morning that the Raiders were in possession of a large stockpile of illegal weapons?"

Deacon and I exchanged a look. Who in the hell would call the ATF with a bogus tip on us? Then it hit me. "Eddy," I grunted at the same time Deacon did.

"I'm sure it's just a mistake. Someone playing a joke on you," Rev argued.

Agent Peterson sneered at Rev. "You boys must think we're a bunch of dumb fuckers. You and I both know you've been running guns out of here for at least thirty years. You've always been one step ahead of us until now. And this time, you're going down."

Two agents ran in from the back. "Sir, we've located the weapons down in the warehouse."

A murmur of disbelief went up among all the Raiders in the room. Rev whirled around and stared at me and Deacon. His face had paled. In a strangled voice, he uttered the words we were all thinking. "Eddy fucking set us up."

Agent Peterson reached out to take Rev by the arm. He brought his hands behind his back and cuffed him. "Nathaniel Malloy, you're under arrest for being in possession of illegal firearms with intent to sell."

Other agents stepped forward to start handcuffing the rest of us. At that moment, the back door flew open again. But this time an agent was ushering in Mama Beth and Samantha. I grimaced at the sight of them, especially Samantha. I never, ever wanted her to see me like this.

"What's going on?" Mama Beth demanded.

Before anyone could answer her, Agent Peterson abandoned Rev and went charging toward them. "Agent Vargas, what the hell are you doing here?"

I glanced from him to Samantha. "*Agent* Vargas? What is he talking about?"

Samantha's eyes pinched shut as if she were in pain.

"Vargas, I asked you a question," Agent Peterson demanded.

"Sam?" I questioned.

When she opened her eyes, she didn't look at him. Instead, she looked at me with an agonized expression. "I'm so sorry, Bishop. I never meant for anything like this to happen."

"All this time you've been a fucking fed?"

"Yes."

"Un-fucking-believable."

"But I swear I've been trying to prove you're not involved in anything illegal—I've been trying to find a way to exonerate you all of any future charges."

My head shook furiously from side to side and I found I couldn't speak. No matter how hard I tried, I couldn't bring myself to believe it. In that moment, my chest constricted so tightly that I had to fight to breathe. I bent over at the waist, sucking in air and wheezing it out. If there truly was a hell on earth, I found myself consumed by the flames.

Samantha was an ATF agent.

The woman I loved was a lie.

The woman I loved had betrayed not only me but my brothers.

Samantha closed the gap between us. "I swear to you that I had nothing to do with what happened today."

"Vargas, you get your ass out of here ASAP and back to the office before you compromise this raid any further!" Peterson bellowed.

With a broken expression, Samantha pleaded, "Bishop, you have to believe me."

I couldn't take it anymore, and I snapped. "You lying bitch! Get the fuck away from me!" I bellowed.

Samantha jumped back as if I had slapped her. Her face crumpled, and tears sparkled in her eyes. Without another word, she whirled around and fled the room.

"Okay, boys, let's go," Peterson barked.

"Call John Morgan," Rev called to Mama Beth. She nodded as she swiped away the tears pouring down her cheeks.

The agent at my side dragged me by the arm out the door. The parking lot that was usually filled with bikes was overrun by the ATF's black SUVs. Each of us was loaded into a separate one. As the door closed, I caught one final glimpse of Samantha as she stood alone by her car. Her body shook from her sobs.

An agent. Fuck. In that moment, I understood what it meant to both love and loathe someone.

EIGHTEEN

SAMANTHA

As I drove down the interstate to the office, I had a hard time seeing the road in front of me for my tears. Although I had initially kept my emotions in check, I finally started crying when I saw Bishop being loaded into one of the SUVs, and half an hour later, I had yet to stop. I had never imagined the course the morning would take. I had been finishing up getting ready when Mama Beth banged on the door. In a panic, she told me the police were all over the compound.

In that moment, I hadn't had the presence of mind to question her on if it was truly the police. We had gone up to the clubhouse immediately. Then my worst nightmare charged at me like a locomotive. My two worlds finally collided, and it was brutal. The look in Bishop's eyes when he found out was heartbreaking. I never imagined someone I cared for would have such hatred and loathing for me. It cut me more deeply emotionally than any physical wound ever could.

I realized how naive I had been to think I could get away with living a lie. How did I think this was going to play out? That I would clear the Raiders and then Bishop would be fine with my being an undercover agent? I was a fool to think that there could be a happily ever after for us. I had gotten so swept up in a sex and love haze that I believed something good could come from a relationship built on lies.

By the time I pulled into the parking lot, my emotions had flip-flopped to anger at the way things had been handled. I wanted answers, and I was going to demand them of Peterson just as soon as he returned from booking Bishop and his brothers.

From my office, I had the perfect view of Peterson's door. I didn't know how long I sat there absentmindedly clicking my pen back and forth. When I saw Peterson entering his office, I leaped out of my chair and charged down the hall. I barged inside without knocking and slammed the door behind me.

"I imagined you would come to me before I came to you," Peterson said as he sat down in his leather chair.

Placing my palms flat on his desk, I demanded, "Why the hell wasn't I notified about a raid?"

Peterson eyed me over his glasses. "I'm sorry, but I was under the assumption that only assigned agents receive sensitive information about a raid."

"Dammit, Peterson, it doesn't matter that I wasn't on the case. You owed it to me for Gavin."

"Right now I think the least of your worries should be about the lack of my communication skills."

With a growl, I pushed off his desk and began pacing around the room. "I know I owe you an explanation."

"You sure as hell do." Rising out of his chair, Peterson walked around his desk. "Can you tell me what the hell you were doing there?"

Pursing my lips, I countered, "You've had surveillance there, so I'm sure you've seen exactly what I've been doing there."

"Up until today, the only involvement we've had has been through phone tapping."

"Then how in the hell did you know about the guns if you didn't have the clubhouse wired up?"

"We received a tip in the middle of the night. Because of the intricate detail of the information given, we deemed it to be reliable. I assembled a small team as quickly as I could. Since it was a weekday morning, I knew we would be dealing with the least number of Raiders on the property. Luckily for us, we got all the officers in one sweep. We're working on the other members as we speak."

My eyebrows rose in surprise. "Just a tip? You didn't have any physical evidence tying the guns to the Raiders besides the tip?"

Peterson crossed his arms over his chest. "Would you like to tell me what you were doing there? Considering the spectacle between you and Bishop Malloy, I'm pretty sure you weren't there in an official capacity."

After jerking a hand through my hair, I sighed. "A week after Gavin's murder I went to see Bishop. We've been talking every day since then."

"Just talking?"

"This past weekend it became more."

"Just exactly how much more?"

I threw up my hands. "I'm in love with him, okay? Somehow along the way as I was getting to know him, I fell in love." Although I hated myself for it, my bottom lip quivered as I added, "And now he despises me."

Peterson exhaled loudly. "How is it possible you fell for a man that you hated so much? Have you forgotten his involvement in Gavin's death?"

I shook my head. "That's just it. He's not who I originally thought he was. None of the Raiders are." At Peterson's skeptical look, I continued. "Yes, at one time they did partake in illegal activity. But then they lost several of their members to violence, and then Deacon became a father and wanted a better, safer life for his daughter. Those factors made them choose to go legitimate. Because I spent so much time with them, I know they're innocent."

"If they are innocent, how do you explain the guns in their warehouse?"

"They were framed."

Peterson scoffed as he leaned back against his desk. "I usually appreciate conspiracy theories, but I'm not in the mood today."

"Bishop told me that there were members of their organization who weren't happy with them going legitimate. He said they were the ones who orchestrated the shooting in Virginia. I think whoever has this bad blood wanted to get back at Bishop and the others, so they planted the guns there and then called the tip in to you guys."

Scratching his chin, Peterson appeared thoughtful. "And where does this animosity for the Raiders come from?"

"I think it somehow all goes back to that deal with the Rodriguez cartel. I think that the Raiders wanted out of the gun business as part of going legitimate, so they gave their gun trade to the cartel. Then someone didn't like getting cut out of the guns."

"That's an interesting theory, but do you think you can prove it?"

My heartbeat thundered loudly in my chest. "If you give me a chance, I can."

"You do realize what a chance you're taking on this case? If it falls apart, your career is over."

While my stomach twisted at the prospect of never rising through the ranks at the ATF, I knew that I had to do everything within my power to see that Bishop and the others weren't falsely imprisoned. "I am aware of what could happen."

Peterson stared me down for a few seconds before he turned and walked back around the side of the desk. As he sat back down in his chair, I couldn't help holding my breath in anticipation. "Look, I know you've had a hell of a time since Gavin's death, but never would I have expected you to go so far as to hook up with Malloy." When I started to defend myself, Peterson raised a hand to keep me quiet. He got up again, then paced around in front of the desk as if he was searching for the right words. "I've always trusted your instinct, Vargas. Always. You've never given me any reason not to. If you're willing to go out on a limb, then you have my support."

I wheezed out the breath I had been holding. "Really?"

Peterson nodded. "I hope you realize how fucking hard it's going to be on me to get you the resources you need."

"I know it's going to be tough."

"It sure as hell is. I'm going to be jumping through hoops like a damn dog."

I smiled at Peterson. "Thank you. I promise I won't let you down."

"You better not, because it'll be both our asses on the line. You've got forty-eight hours to get your shit together before they are arraigned. That's the best chance we have of getting the charges dropped."

Although anxiety threatened to choke me, I bobbed my head at Peterson. "I'll get right on it." I whirled around and headed for the door. "Thanks again, Peterson."

He gave me a small smile. "You're welcome. And good luck."

NINETEEN

SAMANTHA

Although I had been on a lot of dangerous missions in my career, I had never felt the bone-deep level of fear that I did as I pulled into the parking lot of the Raiders compound. With trembling hands, I turned the car off and threw open the door. My shaking knees barely supported me as I made my way to the front door. The immense fear that I felt didn't come from the fact that I was facing down drug lords or gang leaders. No, I was about to piss my pants because I was going to talk to the Raiders women.

For the first time ever, there weren't any guys guarding the door. I had to wonder if they had been brought in as well or if they were lying low because of what had happened. My stomach churned as I jerked open the door and stepped inside.

When the door slammed shut behind me, every pair of eyes in the room was on me. It took about two seconds for Kim to come charging at me, her nostrils flaring like a bull. "You got a lot of fucking nerve coming here!"

I held my hands up in front of me. "I know I do. But I need to talk to you guys."

Mac's old lady, a curvy brunette, snorted contemptuously. "What makes you think we would listen to a damn word you said?" Standing toe-to-toe with me, she then spat in my face. "Fucking traitor!"

Without taking my eyes from hers, I brought my hand up to wipe my face. Part of me wanted to deck her for having the nerve to do something so degrading, but I had to remember where she was coming from. Her husband was behind bars facing gun trafficking charges.

I drew in a deep breath as I surveyed the women I had once considered myself friends with. "Each and every one of you has a right to hate me. At one time, I was a traitor to the club. I admit that I had ulterior motives in getting to know Bishop. But if you would just give me a few minutes to explain—"

"You want to explain how you played Bishop for a fool and then sent our men away?" Kim demanded over the roar of the women spewing hate-filled rants at me again.

"Just give me five minutes. I'm here to help, I swear."

Annabel stepped forward. She held up her hand to silence them. "Let her speak."

At her action, the angry roar became a low grumble. When it became quiet, I started to talk. I told them about my father's murder, about my feelings when I was first assigned the case, how I felt after Gavin's murder, and then finally how I had come to feel about Bishop and the Raiders. Throughout it all, I held their rapt attention.

"What happened today was not because of anything I did or any information I gave my superiors. Yeah, I should have relayed to my superiors what I learned about the club going legitimate. I can't change any of that now, but I have the opportunity to clear their names—to ensure that your men are freed. But to do that, I'm going to need their help."

Alexandra shifted Wyatt on her hip. "Let me guess. To ensure that they cooperate, you need us to talk to them."

I nodded. "You can imagine that whatever I say to them is going to fall on deaf ears. I figured they might actually listen to their wives and girlfriends."

Eyeing me curiously, Alex asked, "Who talks to Bishop?"

"I will."

Kim snorted. "You really think after what happened, you're going to get anywhere with him? The most important thing in the Raiders creed is loyalty. You trampled all over his loyalty."

"I realize that. I hope to be able to apologize to him—to get him to see why I did what I did."

Alex sighed. "Don't be naive, Sam. We're a lot more forgiving than he'll ever be because we're women and we understand what it's like to be desperately in love."

"Who the hell says we're forgiving?" Kim growled.

Alexandra gazed around the group. "I think it's safe to say every one of us here has done something desperate and crazy when it comes to our men. I know I certainly did. What Sam did was completely wrong, but she's trying to make it right—"

"And just why are you doing that? Did you suddenly grow a conscience?" Boone's wife, Annie, demanded.

"Because it's the right thing to do. Your husbands were framed. I would never uphold having innocent men pay for crimes they didn't commit. There's also the fact that the club has turned themselves around. The whole point of our undercover case was to bust them for guns. That's not an issue anymore."

"There's another reason that motivates you even more than setting our men free," Annabel said with a smile. "You love Bishop."

I blinked back the tears that stung my eyes. "Yes. I do. I love him very much."

My declaration sent a hush over the group. Kim made a tsking noise. "I gotta tell you, honey, that you sure have a way of fucking things up."

With a pained bark of a laugh, I replied, "Trust me. I'm aware of it." I swiped away the tears that had fallen down my cheeks. "Everything just happened so fast. I never intended to fall for Bishop, and when I did, I didn't want to be an agent investigating him. I just wanted to be a woman in love with him."

Annabel swept her hand to her chest. "Oh, you poor thing."

Kim gave an exasperated sigh. "Well, the only way you have a chance with Bishop is to see to freeing him and the others. Once he's out, then we can all work on getting him to give you another chance."

My eyebrows shot up in surprise. "You want to give me another chance?"

Kim smiled. "Yeah, I guess I do. At the end of the day, we all fuck up from time to time. Now that you've explained yourself, I can see things differently."

I couldn't help exhaling a huge, relieved breath. "So you all will help me?" A resounding chorus of yeses came back at me. "Great. I can't thank you enough."

"No. Thank you for doing so much to see that our men are freed," Alexandra said.

"Damn straight," Kim said. She then smacked me on the back. "How about a drink before you go?"

I grinned. "I sure as hell could use one."

Shaking her head, Kim said, "Honey, you're going to need more than one if you plan on talking to Bishop."

TWENTY

BISHOP

As I lay back on my jailhouse bunk, I stared up at the ceiling. Counting the many cracks within the plaster was one way I tried to pass the time. It had been thirty-six hours since the ATF busted into the clubhouse and sent my world careening out of control. While I'd had a few misdemeanors in my day, I'd never spent a night in jail. I'd always been bailed out the day I had come in. But now I was facing gun and drug charges, and if the ATF got their way, I wouldn't be getting out for a long time.

Of course the ATF made me think of Samantha, which caused my traitorous heart to ache. I never imagined a woman could wound me so deep, but she did. All the time we had spent together had been a lie. She was a fucking fed working me for a case. I had heard of women playing men before, but I never thought I would be one of the sad saps it happened to. Samantha deserved a fucking Oscar for her acting skills. I had thought she truly cared for me—that we had something special going on. Something like what Rev and Deacon had.

But I was wrong. So fucking wrong. Not only had she screwed me over, but she had screwed over my brothers. Seething anger coiled within me at the reminder of how she acted as though she had cared for them just as she had for me. But she hadn't. All she had wanted was to keep rising in the ranks in the bureau. I was sure our case would win her a fat promotion. While we rotted away in jail, she would enjoy more money and a higher rank. Just the thought caused my fists to clench at my sides and I longed for a way to lash out.

More than anything, I wished I had my brothers to confide in. From the time of our arrest, Rev, Deacon, and I had been separated. The thought being that we couldn't easily come up with stories or plea deals if we weren't a solid unit with our president, vice president, and sergeant at arms. Deacon and Boone had been sent to a jail in another county, while Mac and I remained at the jail where we had originally been brought. As president, Rev was seen as the greatest threat, and he had been put in solitary, away from us.

At the sound of jangling keys, I lowered my gaze from the ceiling to see a guard strolling up to the cell. "Up and at 'em, Malloy."

"What's going on?"

"You got a visitor," the guard replied.

Mac and I exchanged a look. "Mike must have some new information on the case," I said as I hopped down off the bunk.

"As much as the club is paying him, he better come up with a hell of a lot for us," Mac grumbled.

Once the guard swung open the door, I stepped outside and followed him out of the cellblock. After we went down a long hallway, he stopped at a room on the right. When I stepped inside, I found it empty except for a table and two chairs. One of the walls had a two-way mirror, and I couldn't help wondering who was on the other side. After sitting down, I raised my handcuffed fists at the officer. With a shake, I asked, "Aren't you going to take these off me?"

He shook his head. "Powers that be said they stay on."

I narrowed my eyes. "What the hell for?"

"You might pose a danger."

"To my lawyer? That's fucking unlikely, since I need his happy ass alive to get me out of here."

After glancing left and right, the guard said in a low voice, "It ain't your lawyer."

I leaned back in my chair. "If it isn't my lawyer, then who the hell is it? This room ain't for visitors."

Before the guard could answer, the door blew open. Never in a million years did I expect to see the person who walked into the room.

It was Samantha.

Or at least it was a version of her. It sure as hell wasn't the woman I had known before. Gone was the Samantha who wore heavy eyeliner, skintight jeans, and cleavage-baring tops. In her place was a steely professional in a black pantsuit. Her long dark hair was swept back in a bun.

When our eyes met, I shot out of my chair. "Get her the fuck out of here!" I spat.

"Bishop, I need to speak to you," Samantha said in an even tone.

"I ain't got one thing to say to you but maybe *Fuck you*. That's it."

The guard glanced from me to Samantha. She shook her head. "Leave us."

"Miss, I don't—"

Samantha's dark eyes burned with fury. "And I said leave us!"

He held up his hands. "Fine, then."

After he had shut the door, Samantha crossed the room to the table. Her heels clicked along the linoleum floor. Without a word, she pulled out the chair across from me. She tossed a giant folder on the table and then sat down.

We stared each other down for a few seconds before Samantha drew in a ragged breath. "Bishop, I—"

"Look at you. The secret agent woman."

"I'm not a secret agent," she argued.

"Considering what you were doing to me and my club, you might as well have been a spy. Right?"

"I was there to compile what information I could about the Raiders' suspected gunrunning with the Rodriguez cartel."

"You were spying."

"I was doing my job. The one Gavin and I were sent in there to do."

"Gavin? I suppose you mean Marley. Yeah, that was a tough pill to swallow, too. Not only was the girl I was falling for playing me, but it turns out my friend was in on it as well."

A pained look came over Samantha's face. "He was my best friend, Bishop. He was the one who wanted me to give you a chance. He really did enjoy being around you."

Her words caused a deeper ache in my chest. "Whatever. It still doesn't make it right what you did."

Samantha's eyes filled with regret. "For what it's worth, I'm truly sorry."

Man, this girl could act. Bitch. I cocked my eyebrows at her. "You're sorry? You fucked up my life and the lives of my club brothers and all you can say is you're sorry."

"I am very sorry. But the fact is, I didn't fuck up your life. You and I both know your enemies did that."

"Is that so?"

"Yes, it is."

"So what's your point in being here?"

"I came to make things right by seeing you freed from jail."

"Just how do you plan on doing that?"

"By testifying for the Raiders at trial."

What the fuck? She was actually going to help us? She had to have some other angle for wanting to get us off. Narrowing my eyes suspiciously at her, I demanded, "Why would you want to do that? After all, you were working against us."

"That was before I knew the truth about your club—the fact that you were legitimizing the businesses and that you no longer took part in gun trafficking."

I stared at her in disbelief. I couldn't believe she was actually sitting before me and proposing that she help the club. "Tell me something."

"What?"

"Was it all a lie? I mean, was there a single time when we were together that you weren't playing me?"

"Yes, I—"

"Wait, I know. It had to be during the fucking, right?"

Samantha's eyes widened in horror, and she shifted in her chair. "Bishop, please."

"Ah, two words that I'm used to hearing from you. Of course, I was usually inside you when you said them . . . sometimes I was on top, sometimes you were. You begged me to make you come. Which makes me think that was when you weren't lying. I mean, women fake orgasms every day, but I felt you come on my fingers and my tongue."

When Samantha's face flushed with embarrassment, I glanced over at the mirror with a smirk. "Agent Vargas is one hell of a piece of ass in the bedroom. Pretty fucking insatiable, too. No matter how many times she came, she wanted more."

The next thing I knew Samantha's hand came smacking across my cheek. "Fuck you, Bishop!"

I laughed. "Damn, girl, you should get in the ring. If you worked on it, that slap could make a great right cross."

"You cocky bastard. I'm putting my ass on the line for you, and this is how you treat me?"

"I'm sorry for being a little suspicious of you, considering that everything you said to me over the last six weeks was a lie."

"It wasn't all a lie! Everything I told you about my life was the truth. The only fucking thing I withheld from you was the fact that I was an agent."

"That's a pretty huge thing to leave out, especially when it was the only reason you were spending any time with me."

"Only at first. But then I began to care more about spending time with you for myself, rather than the case."

I opened my mouth and then closed it without saying a word. I didn't know how to take what she had just said. I wanted to think everything out of her mouth was a lie, but what if she was telling the truth? What if she truly had started out working me for the case until she began to feel something more for me?

Wanting to change the subject, I asked, "What makes you think I would take you up on your offer?"

"Isn't your freedom enough?"

"I still have to live with myself, and how can I do that if I'm a rat who got into bed with the ATF?"

"Would your brothers honestly think you were a rat for testifying against the man who framed you?"

I didn't know the answer. I hoped they would understand, especially considering that it was Eddy who had framed us. In the end, I didn't have a real argument for not taking Samantha up on her offer. "Fine. I'll say or do whatever I have to so I can get out of here."

Samantha's expression lightened. "I'm glad to hear you say that."

"But let's make one thing clear. It doesn't change a damn thing between you and me. Got that?"

Without answering me, she reached out to pick up the manila folder she had carried in with her. Sam had never been one to avoid eye contact, but right now her eyes were completely focused on the folder in front of her. "I need you to tell me everything you can about who could have framed you."

"There's only one person it could be." At the thought of Eddy, a low growl took me by surprise and seconds later I realized it had come from me. Samantha's gaze snapped up from her paperwork at the sound. "You're in luck, because if you nail this guy, you can have access to the Diablos."

Samantha's eyes widened as she stared from me to the mirror. "The bureau has been trying to get them for a long time."

"Well, you track down Eddy, and you've got the Diablos by the balls, because if I know anything about Eddy, it's that he has no loyalty. He'll sing like a canary if you make it worth his while."

"I see."

Samantha scribbled furiously as I related what had happened with Eddy at the meeting in Virginia. Her pen stilled when I told her that he was one the behind the shooting. She glanced up to look at me. "This fucker has Gavin's blood on his hands?"

"Damn straight."

"I'm going to enjoy nailing him to the wall."

By then I had finished relating everything I knew, including my theory about how the storm and the power being out enabled Eddy to plant the guns. "I'm sure if you had some agents go over the property, you would find evidence of shoe prints or tire treads."

Samantha nodded. "I'll put someone on it." She shuffled her paperwork and then put it back in the folder. "I guess we're finished here."

"I guess so."

"Once we produce the new evidence at the arraignment, it should be less than twenty-four hours before you guys are let out."

"Good."

She rose out of her chair. "I'll let you know if we need anything else from you."

When I nodded, she started for the door. As I watched her leave, I once again felt as if my chest were caving in. There was so much I wanted to say to her, but I was too stubborn. Finally I blurted, "Thank you."

Samantha froze. Slowly she turned around to face me.

"You know, for sticking your neck out for me and my brothers."

"You're welcome," she murmured.

We stared at each other for a few seconds before she hurried out the door. When it closed behind her, I brought my cuffed hands up to rub my shirt above my heart. No matter how I hard I tried, it still hurt like a motherfucker.

TWENTY-ONE

BISHOP

When the van carrying us home from jail pulled into the clubhouse parking lot, I couldn't hold back my emotions, and I let out a giant whoop of joy. Archer had barely put it in park when I flung open the door and hopped out. Raiders came streaming out of the clubhouse. I don't think I'd ever been hugged and kissed and thumped on the back so much in my life.

While the welcome was nice, it still felt hollow to me. Especially as I watched Alex and Annabel run into Deacon's and Rev's waiting arms. Even Boone, who had been married forever, had a happy moment with his wife. It made me miss Samantha, even though I shouldn't, and I fucking hated myself for it. Yet in that moment, I didn't care about all the bad shit that had gone down between us. I just wanted to feel her soft curves against my body, inhale the sweet smell of her peach shampoo, and feel the comfort of her arms around me.

With a grimace, I pushed those thoughts from my head and tried to focus on the party. I wanted a beer the size of my head.

Before we could appreciate the welcome-home party, there were some things we needed to take care of in church. So we headed into our meeting room and closed and locked the door behind us.

Rev took his usual seat at the head of the table. He looked at Archer and Crazy Ace. "Were all precautions taken to ensure that the feds didn't leave any bugs after the raid?"

Archer nodded. "We've each swept the room five times to make sure we didn't miss anything."

"Good." He glanced around the table. "Now, gentlemen. We can begin."

"Feels good to be back in here, eh, boys?" Deacon asked with a grin.

"Sure as hell does," Mac agreed.

"Didn't know when my ass would slide across this leather again," Boone joked.

Deacon turned to Rev. "What's on the agenda?"

"First of all, we need to sign these depositions." Rev waved the manila folder at Crazy Ace. After Crazy Ace took the folder, he passed them out. "Read them and make sure they're accurate before you sign them."

The room fell silent as we read the typed versions of what we had told the ATF about Eddy and the Virginia shooting. Thankfully, we weren't asked to give any information on the Rodriguez cartel. They were one group I wanted in our corner.

One by one we signed. Then we handed the papers back to Rev.

"Okay. Good. Right now that's the only order of business that I have." He shuffled the papers together and put them in the folder. "Who can run these over to Samantha, uh, Agent Vargas?"

At his question, I stared down at my hands. When no one responded, Rev cleared his throat. "Bishop, why don't you take them?"

"No fucking way," I replied.

"It might do you some good to see her. Maybe you guys could talk," Rev suggested.

I jerked my gaze up to stare at him. "Are you fucking serious?"

"Yeah. I am."

"You're actually sitting there advocating for me to talk to the woman who betrayed me?"

"Look, I'm not saying it doesn't make me fucking furious that at one time she was sniffing around here for dirt on us—"

"Exactly," I said.

"But there's also the fact that she was spending most of the time here trying to clear us," Rev argued.

"Un-fucking-believable."

Deacon sighed. "Look, B, she's really putting her ass out on the line for you and for us. You can argue that she's doing it because we're innocent, but there's also the fact that she cares about you."

Crossing my arms over my chest, I demanded, "Could you forgive a woman for doing something like that?"

He snorted. "How quickly you forget that Alexandra hand-cuffed me to a bed in her efforts to take Sigel down. While it pissed the ever-loving shit out of me, she did it because she loved me, and she wanted to protect me."

"It's different with Samantha and me."

Deacon cocked his eyebrows at me. "Are you so sure?"

I gazed around the table at the guys. They each gave me a look that told me I needed to take the depositions. "Fine." I shoved out of my chair and snatched the envelope from Rev. Without another word to the guys, I headed out of the room and to my bike.

It took a good half hour to get to Samantha's office building. Once I got to her floor, I had to look for help in order to find her office. It wasn't an easy thing, since a lot of the agents and staff had gone home. A guy who looked like a wrestler in the WWE stood outside Samantha's door. "I need to give these to Agent Vargas."

"I need your ID first."

"Damn. Do agents always have bodyguards on hand?"

"Whenever there's a threat, we do."

I cocked my head at him. "Vargas has been threatened?"

He eyed my driver's license. As he handed it back, he replied, "I'm not at liberty to say."

"That answers my question." I then knocked on the door.

"Come in," Samantha called.

My stomach clenched nervously, which made me feel like a pussy. I pushed through the door. Sitting at her desk, Samantha once again looked polished and pressed like ATF Agent Barbie. Our eyes met, and we stared at each other. She broke the stare by rising out of her chair. "Can I help you, Bishop?"

"Yeah. You can tell me what Hulk Hogan is doing outside your door."

"It's nothing you need to be concerned with."

I narrowed my eyes at her. "Let me guess. It's confidential or whatever bullshit it is you don't tell civilians like me."

"It's something like that." While she appeared cool, calm, and collected, I could tell that deep down she was on edge.

"Whatever." I tossed the folder with the depositions onto her desk. "Rev asked me to bring those over. It's all the officers."

"Good. Thank you."

"Yeah, whatever. You're welcome."

"So you got home today?"

"A little while ago."

"I'm glad to hear they didn't drag their feet on letting you guys out."

"No. It was pretty quick."

As we stood there talking like strangers, I couldn't help shaking my head.

"What is it?" Sam asked.

"I was just wondering how the fuck we got to this point of being like strangers."

She looked down at the floor. "Oh."

"I guess if we're acting like this, there wasn't much there to begin with, huh?"

"I disagree," Sam said.

"Do you?"

"I think there's always been something strong between us. Even from the first time we met."

"Maybe. But for the most part it was all about the physical."

"There was always a strong physical attraction between us, but that wasn't it."

"The physical's the one thing that never changed."

"What do you mean?"

"You know, the fact that you changed when you lied to me."

Samantha rolled her eyes. "I lied to you about one thing—one fucking thing."

"It was a pretty big thing."

"Everything else was me, Bishop. Through all the long conversations on the phone and at dinner, that was me. Whenever I was with you at the clubhouse, that was me."

"The most important thing in my world is loyalty, and you trampled all over that."

Her dark eyes flashed. "Fuck you, Bishop!"

With a smirk, I said, "Wouldn't you love to one last time? To have me make you come like I always did."

"You should leave. Now."

"And not be a good boy and satisfy you?"

Samantha's expression was one of disgust. "I hate you. I seriously despise everything you are."

"But you still want me."

She cocked her eyebrows. "Considering the bulge in your jeans, I'd say you want me pretty bad, too, although I'm sure you hate yourself for it. Just like I do."

Yeah, I do. "I want the old Samantha—the woman who made me fall for her."

"We're the same person, you arrogant, stubborn prick!"

That was my undoing. As I crossed the room in two long strides, Samantha started around the side of her desk. We crashed together and the next few minutes were a complete blur, a tangle of lips, arms, and legs. She brought her hand between us to cup my throbbing dick. It had been rock hard before she even touched me. "Please," she murmured against my lips.

Taking her by the shoulders, I turned her around and bent her over her desk. I pushed the hem of her skirt up and almost came in my pants at the sight of her sexy garters. I tore her flimsy panties down her thighs. My hands quickly unbuttoned my jeans and shoved them down.

When Samantha tried to turn to face me, I shook my head. "No. We do it this way. It's only fucking." Placing my hand on her shoulder, I pushed her down. I used my free hand to guide my dick to her pussy. Finding her wet and ready for me, I plunged into her, causing both of us to shout. Oh fuck, I was going to miss her pussy. So warm. So tight.

When I began pounding relentlessly in and out of her, Samantha gripped the front of the desk.

"Agent Vargas? Are you all right?"

"I'm fine," Samantha panted.

"Do you need me to—"

"Just stay outside, Tomkins."

"I have my orders, Agent."

"She's more than fine, because I'm fucking her brains out. Okay?" I shouted.

When Sam moaned in pleasure, Tomkins finally got the message and left us alone. The only sound from then on was our sweat-slickened skin slapping together. As I got close to coming, I realized Samantha hadn't come yet. Part of me didn't give a fuck if she got off, but the other part of me didn't want her to remember our last time as me not getting her off. So I reached around to stroke her clit. Over and over, I massaged it until I felt her walls tensing around me. "Oh, Bishop!" she cried as she went over. Then I brought both of my hands to grip her hips. I pulled her back against my thrusts. It wasn't long before I came, cursing and then shouting her name.

Panting, I collapsed over Sam's back. I stayed that way for a few seconds while I caught my breath. When I realized what we had just done, I winced. "Fucking hell," I muttered. I quickly pulled out of Sam, and once again winced at the fact that I hadn't put on a condom in the moment.

My emotions were skidding out of control. When I started to help Samantha up, she drew herself away from me. "Sam, I'm—"

"Just leave."

"But—"

She shoved herself off the desk and pinned me with a death glare. "You got what you wanted—to fuck me again—so leave."

I wanted more than anything to pull her into my arms. I wanted to sit her down and tell her that somehow we would work things out. I wanted to tell her I was sorry for being the stubborn prick she had called me.

But I turned and walked out the door. That was it. The last time I would see her, touch her. It was the way it had to be.

TWENTY-TWO

SAMANTHA

After the door slammed shut behind Bishop, I calmly went about putting my clothes back together. Once I finished, I collapsed into my chair. Placing my head in my hands, I began to cry with abandon. Harsh sobs tore through my body with such intensity I didn't know if I would ever recover.

I didn't know how much time had passed, perhaps five minutes or maybe ten. I was too lost in my grief to notice. In some ways, it felt like losing Gavin all over again. As if I was somehow destined to always lose the ones who I loved to the MC world.

At the creak of the door, I kept my head buried. "Give me five minutes, Tompkins. Then you can walk me out."

"You'll make time for me now," a raspy voice said from the doorway.

I snapped my head up. Although I'd only seen pictures of him from his file, I knew without a doubt that it was Eddy Catcherside. "Where's Tompkins?"

With a vicious sneer, Eddy said, "I'm afraid that Tompkins is indisposed. Indefinitely."

While my mind wanted to spin in a hundred different directions, I worked to keep my focus. My life depended on it. There was nothing else I could do for Tompkins, but I could save myself. In the top right drawer of the desk was a gun, and I needed some way to get to it.

"Agent Vargas, I can't allow you to testify for the Raiders. They have to go away, and I have to get access to their gun trade. But first, you have to go away."

He raised his hand to reveal a knife with a long blade that caught the light. When I started to reach for the desk drawer, he dove at me. Frantically, I struggled to open the drawer and get the gun. Before I could, the knife pierced me in the arm. A scream tore from my lips with the onslaught of pain. I didn't have time to recover before he stabbed me again in the chest and then in the stomach.

In agony, I collapsed onto the floor and tried to block some of Eddy's hits. But I began to grow weak and soon couldn't lift my arms. It was then I heard a shout from the doorway. As hard as I struggled to keep my eyes open, it was futile, and I felt myself slipping away.

TWENTY-THREE

BISHOP

I felt like the biggest bastard imaginable as I made my way out of Samantha's office building. What the hell had I been thinking? Well, I guessed I knew what I had been thinking—I had once again let my dick control my decision-making. Just the thought of the angry sex we'd had caused my cock to throb for a second round.

When my phone rang, I dug it out of my pocket. It was Rev. "Yes. I got the depositions delivered. I'm not a total idiot."

"That's not why I'm calling."

"What is it?"

A pause came on the other end. "Was Samantha okay when you saw her?"

I didn't think Rev would want me to answer that question honestly, so I replied, "Yeah. Why?"

"She wasn't alone?"

"No. She had a bodyguard outside her door."

"Oh. Good."

"Rev, what the fuck is going on?"

He sighed. "Eddy's gone off the grid again, even from the Diablos. And I'm worried about what he said before he disappeared, B."

Anxiety spiked in my bloodstream as I gripped the phone. "What?"

"He said that without Samantha's testimony, there wouldn't be a case against us Raiders, so she needed to disappear. Then we would be behind bars, and he and the Diablos could take on the Rodriguez cartel for the guns."

"Fucking hell."

I didn't hear anything Rev said next. Instead, that eerie sixth sense feeling of dread pricked up my spine. "I have to go," I spat. After I hung up, I sprinted back into the building. When the elevator didn't budge, I hit the stairs to Samantha's fifth-floor office.

When I burst out of the stairwell, I froze at the sound of Sam's screams. Then I raced forward on a burst of speed, zigzagging my way through the maze of desks. I barreled into Sam's office, only to find her crumpled on the floor and Eddy stabbing her.

"Over here, motherfucker!"

My outburst momentarily stunned Eddy, and it gave me the leverage I needed to tackle him. After we tumbled to the floor, I drove my fist into his jaw and then his cheek. He was the extreme opponent I needed to take down in the ring, except the stakes were so much higher here.

Eddy launched three punches back at me before I began pummeling his face with both my fists. Over and over, I beat him as I screamed in agony.

The next thing I knew I was being lifted up and dragged away. When I came to myself enough to realize what was going on, paramedics were dragging a gurney into the room. "Samantha?" I pushed away from the two men holding me and stumbled over to the desk. "Oh Jesus, Sam," I moaned.

She lay in a pool of blood with jagged cuts along her arms and legs. The worst were the wounds in her chest and abdomen. Tears seared and burned my eyes like acid as I dropped to the floor beside her. I took her limp hand in mine and brought it to my lips. The metallic taste of blood entered my mouth, and I didn't know if it was Sam's or Eddy's or mine. "Oh, Sam, I'm sorry. I'm so, so sorry."

"Sir, you have to move so we can work on her."

No, I can't leave her. I did this to her. It's all my fucking fault. But she needed the paramedics. She needed for them to be able to save her life. Once again, they asked me to step aside. I wasn't sure my legs would hold me, but somehow I scrambled to my feet. *Jesus, I'm so sorry, Sam. I'm so fucking sorry.*

After one of the paramedics checked her, he said, "She's holding on, but we have to get her the hell out of here. She's losing too much blood."

I watched helplessly as they put Sam's body on the gurney. "Sir, do you want to ride along with us?" one of the paramedics asked.

"Y-yeah. Yeah, I do," I croaked.

"Then let's go."

As the wheels of the gurney rattled along the floor, I fell in step with the paramedics. All I could do on the elevator ride down was pray. I needed her to live more than I'd ever longed for anything in the world. I needed to be able to make things right between us.

Most of all, I needed to tell Sam I loved her.

TWENTY-FOUR

SAMANTHA

My eyelids fluttered as I regained consciousness. When I finally opened my eyes, I realized I wasn't on the floor of my office. Instead, I was laid out on a hospital gurney in the ER.

The curtain opened, and a doctor stepped inside. "Miss Vargas, I'm glad to see you've come around. We're just about to move you to a room." He extended his hand, to which I brought my IV-shackled hand up to shake. "I'm Dr. Harrelson. I'm the doctor who took care of your injuries."

"My injuries?" I rasped.

"Yes. You were admitted with multiple stab wounds."

Everything that had happened came back at me in a rush that caused a wave of dizziness. Bishop had come and brought the depositions . . . we'd had sex . . . then Eddy had shown up in a rage and attacked me. The last thing I remembered besides the pain was Bishop and Eddy fighting. I gasped. "The man who saved me—is he okay?"

Dr. Harrelson nodded. "Yes. He's right outside the curtain if you'd like to see him. We've barely been able to get him to leave your side."

Overwhelmed with emotion, I could only nod. Dr. Harrelson dipped behind the curtain. When he reappeared, Bishop was with him. He had some cuts and bruises along his face. At what must've been the fear in my eyes, he held up his hands. "Don't worry. I'm fine."

"Are you sure?"

"You forget that I'm used to getting hit in the face when I'm boxing."

"I'll leave you two," Dr. Harrelson said. When we were alone, I motioned to the chair next to the gurney.

Bishop sat down on the edge of the chair. "Doc says you have to stay in the hospital for a few days, but you're gonna be fine."

"I'm glad to hear it."

"Are you hurting? Do you need some pain medicine or something?"

I shook my head. As he fidgeted in the chair, I realized how nervous he was. "Do you want to talk about the elephant in the room? And I don't mean me being stabbed."

"Eddy's dead."

After sucking in a harsh breath, I said, "That wasn't what I meant, but it's good to know."

"It was a long time coming for that fucker."

"Did you kill him?" I questioned in a low voice. I hated to ask it, but I had to know.

"Yeah. I did." A look of dark pride gleamed in his eyes. "With my bare fucking hands."

"Oh no, Bishop."

He shook his head. "Cops talked to me a few minutes for my story and then let me go. There won't be any charges."

It took a moment for me to process it all. Bishop had killed a man to defend not only himself, but me as well. Just as he had taken a personal risk to his own safety to protect me in Virginia when the Diablos attacked. Given that I had sought justice in the courts my whole career, it was still a little hard to swallow the fact that Eddy had died at Bishop's hands. On the other hand, Eddy had been responsible for Gavin's death. In a sense, I took some comfort in the old adage of an eye for an eye.

I sighed with relief. "Thank God."

Bishop rubbed his palms together. "You scared the hell out of me tonight."

"I did?"

He nodded. "When I busted in your office and saw what Eddy was doing . . ." He closed his eyes with a pained expression. "I thought you were going to die. I didn't want to lose you, and I especially didn't want you to die with things still strained between us."

"You didn't want to lose me to death . . . or in your life?" My heartbeat accelerated so fast I was sure the heart monitor I was attached to was going to go off.

"Both," Bishop said, and his voice cracked.

"I'd give anything if you meant that—if you wanted to give us another try."

"I do, Sam. After what happened tonight, I realized that I don't want to live a life without you in it."

Tears stung my eyes at his words. "Oh, Bishop. I love you."

He smiled. "Even after the way I've treated you?"

Regardless of what had gone down between us, I did love him, and I had for some time. But he did ask a valid question. One he probably needed assurance from more than I did. I had already made the sacrifices necessary to prove to myself I loved him. It had been a tough road, considering that through association with him, I'd lost my very best friend. I missed Gavin so much, and some days it was hard to get out of bed. But in his gentle yet strong way, Bishop had been such a comfort to me. He had given my life purpose . . . and it was a life I wanted him to be a part of.

"Yes, yes, I love you."

Bishop took my hand in his. "I promise I'll make it up to you all the times I was such an asshole."

I laughed. "Okay. I'll let you."

He rose out of his chair to lean over and kiss me. "I love you, too," he murmured against my lips.

Once again, I fought the tears as I felt as if my heart would explode from happiness. Surprisingly, it didn't set off any alarms. As Bishop sat back down, he frowned slightly.

"What's wrong?"

"I was just thinking that I love you so much that I wish we could start over. Like we could forget the past of you being an agent and all that bullshit."

"All we can do is try." When I pulled my hand from his, he stared at me in surprise. I then held it out for him to shake. "I'm Samantha Vargas. I'm an agent with the ATF."

"Bishop Malloy—sergeant at arms of the Hells Raiders."

As we shook, I smiled. "That's a start."

EPILOGUE

SAMANTHA

My fingers flew furiously over the keys as I typed up my latest debriefing. As I relived the takedown, I couldn't help smiling. After all, it wasn't every day that you apprehended a gun trafficker who carried his shipment in a clown-decorated ice cream truck.

It also made me think of Gavin and how he would have hated the case. The one thing he was afraid of was clowns. A year might've passed since his murder, but I still thought of him and missed him every day.

A knock came at my door, but I didn't look up. "Yeah?"

"Are you still here?" Peterson asked.

"Just finishing up."

"You should have left an hour ago."

I glanced up at him. "Since when do bosses encourage their employees to be slackers?"

Crossing his arms over his chest, he countered, "When that employee has a wedding rehearsal in less than two hours."

After hitting SAVE on the file, I held my hands up in defeat. "Fine, fine. I'm leaving now."

"Good. If I had to see one more text from your future sister-in-law about where you were, I was going to scream." At my laugh, he narrowed his eyes. "Just exactly how did she get my number?"

"You're in the wedding party, and as the wedding planner, Alexandra needed your contact number."

"I see." He motioned me with his hand. "Come on. I'll walk you out."

I had to smile at his overprotectiveness. Even though it had been close to a year since Eddy attacked me, Peterson still insisted on walking me out if he was in the building when I left at night. He would also be walking me down the aisle tomorrow at Bishop's and my wedding. Although I could have asked my older brother, Steven, or my stepfather, Peterson had really been a father figure to me over the years.

We took the elevator down to the parking garage, and then Peterson walked me over to my car. "See you in two hours."

"Drive safe."

"Yes, Daddy."

Peterson gave me a wry grin. "You better watch that. I might just get a kick out of it in a dirty-old-man way."

I laughed. "Get out of here."

He waved and then headed down the row to his car. Just as I started the car, my phone rang. I smiled at the ID. "Hello, Future Husband."

A chuckle came from the other end. "Hello, Future Wife. You leaving work?"

"Yep. On my way to the clubhouse now."

"Good. I've had Alexandra and Annabel on my ass most of the afternoon."

"Oh man, double trouble there."

"Damn straight."

Since I lacked the girly girl gene for interest in wedding planning, Alexandra and Annabel had taken over the details. Whenever they tried to make it too much, Bishop and I would veto them. In the end, we decided to get married in the same place that Annabel and Rev had. It made sense to do it at Tohi Ama. It was where we had spent our first night together. The place where we started our relationship. It made sense that we would become man and wife there as well.

"So I picked up your mom and stepdad at the airport. Your brother and sister and their families won't get in until later tonight, which will be better for you to make the introductions."

"Thanks for doing that. How are they?" What I meant to ask was how they were adjusting to being at an MC clubhouse surrounded by bikers. My mom, who still harbored a lot of prejudice against bikers, had had a hard time when I told her about Bishop. She hadn't wanted to accept our relationship for a long time, and I think she hoped I was just sowing some wild oats or something rebellious like that. She couldn't understand how someone with my history could ever trust, least of all love, a biker.

But as the months went on, Bishop and I remained serious. When we got engaged, she tried through numerous phone calls to talk me out of it. Over and over again, I tried explaining to her that the Raiders had gone legitimate, and while Bishop and his brothers had killed in the past, they were nothing like that anymore, least of all like the man who had killed my father.

It had taken a face-to-face meeting for her to actually start to warm to Bishop. We had gone down after Christmas and spent New Year's with my mom and stepdad. Bishop was extremely patient with her and kept his temper when she was openly hostile. Finally, it all came to a head over dinner one night at my mother's favorite restaurant.

After Bishop picked up the check, he turned to my mother. "Mrs. Bennett, there's something I need to say to you."

My mother pursed her lips at him as she reached for the last of her wine. "What is it?"

Bishop drew in a deep breath as my stepfather and I leaned forward anxiously in our chairs. "I've spent most of my life dealing with people thinking I'm the scum of the earth because I wear a cut and ride a Harley. I've learned to accept that. And while my brothers and I weren't always model citizens, I can swear to you on my life that we are decent, law-abiding men now."

My mother waved her hand dismissively. "Yes, yes, Samantha has told me that a hundred times. But it still doesn't change anything for me."

"I hate to hear you say that. I want you to be able to be happy that your daughter is in love and that she is loved in return. I will work until my fingers bleed to provide for her a safe and stable life. I will always put her life before mine."

I reached over and squeezed Bishop's hand. "Just like he has done not once, but twice."

"Twice?" my mother questioned in surprise.

While she knew what had happened with Eddy, she had no idea what Bishop had done during the Diablos' attack. Her hardened expression relaxed when I told her about Bishop throwing himself on top of me. "I see," she murmured.

"More than anything in the world, we would like your blessing," Bishop said.

My mother played with a piece of lint on the tablecloth. "I can't say that I'm ever going to feel completely comfortable with Samantha being a biker's wife and being involved with outlaws—"

"Former outlaws, ma'am," Bishop argued with a grin.

She nodded. "But at the same time, I don't think she could find a man who would love her more than you do."

Although I was never one to cry, tears pooled in my eyes. "No. I couldn't."

"So all I can say is I'll try."

"Thank you, Mrs. Bennett." With a wink, he added, "Just you wait. I'll win you over before you know it!"

And he did. By the time we left to go home, my mother had made huge strides in coming to accept Bishop. Of course, he was only one biker. Now she was about to face a roomful of men in cuts.

"I'd say it's going okay. I steered them down to Mama Beth's, since I thought it was a safer bet than keeping them out of the road-house."

"Good thinking. I'll go straight there when I leave. I'll have Peterson with me. He's still a little skeptical about this whole marrying-in-the-woods thing."

Bishop laughed. "That doesn't surprise me." At the sound of voices in the background, Bishop sighed. "Look, I gotta go. I'll see you in a little while."

"Okay. Bye. I love you."

"I love you, too."

No matter how many times he said it, I never got tired of hearing Bishop say he loved me. There was a time I thought I'd never get to hear the words, so that made them even sweeter. I was thankful he wasn't the type of man to shy away from saying how he felt.

As we started into the clearing at Tohi Ama, the sun sat low on the horizon, sending streaks of pink, orange, and purple across the sky. I couldn't imagine a more beautiful evening, and furthermore a more beautiful location to have my wedding ceremony tomorrow. "Okay, once the bridesmaids are in place, then we'll cue the wedding march, and, Samantha, you'll come down the aisle."

"Now?"

Alexandra waved her hands wildly. "No, no, no! It's bad luck to walk down the aisle during the rehearsal. Mr. Peterson can walk down the aisle, but you need to come around the chairs."

"I stand corrected," I replied with a grin. Alexandra was taking this wedding stuff way too seriously. But the last thing Bishop and I needed was more bad luck, so I decided to humor her for the both of us. After bypassing the aisle, I rejoined Peterson at the altar, where Bishop waited. Both Rev and Deacon were his best men, and Mac, Boone, and Breakneck evened out the groomsmen.

Besides my sister, Sophie, my bridesmaids represented the world I was entering, and there was no one from my past before Bishop. Alexandra, Annabel, Kim, and Annie filled the spots. It was a no-brainer that Willow would be the flower girl, and Wyatt was going to try his best at being the ring bearer. Since he wasn't quite two, it was going to be interesting seeing how he did.

"Now we'll practice the vows."

The minister, who was a Raider from out of town named Fuzz, went over the parts of the service with us without our actually saying the vows. That would be reserved for tomorrow. "And then it'll be the 'by the power vested in me' jazz, and you may now kiss the bride."

Bishop drew me into his arms and brought his lips to mine. I melted into his embrace, letting my hands run up and down his back.

At Fuzz's whistle, we pulled apart. "Now, that's enough of that. You weren't supposed to practice that part," he said.

Bishop grinned. "But I needed to make sure I get it just right for tomorrow."

"Like you need practice," I mused.

Alexandra stepped forward again. "After the kiss is the processional and the service is done. Once we do some pictures, we'll move on to the reception."

"Speaking of the reception, I'm starved. Let's head back for dinner," Bishop said.

Back at the clubhouse, we had a sit-down dinner of homemade BBQ and sides. It wasn't fancy or classy, but I loved it all the same. Bishop and I were making a dent in an enormous piece of chocolate cake when a scream of pain echoed through the room. Two tables down from us, Kim's daughter, Cassie, was bent over, huffing and puffing. Considering the special circumstances of her pregnancy—she was the surrogate making Rev and Annabel's dreams of parenthood come true—everyone's attention was immediately riveted to her. Turning over their chairs in a rush, Rev and Annabel sprinted over to Cassie.

"Are you okay?" Rev questioned.

"Is it Braxton Hicks?" Annabel asked.

Cassie looked up and gave a grim smile. "My water just broke."

"Holy shit!" Rev shouted as Annabel started to cry happy tears. "We need a doctor! Where the hell is Breakneck?"

"I'm right here," Breakneck replied with a grin. Rev was so beside himself he hadn't realized Breakneck was sitting next to Cassie.

"Oh, sorry," Rev said sheepishly.

Breakneck rose out of his chair. "First thing we need to do is to take a deep breath and calm down."

"But—" Rev started to argue.

Breakneck shook his head. "You have to calm down. This will go a lot easier for you and especially for Cassie if you're calm."

With a reluctant nod, Rev asked, "Okay, what else?"

"We need to get her to the hospital. Cassie, do you have your suitcase?"

"It's at Mom's."

Kim shot out of her chair. "I'll go get it."

After she raced out of the room, Breakneck said, "Then let's get you to the car."

Bishop and I got up and followed the crowd outside. Once Cassie had been eased into the front seat of Rev's SUV, Rev turned to Bishop. "I can't drive."

"What?"

He held out a hand to show that it was visibly shaking. "I'm too fucking nervous to drive."

While I bit back a smile, Bishop wasn't quite so thoughtful. He busted out laughing. "Seriously, dude? After everything we've been through, you're losing it now?"

"This is my child, B. A child we've been through hell to get," Rev argued.

Bishop's expression grew serious. "I get it. I'll be happy to drive you."

"Do you want me to wait here?" I asked.

Shaking his head, Bishop said, "Of course not. Hop in."

"But aren't we going to be a full house with five of us?"

"You, Rev, and Annabel can squeeze into the back."

"If you say so."

When we opened the back door to get in, Cassie turned to us with tears in her eyes. "I'm so sorry to have ruined your night."

I leaned forward in the seat to pat her back. "Oh, honey, you haven't ruined our night. You just made it a whole lot more special by having our future nephew or niece come into the world."

"Exactly," Bishop said as he cranked up the engine.

Deacon and Alexandra waved to us as they got in their car. We then led a caravan of cars to the local hospital. Bishop roared up to the ER entrance and screeched to a halt. Before the car was in park,

Rev was out the car door and running inside to get a wheelchair. When he returned, he and Annabel got Cassie into the wheelchair and then Rev wheeled her inside.

After a flurry of activity at the front desk, the mechanized doors opened up, and Cassie was whisked away with Rev, Annabel, and Kim. At the sight of us standing around, a nurse said, "You all should go on up to maternity to wait."

Our herd then moved on to the fourth floor, where we took up half the room and got settled in to wait. Deacon and Bishop played cards while I helped Alexandra with Willow and Wyatt. Hours went by. Wyatt fell asleep in my arms, and finally Willow went to sleep in Deacon's.

It was a little after two a.m. when the doors opened up and Rev appeared with a beaming smile and a tiny bundle. "It's a girl!" he cried.

A whoop of joy went up in the room. Rev and Annabel had wanted the sex to be a surprise until delivery. Everyone started hugging and swiping tears from their eyes. Then we gathered round to ooh and aah at the baby, who looked an awful lot like her father. "What's her name, Daddy?" Bishop asked.

"Natalie Elizabeth . . . for me and Mama Beth."

Mama Beth grinned. "Good choice, son."

"You're welcome," Rev said. He then passed Natalie into Mama Beth's waiting arms. With tears in her eyes, she kissed her newest granddaughter, then handed her off to Deacon, who then gave her to Bishop.

"I better get her back to the room. You can come back and see Cassie in a little while. She did amazing."

After Rev left, Alexandra took Wyatt from me so they could go home. "We better head out, too. Big day tomorrow," I said.

"Yes, the day I get saddled with a ball and chain," Bishop teased.

I smacked his arm playfully. With the elevator full of our family and friends, we took the next one down alone. "You looked awfully natural with Natalie," I mused.

"I've had a lot of practice with Wyatt."

"Think you've had enough practice to do it for yourself?"

Bishop's brow lined in confusion. "What do you mean?"

"This isn't exactly the place I had in mind to tell you, but it just feels right." I wrapped my arms around his neck. "Bishop Malloy, you're going to be a father."

His blue eyes widened. "Wh-what?"

I grinned. "Remember how we decided to go off my birth control a few months before the wedding to give it time to be out of my system?"

"Yeah . . . And?"

"And I'm pregnant."

The elevator doors opened, and Bishop ambled out. "A baby . . . You're pregnant."

Considering the rough-and-tough man he was, his reaction was pretty priceless. "Are you okay?"

He turned back to me and blinked. It took a few more seconds for a beaming smile to light up his face. "Okay? I'm fucking amazing!"

He pulled me into his arms and squeezed me tight. "You just gave me the best wedding present anyone could ever ask for."

"I'm glad to do it."

"I hope it's a girl, and she looks just like you."

I laughed. "I have a feeling it's going to be a boy."

"Oh Lord, another Malloy to raise hell."

With a shake of my head, I argued, "No. The Malloy boys' days of raising hell are over. The last one officially becomes an old married man tomorrow and a father in seven months."

Bishop grinned. "You're right. My son will have a different future."

"But I'm sure he'll want to ride bikes and patch in to the Raiders."

"You don't mind?"

I stared into Bishop's eyes. At one time, the prospect of a child of mine joining an MC would have been absolutely unthinkable to me. The last thing on earth I would ever have wanted was for my son to be a biker. But times change and people change.

"No. I don't mind. We're going to need a good, solid generation of Raiders to keep the new traditions alive."

"I totally agree."

Bishop slid his arm around my waist and led me to the car—and to the new future that awaited us as husband and wife and mother and father.

Katie Ashley is the *New York Times* and *USA Today* bestselling author of the Vicious Cycle, Proposition, and Runaway Train series, as well as several New Adult and Young Adult titles. She lives outside Atlanta, Georgia, with her daughter, Olivia, and two very spoiled dogs. She has a BA in English, a BS in secondary English education, and a master's in English education, and spent eleven years teaching middle school and high school English until she left to write full-time.